Praise for
Canine Christmas

"Two paws up. *Canine Christmas* provides as much pure pleasure as a good old-fashioned belly rub."
    —DAVID HANDLER
        Edgar Award–winning author of
        The Man Who Loved Women to Death

"A witty, deliciously mysterious romp through Christmas in Dogland."
    —ELLEN HART
        Lambda Award–winning author of
        Murder in the Air

"Move over, Jane Austen. These canine scents and sensibilities unearth a lot more than pride and prejudice. Murder, for example. Yule love these tails."
    —ABIGAIL PADGETT
        Author of the Blue McCarron novels

Presented by Jeffrey Marks
Published by Ballantine Books:

CANINE CRIMES
CANINE CHRISTMAS

CANINE CHRISTMAS

Presented by
Jeffrey Marks

BALLANTINE BOOKS • NEW YORK

A Ballantine Book
Published by The Ballantine Publishing Group
Compilation and introduction copyright © 1999 by Jeffrey Marks

www.randomhouse.com/BB/

Library of Congress Catalog Card Number: 99-90725

ISBN 0-345-43657-1

Manufactured in the United States of America

First Edition: December 1999

10   9   8   7   6   5   4   3   2   1

Contents

Introduction

Jeffrey Marks

Home for the holidays. The words evoke images of happy families gathered around the fireplace anxiously awaiting the arrival of Santa, with eggnog prepared, and gifts wrapped under a decorated tree. Songs revel in merriment, and television specials concoct a happy ending in thirty minutes or less.

However, we all know about the dark side of the Christmas season as well: merchants who start their commercial escapades at Halloween, the mall sales and Muzaked carols in mid-November assaulting hordes of people in every corner. Christmas ranks as the most stressful annual event on our calendar. The increased crowds, the inflated prices, the expectation of gifts, the parties, and the obligatory ho-ho-ho spirit—they all take a toll. As Christmas can summon the altruistic spirit of a reformed Scrooge, it can also summon depression, avarice . . . and the basest forms of humanity: con artists, pickpockets, and those with homicide in their hearts.

This year won't be the first incidence of a felonious Noel. One of the earliest signs of a contentious holiday came just after the birth of Christ. Herod demanded the death of all infants under the age of two to rid himself of the Christ child and to protect his claim to the throne. While the Holy Family slipped into the night en route to Egypt, thousands of innocents were slaughtered by this edict. Malice as an accompaniment to the year-end holiday season has a long and bloody history.

Small wonder that so many mystery authors set novels and stories in the confines of a Christmas setting. From Agatha Christie to Ellery Queen, crime writers have recognized the blackness in men's souls—which is not diminished by a special date on the calendar.

To continue the tradition, please begin your investigation of the stories in this volume. The crimes, all purely fictional, continue apace—but here's the special attraction: they are always accompanied by the appearance of man's best friend.

So lean back in the easy chair, let the fire warm your toes, sip that eggnog, and enjoy these fifteen tales of mischief, mistletoe, and murder. And be sure to slip something extra in the stocking for your dog.

Clicker Training

Parnell Hall

PARNELL HALL is the author of the Stanley Hastings private eye novels (beginning with the Edgar Award– and Shamus Award–nominated *Detective*), the Steve Winslow courtroom dramas, and the Puzzle Lady crossword puzzle mysteries. He lives in New York City with his wife, his two sons, and Sophie, his Portuguese water dog.

"That's a nice poodle."

"She's a Portuguese water dog."

"Whatever. She's a fine looking animal."

"Thank you."

I said it through gritted teeth. I wouldn't have minded so much if it wasn't the third or fourth time we'd had the exact same conversation. But either Mr. Abercrombie had a worse memory than mine—hard to imagine— or else he was determined to pretend to forget due to a bizarre sense of humor of the type that was apt to be funny only to him. In either event, I was finding it rather tiresome, particularly since my wife and I had only checked in the night before.

The Stone Inn—the unlikely name of the sprawling, three-story, white, wood-frame house that to the best I could determine did not have a single stone in it—was one of the few bed and breakfasts not booked solidly through Christmas in all southern Vermont, due to the fact there had been three straight weeks of light, dry, powdery snow, resulting in gorgeous, idyllic New

England landscapes and the best skiing conditions in twenty years.

My wife and I don't ski. We were in Vermont because our son Tommie was spending his Christmas vacation in France on a school trip—don't ask. (In my day a school trip meant going down to the firehouse to see the firemen polish the fire engine.) So for the first time in years our apartment would seem rather empty over the holidays, and we wanted to get out of town.

To be sure, the snow was a lure. We don't get snow much in New York City these days, what with global warming, and as a New England boy born and bred, I miss it. So we opted for Vermont.

The Stone Inn was not our first choice. In a guide book that gave up to four stars, it got one. Nonetheless, we had chosen it on the basis of two important criteria: it had a vacancy and it took dogs.

Mr. Abercrombie, it occurred to me uncharitably, had probably chosen it because it was cheap.

Abercrombie was a plump man with a bulbous nose, twinkling eyes, rosy cheeks, and a predilection for heavy knit sweaters with reindeer on them. So far he had exhibited only two, still that was enough for me to fantasize dozens more carefully packed in an enormous suitcase.

But I was talking about the dog.

The morning after we had arrived we were all sitting around the spacious living room after a rather feeble breakfast of French toast and coffee, garnished with an occasional grape, served by the stout Austrian man whose stout Austrian wife had prepared the sumptuous repast. The two of them presumably owned the Stone Inn and were responsible for racking up its impressive total of one star. Such as it was, that was breakfast. The Stone Inn was a bed and breakfast, and since we'd slept there and had breakfast, we'd gotten what we'd paid for, and now we had all adjourned to the living room, where Alice and Zelda were holding an impromptu lecture on clicker training.

Alice is my wife.

Zelda is the dog.

"Pure clicker training," Alice was saying, "is very nice, because basically the dog teaches herself. The dog offers you a behavior, you click the clicker. The dog hears the click, realizes she's done the right thing. The dog repeats the behavior to hear the click again."

"Why?" said a young woman with sandy hair and a rather well filled out ski sweater, if aging married men are still allowed to notice such things, sexist notions dying hard. The woman was presumably the wife, girlfriend, or sister of the young man in the green fleece pullover who had blond hair, wore wire-rimmed glasses, and looked too all-American to be true. They were sitting on a love seat in the corner, which made me think they probably weren't brother and sister, but I've been wrong before.

Also in the audience were a middle-aged couple, he bald, she white haired, whom I shuddered to think were probably no older than I; an elderly man with wizened hands, an emaciated face, and an alarming death rattle when he opened his mouth, who damn well better have been older than I; and a man I classified as a sailor, though I hadn't a clue why, unless it was his large, black beard that I somehow associated with sailing through some elusive, subconscious, psychic connection of which I was not aware.

Alice and I had been introduced to all of these people during breakfast, but I, who retain names like a sieve, could remember only Abercrombie's, either because he grated on me so or because of the association with Abercrombie and Fitch.

"Why?" Alice said. "Because of the food. We call it clicker training, but it's really click/treat. You click the clicker and give the dog a treat. The dog quickly comes to associate the click with food."

Alice plunged ahead, in full lecture mode. "Take a puppy, never been trained before. You want to teach her to sit. So you wait till she does. The puppy sits, you click. And give her a treat. But you don't feed the puppy where she's sitting. You hold the treat so she has to get up and get it. Now she's standing. When she sits again, you click. And treat. It's amazing how quickly the puppy realizes, If I sit, they'll click me and I'll get a treat."

"Why click at all?" the bearded sailor-type said. He had a cultured voice which, I had to admit, didn't sound a bit like a sailor. "Why not just give a treat?"

"Because you can't do it fast enough," Alice said. "When the dog sits, you feed her. But by the time you reach out and hand her the treat, it's several seconds after she sat. The dog is smart, but not that smart, to have to think back and say, Oh, they're feeding me, is that because I just sat? But the click is instantaneous. It pinpoints the action. And promises a treat."

"Then how come your dog isn't sitting all the time, trying to get a treat?" the young woman in the sweater said.

"Because you change the game," Alice said. "After the dog learns the behavior, you add the word *sit*. Or a hand gesture. Then you only click and treat when the dog does the behavior when you ask her to."

"So, what can she do?" the bald man said. (The one I was afraid was younger than I.)

"Oh, lots of things," Alice said. "Though I don't teach Zelda tricks so much as general obedience."

The middle-aged woman smiled and said, "Zelda?"

"Yes," Alice said. "After F. Scott Fitzgerald's wife."

I smiled and said nothing. Alice might think that, and we would never disillusion her, but my son Tommie and I both know she was actually named after a Nintendo game.

"Zelda," Alice called in a high lilting voice.

Zelda, who had been curled up happily in front of the fireplace, raised her head at the sound of Alice's voice. She certainly looked intelligent, though maybe I'm biased. Zelda is a black dog with white markings on her paws and chest, and long curly hair. Portuguese water dogs don't shed, they have to be groomed like poodles—though they are *not* poodles, thank you very much, Mr. Abercrombie—and Zelda was overdue for a haircut, which meant she had a luxurious coat of loose curls and looked positively gorgeous. It also meant you couldn't see her eyes, but, trust me, the dog was very bright.

Alice stood up, said, "Zelda, come."

Zelda trotted over to Alice.

Alice said, "Go round."

Zelda walked around behind Alice's back.

"Sit," Alice said.

Zelda sat at her side.

"Down," Alice said.

Zelda lay down.

"Stay."

Alice walked across the room, turned, and faced the dog.

"You haven't clicked," the elderly man said. It came out as a wheeze, but confirmed the fact he was still alive.

"Because the sequence isn't over," Alice said. "After the dog learns, you chain behaviors. Zelda will follow a whole sequence of commands in order to hear a click. Zelda, come."

Zelda trotted over to Alice and sat in front of her.

Alice clicked and reached in her pocket for a treat.

"You didn't ask her to sit," the young woman pointed out.

"Yes, I did," Alice said. "I gave her a hand signal."

"Can you teach her a new behavior?" the young man asked. It was the first time he'd spoken, and he sounded young.

"Sure thing," Alice said.

Alice looked around the room. In the far corner was a Christmas tree, with strings of lights and colored balls and tinsel. It had presents underneath and a star on top. So far Zelda had given it a wide berth.

"See the Christmas tree?" Alice said. "Zelda's afraid of it because she's never seen one. It's only her second Christmas, and last year she couldn't go because we went to Stanley's mother's, and his mother has cats. So she's cautious about it, because she's not entirely sure what it is. From her experience, trees do not grow indoors or have lights."

"So?" the young man said.

"So, I can use clicker training to teach her something to overcome the fear."

Alice walked over to the Christmas tree.

"Zelda, come."

Zelda trotted over.

Alice pointed to a Styrofoam ball hanging from a lower branch. "Touch."

Zelda looked up at Alice.

Alice pointed again. "Touch."

Zelda took two steps, reached out, touched the Styrofoam ball with her nose.

Alice clicked. "Good girl," she said, and gave Zelda a puppy biscuit. As soon as Zelda had eaten it, Alice pointed to the ball and said, "Touch."

Zelda touched it again, much quicker this time.

Alice clicked, gave her a treat.

This time, when Zelda finished the biscuit, Alice said nothing. She stood there, arms folded.

Zelda looked at her for a moment, then turned, took two steps, reached out, and touched the ball with her nose.

Alice clicked and gave her a treat, while the people in the living room laughed and applauded.

"That's a smart poodle," Abercrombie said.

I gnashed my teeth.

Later that morning, we took Zelda out in the snow. She loved it. She ran, she jumped, she rolled. She had a wonderful time. The only thing missing was another dog to play with.

That problem was solved right after lunch. Alice and I got back from the local soup and sandwich shop downtown to find a Labrador retriever had checked in. Of course, the Lab had not checked in by himself—his mommy and daddy were with him. Which is how we dog people refer to the owners of other people's dogs. And, yes, our own, too. Alice is Zelda's mommy, and I am Zelda's daddy. And we know it's silly, but only to an extent. When Alice says to Zelda, "You wanna go for a walk with daddy?" I hardly even notice.

Anyway, the Lab's mommy and daddy were a nice young couple, who laughed affectionately as their dog catapulted from the backseat of their Subaru, bounded up to Zelda, and took off with her across the lawn. They whirled and rolled and frolicked and frisked, biting at each other's ears and tail in a playful friendly way, then raced down the hill over the frozen pond.

I must say, that gave me a turn. But as if he read my mind, my gracious host, Mr. Stone Inn himself, was at my side, grunting away in a thick Austrian accent through which I could barely discern enough words to determine that what he was attempting to assure me was that the pond had been frozen for weeks, and the dogs were in no danger.

Unfortunately, while he was outside calming my fears, Mrs. Stone Inn, his ill-cooking wife, was inside rejecting our new arrivals. Evidently there was no room at the inn—a common Christmas theme—and Zelda and I barely had time to learn the golden Lab's name was Sandy before he was gone.

Heartbreak.

Do dogs get depressed? In a word, yes. Zelda missed Sandy, not enough not to eat, but enough to mope around the inn and give everyone a good idea where the word *hangdog* came from.

"Can't you clicker train her to be happy?" the bald,

middle-aged man asked when I ran into him after dinner on my way to take Zelda for a walk.

"That's the one thing that doesn't work," I told him.

And it didn't. Zelda was decidedly moody the rest of the evening, went to sleep early, and did not even go out for her eleven o'clock walk.

Which is why she was up at the crack of dawn.

She woke me with a woof, as is her custom. Not a loud bark, but just a low, squeaking woof, as if to say, Excuse me, I don't want to wake the neighbors, but if it's not too much trouble, do you suppose we could go out?

I raised my head from the foam rubber pillow of the rickety four-poster bed with the broken box springs and lumpy mattress, all of which Alice had commented on at great length the night before. By what little light was coming in the window, I grabbed my watch from the night table and determined it to be six-fifteen. I sighed, swung my legs out from underneath the covers, set my feet down on the cold, uneven, wood floor, and reminded myself, as I always do on such occasions, how much I really enjoy having a dog.

I put on my pants and shirt, socks and shoes, sweater, coat, mittens and hat, and took Zelda downstairs to find the body of the elderly man stretched out under the Christmas tree with a bloody length of pipe next to his left ear.

He was clearly dead. He was lying facedown, with his head bashed in, his arms and legs at grotesque angles, and a Christmas tree ornament on his back.

I am utterly ashamed to admit the first thing that occurred to me was now there would be room for the people with the golden Lab.

The policeman did not look happy. Evidently murders during the holiday season cut into his family time. A little man with shrewd eyes, a jutting jaw, and a thin mustache, he stood in front of the Christmas tree where the body had lain and told the assembled suspects, the Hastings included, what he intended to do. We had already had a preview of how he intended to do it. He had spent the morning striding around the Stone Inn as if he owned it, barking orders at the state troopers, emergency medical technicians, newspaper reporters (whose exit had been speedy), and employees and guests alike. As a result, the medical examiner had been summoned, the body had been inspected and removed, the crime scene had been processed and photographed, and the living room was once again open to the guests, just as it had been the day before, with the exception of the chalk outline on the floor.

The policeman pointed to the outline and stated unnecessarily, "A man has been killed." He paused, as if for dramatic effect, and went on, "The man is Vincent Lars of New York City. He was eighty-two years of age. He was retired, lived alone, was up here to the best I can determine to spend Christmas in front of a roaring fire." He snuffled his nose, which crinkled his mustache. "That will not happen. It is up to me to determine why. We know how. He was struck from behind with a piece of pipe. The pipe was discovered next to the body and processed for fingerprints. There were none. It is yet to be determined where this pipe came from, though the cellar and the toolshed are likely sources. The toolshed is somewhat less likely, as there appear to be no footprints leading to it in the snow."

The policeman paused, shook his head. "Don't you hate a crime where snowy footprints are a clue? I certainly do. So far, the only snowy footprints belong to Mr. Stanley Hastings, who, after finding the dead body, saw fit to walk his dog."

Here the policeman fixed me with a steely gaze, which I thought was undeserved. I had called the police first, and Zelda had needed to go.

"At any rate, we are not going to rely on snowy footprints. We are going to determine the truth the old-fashioned way, by interrogation. I am going to question each and every one of you, and I am going to take you one at a time."

I went last, which hardly seemed fair, seeing as how I'd been the one to find the body, but it did have two advantages. It meant by the time he got to me he'd already heard everyone else's story. And it gave me time to talk to Alice.

"So," the policeman said. "You're a private investigator?"

I smiled, in my best self-deprecating way. "Not so you could notice. I'm actually an actor and a writer. I don't get much work, so I support myself chasing ambulances for a negligence lawyer. I interview accident victims and photograph cracks in the sidewalk. It's mostly trip and falls."

He frowned. "I thought it was *slip* and falls."

"It is. I say *trip and fall* by force of habit."

"What habit?"

I blinked. I couldn't believe he'd asked that. "The habit of being wrong," I said. "I'm frankly a poor detective, the last one on earth I would personally hire."

"Yet your wife says you've assisted the police on occasion."

"I wish she hadn't. I wish you'd treat me like any other witness."

"Or any other suspect?"

"If you prefer."

"All right. Would you care to tell me how you came to find the body?"

"You already know that. I got up to walk the dog."

"This was standard practice?"

"What do you mean?"

"For you to walk the dog and not your wife."

"I very seldom walk my wife."

He blinked.

I put up my hand. "Sorry. I know this is serious. We

share the duty of walking the dog. This morning it was my turn."

"Why?"

"Because Zelda woke me."

"Zelda is the dog?"

"That's right."

"What time did she wake you?"

"Six-fifteen."

"Was that earlier than usual?"

"I'll say."

"Why do you suppose she woke up?"

"I don't know. I suppose it was being in new surroundings. Oh, I see. You mean did she hear something? It's a possibility. Did you pin down the time of death?"

"Not with any accuracy. But I doubt if it was six-fifteen."

"I'm glad to hear it."

"You shouldn't be. If you were here in the house just like everybody else, you could have killed him at any time. In point of fact, I would find it very unlikely you killed him in the presence of your dog."

"Thank goodness for small favors."

"Again, that doesn't let you out."

"No, but common sense should. Why would I drive here all the way from New York with my wife and dog to kill a man I never met?"

He shrugged. "Why would anyone?"

"They wouldn't," I said. "Obviously the killer has some connection. You have only to find it."

"That's what I'm trying to do."

"Really? How you doing so far?"

He frowned. "Mr. Hastings, I find your manner insolent."

"You're right," I said. "I'm sorry. I've had no sleep, and a considerable shock. But that's no reason to take it out on you. I'm just getting impatient with your preliminary questions which I happen to know have no bearing on the crime."

"Oh? And how do you know that?"

"Because they're all tangential, and they don't relate to the actual killing."

"You want me to ask you questions about the actual killing?"

"I thought that was the point of your investigation."

"It is. And you are a key factor in that investigation, having found the body."

I winced. "I wish I hadn't found it."

"Because of the shock?"

"No. Like I say, because it clouds the issue. All you want to ask me about is finding the body."

"Oh, is that right?" he said, ironically. "And what is it you'd like me to ask you about?"

"I told you. The killing."

"I see. You feel you could shed some light on the matter?"

"Yes, I do."

"Very well then, Mr. Hastings. What do you know about the murder?"

"I know who did it."

We were once again assembled in the living room, just as we had been the day before when Alice had given the demonstration with the dog. With a few exceptions. Alice and I shared a couch with Abercrombie this time, our chairs having been taken by Mr. and Mrs. Stone Inn, who had been invited to join the proceedings. Zelda lay curled up at our feet.

Aside from that, everything was pretty much the same. The young couple were on their love seat. The middle-aged couple were on a couch. The bearded man sat in an overstuffed chair.

The elderly gentleman wasn't there, of course, but the policeman was. He stood on the chalk outline in front of the Christmas tree and addressed our little group.

"Ladies and gentlemen, I have talked to you all. And I am happy to say I have made some progress. That has been largely due to one man, Mr. Stanley Hastings, who, as you know, found the body because he happened to walk his dog." Here he bowed to Zelda. "That was at six-fifteen this morning when the alarm was raised."

He paused, smiled. "By a happy circumstance, he also happened to walk the dog during the night. I'm going to let him tell you what happened then."

All eyes turned to me. Not that anyone knew the name Stanley Hastings, but they all knew the dog.

I didn't bother getting up. I sat on the couch, patted my dog. "Last night Zelda went to sleep early," I said. "Which is not surprising. It's a new environment, it's new people, it's overstimulating, and she doesn't get her normal naps. At any rate, she went to sleep early and didn't get her usual last walk. Which is why she woke me in the night. She woke up and needed to go out. So I pulled on my clothes and hurried downstairs. I was not fully dressed. Because, frankly, I wasn't going to *take* her out, I was going to *send* her out. I was cold and half-asleep and didn't want to wake up any more than I had to. Anyway, I didn't have her leash on, since if I wasn't going out with her, there was no point. I brought her downstairs, let her out the back door.

"Only she didn't go right out. Instead, she trotted over and looked in the living room door." I pointed. "Right over there. Stuck her head in, looked in the direction of the Christmas tree. I called her, and after a moment or two, she trotted over and went out the back door."

"Uh-huh," the policeman said. "And what do you conclude from this?"

"There was someone in the living room who attracted her attention. Most likely the decedent and his killer."

"Did you hear sounds from the living room?"

"No, I didn't. Frankly, I didn't hear a thing."

"And what makes you think they were there?"

"Zelda's actions." I shrugged. "And the resultant corpse."

The policeman held up his finger. "Aha. The corpse. How do you know *that* wasn't what attracted the dog's attention? The body could have been lying there, and the murder could have happened some time before."

"I don't think so."

"Why not?"

"Zelda's actions. This morning, when we found the body, she trotted right over to it, sniffed it. If it had been there last night, that's what she would have done. But she stopped in the doorway. Cautiously. Which is what she would have done if there had been two people in there not on the friendliest of terms. Dogs are very sensitive. They read body language well. It is my contention that Zelda got a look at the decedent and his killer very shortly before the deed."

"Oh, that's ridiculous," said the bearded man I thought was a sailor but who had turned out to be a life insurance salesman. "It means nothing of the kind."

"Oh, you think not?" the policeman said. "Well, I think it might. Mr. Hastings has a theory, and a very interesting one." He gestured to me. "Why don't you tell them what it is?"

"It's very simple," I said. "Zelda is very smart. She saw two people arguing. Then she saw one of them dead. She can make the connection one person harmed the other."

This time it was the middle-aged man who spoke. "I think that is a little much. Mr. Hastings, are you telling me the dog knows who committed the crime?"

"I wouldn't go that far," I said. "She doesn't know she knows it. All she knows is two people didn't like each other and one is dead. She doesn't really know the other person killed him. That is a leap *we* have to make. *But she knows who that other person is.*"

"Oh, for goodness' sake," Abercrombie said. "You expect us to believe that?"

"No, I don't," I said. "But I can prove it."

For once I silenced Abercrombie. He gaped at me, his mouth open.

I stood up and took a little metal clicker out of my pocket.

"Zelda," I said, "go round."

Zelda got up and circled me.

"Sit," I said.

Zelda sat at my side.

"Down," I said.

Zelda lay down.

"Stay," I said.

I walked to the middle of the room, turned around. Zelda was still lying there.

"Zelda, come," I said.

Zelda got up, trotted over to me.

"Sit," I said.

Zelda sat and I clicked. I reached in my pocket and handed Zelda a puppy biscuit. She chomped it gratefully, looked up at me expectantly.

"Zelda," I said. "Walk with me."

Zelda walked at my left side back across the room.

I stopped, said, "Zelda, sit."

Zelda sat at my side.

I said, "Zelda. Touch killer."

There was a stunned silence in the room.

Zelda looked up at me expectantly.

Raising my voice slightly, in a high pitched tone dogs like, I repeated, "Zelda. Touch killer."

Zelda's eyes traveled around the room. Then she got up, turned, trotted over to the love seat, and put her head in the young man's lap.

But it was the young woman who sprang up. "No! Stop it!" she cried. "Get her away from him! Danny didn't do it! It was an accident!"

I must say, Danny no longer looked like the all-American boy. From the expression on his face, and the daggers he was darting at the young girl, I got the impression if it weren't for the others in the room there might have been another "accident."

Of course, it was just a trick. Zelda didn't see the young man arguing with the old one. Because I never took her out during the night. She slept straight through till six-fifteen. No, I must admit that was a slight fabrication for the purposes of trapping a killer. Which worked pretty well, I might add.

You're probably wondering how I knew Danny was the killer. Actually, I didn't. I didn't even know he was Danny.

But Alice told me. Alice is good that way. She told me and then refrained from telling the policeman, in order to make me look good.

Actually, she would have told the policeman, had he bothered to ask her. But he didn't, and Alice made up her mind if he was as obtuse as that, she wasn't going to volunteer it. She said she thought he would take it better coming from a private eye. But I know better. At any rate, that's what she did.

But how did Alice know? Well, her powers of observation are as acute as mine are virtually nonexistent. And while the policeman was telling us all about the crime, she was watching the people in the room.

Danny, to his credit, betrayed not a thing. Alice knew he was guilty from watching the girl. From the way the girl was watching him. Just the way she looked. Of course, there was nothing specific.

Which is another reason Alice didn't want to tell the policeman. She figured he'd put it down to women's intuition, vivid imagination, flight of fancy, what-have-you.

And as for the motive, we didn't have one. I made it up. Turned out it was right on the nose, but then even I can't be wrong all the time. I figured most likely the old man and the girl were related in some way the old man would never have dreamed to suspect. And that Danny and the girl had followed him here deliberately in the hope of making something out of the connection.

I don't believe murder was ever intended, at least not by her. But when the opportunity presented itself, Danny took it. Not being particularly smart. Not figuring the relationship, though tenuous, could be traced. Particularly if the young woman presented herself as an heir. Though, to be fair, had they survived questioning, gone home to New York, and months later accepted a behest, probably nothing would have come of it. Because the actual connection, grandniece twice removed, whatever that means, was not particularly likely to come out.

Except for Zelda.

And how did Zelda identify the murderer?

Clicker training, of course.

Alice and I spent a half hour with her alone in the living room training her what to do. Of course, we didn't teach her to touch the killer. She had no idea who the killer was. Or Danny, for that matter. No, we clicker trained her to touch the love seat. As soon as she learned it, we added the command, "Touch killer." Which was fine with her, and she learned it well. Any time we want a love seat touched, that's all we have to say.

I doubt it will come up often.

But it certainly saved the day.

And it certainly made a big impression on the other guests.

Abercrombie was exuberant. "Would you believe it?" he said, triumphantly. "The poodle solved the crime!"

I didn't bother to correct him.

The Emerald Collar

Leslie O'Kane

LESLIE O'KANE is the creator of two mystery series. The longest going involves Molly Masters—full-time mother of two, part-time creator of faxable greeting cards, and occasional reluctant sleuth. (Molly's most recent criminal investigation is detailed in *The Fax of Life*.) Ms. O'Kane's newer series, beginning with *Play Dead*, features dog psychologist Allie Babcock, who lives in Boulder, Colorado—where the author also makes her home, along with her husband, two children, and a cocker spaniel.

Jarrod Miller, his face still flushed from his having come in from the cold, glanced up at the small window of my basement office in downtown Boulder. The already minimal view that the window afforded was blocked by the snow that had blown into the window well. Beside him, his scruffy little mixed breed dog, Patch, so named after the dark pattern of fur on half of his face, let out a sad whine.

"You've got to do something about my dog, Miss Babcock," Jarrod began. "My wife insists I either solve this problem now, or she'll have Patch put in a kennel until after Christmas."

"Have you had a lot of houseguests lately?" I asked, guessing at the likeliest cause of dog problems at this particular time of year. The onslaught of visitors often makes dogs anxious; they suddenly find themselves forced to share their territory and their human "pack." Patch, however, was one of the calmer dogs I'd seen lately, and considerably more so than his owner, who was rocking slightly in his seat and tapping one foot. Patch's chin rested lazily on his owner's nontapping foot, and his eyes were half-closed.

"No, Miss Babcock, that's not it at all."

"Please call me Allida."

Jarrod nodded, then crossed his arms. "Patch . . . keeps lifting his leg on the Christmas tree. It upsets the wife and kids. We've already got presents under there, and they're getting so yellow and washed out that you can hardly read the tags. Plus, he's always shorting out the kids' model electric choo-choo."

This was such an unexpected problem that I had to stifle a chuckle. Though I'd worked as a dog psychologist for less than a year now, it had been easy for me to surmise that laughing at a client's problems was no way to endear myself to them. "I'm assuming that this is a live evergreen?"

"I don't know if it's *still* alive. I think the water in its tree stand has wound up being too acidic, thanks to Patch. The thing's shedding needles like crazy."

"I hope you've moved the presents."

"Of course."

"Jarrod, my first hunch would be that some other dog marked this particular tree when it was still in the lot. If so, Patch would be bound and determined to counter that with his own scent, especially since the tree is in his territory now."

Jarrod leaned forward, putting his elbows on his knees. He was still wearing his unzipped parka and was casually dressed in dark thick corduroys and a pullover. "What do we do to get rid of this other dog's scent? Spray the trunk with perfume?"

"I'm honestly not sure. I've never tried to . . . de-scent a tree trunk." By my way of thinking, there was no sense in trying to cure—or, more correctly, redirect—a dog's problem behavior if it could be easily circumvented. "Would you consider getting an artificial tree, or simply banishing Patch from that particular room?"

He rubbed his chin thoughtfully. So far, Jarrod struck me as an intense man, hands always in motion, unsure of where to focus his gray eyes. "I wouldn't have a problem with the first suggestion. I mean, this tree we've got now has . . . lost its luster anyway. I've only stuck with live trees because I like the scent of pine needles. But it's only a matter of time now till the thing smells more like an outhouse than the great out-of-doors." He gave Patch a pat as he spoke, as if to reassure him, though Jarrod only succeeded in waking him from his slumber.

"He hasn't been doing any other marking of territory inside the house, has he?"

Jarrod sighed and dragged both his palms over his curly red hair. "No, fortunately, the tree seems to be it."

"An artificial tree could do the trick then. Though I have to warn you that this is a first for me. I've worked with dogs that became so determined to take over their pack . . . their family, that is, that they peed on their masters' beds, but never a dog that did so exclusively on the Christmas tree."

"Yeah? Well my neighbor said you were great. Apparently you worked with him and his Jack Russell terrier, Kudos."

"Oh, yes. I remember Kudos. Smart dog." His owner had hired me to help train him for special tricks. I rarely took strictly dog-training gigs but had grown so fond of Kudos that I made an exception. I suspected that the owner, whose name I'd since forgotten, had aspirations of earning millions by hiring Kudos out as the next TV trickster dog. "How's he doing?"

"Oh, business is booming. He owns that jewelry store down the street a ways, and with Christmas coming up, he's doing a brisk business."

"Oh, good," I murmured to be polite, but I'd actually meant to ask how Kudos was doing, not his owner. Jarrod had jogged my memory, though; Kudos's owner was Ben Richards, the proprietor of Richards Jewelry Store.

As if he could no longer contain his energy, Jarrod leapt to his feet, kicking his dog slightly in the process. "Hey! You're a woman. I should show you this. Get your opinion on it." He pulled a small, nicely wrapped box out of the pocket of his forest green parka. Fully awake now, Patch jumped up to put his front paws on Jarrod's legs and started sniffing at the package. He even attempted to lick the wrapping paper. Jarrod, however, plopped back into his chair as abruptly as he'd risen. He kept having to push his now persistent dog away with one foot while scraping with his thumbnail at the tape on one end of the wrapping paper. He extracted a velveteen jewelry case, leaving a neat shell of the wrapping paper, which he returned to his pocket.

"Your dog sure likes your wife's present."

Jarrod chuckled. "No kidding. I don't know what the story is with him. He's been like this ever since I got the necklace. Maybe he thinks it's a new dog collar."

"Do you keep doggie treats in that pocket? If so, the scent could have rubbed off onto the box."

"I never keep treats in this coat."

With Patch yipping and trying to snatch the box, Jarrod snapped open the lid and held out the case to me. "Tell me what you think."

I found myself holding one of the prettiest necklaces I had ever seen. It was yellow gold in a serpentine chain that widened to a triangular shape at the center, where a series of diamonds and emeralds were set into the gold. I'm not usually drawn to such flamboyant jewelry, but this piece had an undeniable elegance. "It's absolutely beautiful," I said honestly.

"Thanks. Joan had better flip. It's worth ten grand." He smiled proudly. "Decided it was high time to splurge on my wife."

"This is quite a splurge." Apparently he had a large amount of disposable cash. Too bad for my sake that his dog's problem was likely only going to require this one session.

He shrugged and said proudly, "Ah, she has a different interpretation of marital fidelity than I do. If it'll get her off my back for a while, it's worth it. Besides, Ben gave it to me for half price. That's my neighbor. Kudos's dad. Owner, I should say."

Get her off my back? I thought sourly. What a lousy sentiment behind such a nice gift. I handed him back the necklace, which, as he'd said regarding his tree, had "lost its luster" for me. Patch, however, was still whining and sniffing at the necklace. "Maybe this has been scented with Eau de Pork Chop."

"I hope not. It'll be around my wife's neck in six days."

"I'm sure she'll feel like a million bucks wearing such beautiful jewelry." So long as Patch wasn't dangling from it, jaws clamped on the emeralds, at the time.

Jarrod grinned and slipped the box back into its wrapping and then into his pocket. "Thanks." He looked at me expectantly, and I realized we needed to bring this session to a close.

"Does Patch have any other behavioral problems you'd like me to work on with him? Besides the tinkling on the tinsel, I mean?"

"Ah, no. He's a good boy, aren't you, Patch. Just this tree thing, which seemed to . . . come out of nowhere. Didn't seem to be anything I could do to get him to stop. And it never occurred to me that the tree might have come pre-dog-owned. But what's strange is, he didn't start lifting his leg on it till last week. We'd already had it in the house for a week by then."

"Really? Frankly, that weakens my theory that your just getting an artificial tree will do the trick. You haven't had any other dogs in the house lately, competing with Patch for turf?"

He was already shaking his head, so I quickly added, "Or how about a new kitten or cat?"

" 'Fraid not."

"What would you like to do, then, Jarrod? Do you want to try to keep this tree and see—"

He held up his palms, cutting me off. "No matter what, it's got to be replaced. Trust me. Nobody would want a Christmas tree that their dog treats like a fire hydrant. I'll go ahead and get an artificial tree, right now, even, and we'll take it from there."

He rose, and I stood up as well. We hadn't taken close to the full hour, but there was little left to discuss. Patch's tail wagged in excitement at the departure that he sensed was imminent, and he rushed over to me for a pat, which I happily obliged. "What a good dog Patch is," I assured the little dog as I scratched his ear. There had never been a time in my thirty-three years when a dog or two or three hadn't played a significant role in my life.

Jarrod asked how much he owed me and then wrote out a check. "Let's hope this plastic tree does the trick."

"We'll see if a second session is required or not. We can keep our fingers crossed. In any case, it's less than a week till Christmas, so you won't need to be protecting your tree from Patch much longer."

"Okay. I'll keep you posted."

Two days later, Jarrod was on the phone with me, very upset. "It didn't work. Patch is still peeing on the stupid tree. Only now, since the trunk is plastic, it's splattering more."

"I'm sorry to hear that. Isn't there some way you can block off that room from Patch?"

"No. It's in the family room. That's where we like it. Joan suggested we try moving it to a smaller room that we can close off, but that just doesn't feel like Christmas. I want you to teach him not to do this."

"Jarrod, I don't think that there's any way I can get those kind of results in the four days between now and Christmas. I would almost have to catch him in the act, and I'm assuming that you already stop him from running up to the tree when you're there in the room with him."

"Yeah, and know what else? We've had to lock the dog door. Yesterday, all of a sudden, I'm minding my business, and in rushes Kudos from next door. He grabs a present from under our tree and tries to rush outside with it. It was that five-thousand-dollar necklace I showed you the other day. If it had been a yo-yo or something, sure, that's cute. But not when it costs half a used car."

"What happened? Did you get it back from him before he got back outside?"

"Yeah. I had to chase him around the Christmas tree, though. And when I got it back from him, know what he did? He lifted his leg on the tree! Like, what? It's not bad enough that our own dog does this? Now it's half the neighborhood's dogs?"

"That's . . . terrible." And extremely unusual. This was not something that had been covered in any of the behavioral courses I'd taken at the veterinarian school at Fort Collins.

"Can you do something? Please? Patch is really used to having access to the open dog door. I'm afraid this . . . peeing business is just going to get worse."

"Maybe I could make a home visit today and see if I can make some suggestions."

"Good. And maybe you can talk to Ben Richards for me, too. He went ballistic when I told him about what his dog had done. Said that that wasn't possible and that I was slandering his dog."

We set an appointment for later that day, said our goodbyes, and hung up. How could I work in a friendly conversation with Ben Richards in the meantime, whom I hadn't seen in months? I still needed a gift for my mother. Jewelry from Ben's shop might be just the answer. Meanwhile, if he would talk about his dog and Patch, maybe I'd get some clue as to what was going on.

* * *

The bell over the door to Richards Jewelry Store jingled merrily when I entered. Ben was doing a brisk business, which was nice to see. As is often the case, I liked his dog considerably more than I liked Ben himself, but I always rooted for small independent businesses to succeed. Too many in Boulder had given way to chain stores.

Ben nodded in greeting, and I scanned the various items in the glass-enclosed displays. To my considerable curiosity, there was an emerald necklace on sale for $5,000 that looked identical to the one Jarrod had shown me. I studied it, but saw no differences.

Ben made his way over to me behind the counter. "Looking for a high-end gift, I hope?" he asked, giving me a toothy grin.

"Not unless you're willing to divide the price by a hundred. I was just surprised to see this here. Did Jarrod return this for some reason?"

"No, I made two of them. I do that with some of my favorite designs. There are slight differences between the two necklaces though, because, as my advertising says, the personal touch is that every item I sell is one of a kind. Rest assured, Allie, that if you purchase this necklace, no one else will be wearing a carbon copy."

"That would be comforting, I suppose, but do you have any two-of-a-kind fifty-dollar items?"

"No, but I've got some nice earrings for around a hundred."

"That's still twice what I was hoping to spend. If Mom had only one earlobe we'd be in business."

Again, Ben flashed his toothy, salesman smile. "Why don't I show you what I've got, and let me see what we can do for you."

He returned with such a beautiful pair of earrings that I didn't bat an eye at doubling my budget, knowing even my non-jewelry-wearing mother would be delighted. Ben started to ring up the purchase on the cash register for me, then stopped and peered at me. "You mentioned Jarrod a minute ago. I take it he showed you the necklace?"

I nodded. "Yes. It's lovely."

"Thanks." He sighed. "You know, I try to be neighborly. That's why I recommended you to him, after all. But, between you and me, the guy's losing it. Despite what he says, my dog does not go into other people's homes uninvited. Kudos was home in our fenced yard."

"Maybe he dug under the fence, or squeezed between a loose slat."

Ben shook his head and said adamantly, "Not on his own, he didn't. Jarrod's trying to frame Kudos. I inspected every inch of that fence the day before this alleged incident. I was stringing up Christmas lights along the top and sides of the fence, you see. No holes. I go out after he calls, and guess what?"

Ben was speaking with such intensity that the couple of potential customers who'd recently entered shifted their attention to us.

"A hole?" I suggested with a shrug.

He nodded, his eyes flashing in anger. "Right underneath the center of the fence. Despite the fact that the ground's frozen. Who does he think he's fooling? Does he think my Kudos rented himself a jackhammer?"

The image and accompanying wordplay of a Jack Russell operating a jackhammer distracted me. Ben leaned closer. "I'm telling you, Allida. Ida and I both know something is going on. Jarrod Miller has never done a decent thing for his wife in the ten years they've lived next door to us. Now he buys her a fabulous necklace. And suddenly he accuses my dog of breaking and entering!"

The jingling bell behind me indicated that the door was being opened. I gave a quick glance and noted that his wife was entering and that the other customers were leaving. "Nobody's making any such accusations," I said. "Entering and peeing, maybe, but there was no breaking."

"This isn't funny, Allida. Something happens to that necklace now, and I'm going to be the first suspect! Me and Kudos are, that is."

Ben's wife, a thin, pleasant-looking woman who, like her husband, appeared to be in her mid-forties, put on a plastic smile and all but raced behind the counter to stand beside her husband and pacify the situation. "Oh. Allie. Hello. Doing some last minute shopping?"

"Yes, for my mom. How are you, Ida?"

"Fine. Great, even," Ida answered with a smile.

"Allie's working with Patch now," Ben grumbled, giving his wife some sort of significant look—widening his eyes.

Her smile faded only slightly as she shifted her vision to me again. "Oh, that's right. Joan told me. Jarrod's wife, I mean. We're good friends. Or at least, I hope we still are. Honestly. You'd think Kudos should have been named Bandit, to hear them tell it."

"*Them?*" Ben repeated, his eyes once again flashing in anger. "You were talking to Jarrod?"

"Joan was there the whole time," Ida said through her forced smile. She blushed a little as she returned her gaze to me. "My husband doesn't trust Jarrod. He's something of a compulsive ladies' man. I hope you didn't have any trouble with him."

"No, he wasn't acting compulsive toward me at all."

"Here you go, Allida," Ben said, handing me a nicely wrapped small package. The wrapping paper was identical to the one that had been on the box that Jarrod had shown me, though this box was smaller.

"Thanks. I'm sure this will all blow over, once the stress of the season is gone."

"Oh, I'm sure you're right," Ida said with a big smile. She glanced over, noted Ben's glum expression, and elbowed him in the ribs. "Isn't she right, dear?"

"Women always are," Ben said through the toothy smile he'd once again donned.

They wished me a Merry Christmas and waved goodbye to me. It felt uncomfortable when I turned and saw them watching me cross the street. There were some strange vibrations between those two. Could Jarrod and Ida have had an affair? That might explain why Jarrod had built a dog-sized tunnel under the fence. Jarrod could have wanted to lure Kudos into his yard as an excuse to see Ida.

On second thought, Patch had been oddly obsessed with the necklace box. Then later, Kudos had rushed in through the dog door and grabbed the same box. It would have been possible for the Richardses to treat their wrapping paper with some sort of scent that their dog was trained to recognize. That would make for an interesting scam operation; the Richardses could sell high-end items and train their dog to bring them back. Then they could either resell them or remake them into a new bauble.

Or, more likely, this was the by-product of my over-taxed mind. I'd been working too hard lately and was subject to the same kind of holiday stress as everyone else. I stuck Mom's earrings in the pocket of my coat and vowed not to think about Jarrod and Patch or Ben and Kudos again until I could judge for myself how serious the situation was.

A couple of hours later, having worked with a fearful schnauzer given to biting the nearest ankle if there were any sudden noises—not the kind of dog you'd want at your New Year's Eve party—I parked on Fourth Avenue alongside Jarrod Miller's house.

The neighborhood featured small older homes without garages, though nowadays the homes were often bought up by young professionals who rebuilt and expanded as much as their property lines would allow.

This is what Ben and Ida Richards had done. The Millers' house was much smaller.

The woman who answered the Millers' door said she was expecting me and introduced herself as Jarrod's wife, Joan. She also explained that the kids were on sleep-overs and that Jarrod had called to say that he was going to be a little late.

We discussed Patch's "bladder problem" while she showed me the tree. They had blocked it off, to an extent, having built a low, makeshift wall out of the Christmas packages. Joan said that though she hadn't actually "caught Patch in the act," Jarrod had, and she showed me the physical evidence on the various gifts that she hadn't "gotten a chance to rewrap yet." Strangely, I wasn't detecting any odor whatsoever, but then, sniffing out such things was not within my typical job description. Fortunately.

Joan was a nice enough woman but a bit hyperactive for my taste. She reminded me of a nervous Chihuahua. She had a pixielike hairstyle, freckles, and was always crossing or uncrossing her legs as we spoke and fidgeting with her dark bangs.

"This has been just the . . . the darnedest thing, Allie," she said, immediately opting to use my nickname. "I just don't know what's gotten into Patch. He used to be so well behaved. Now he's been sneaking out one particular present and trying to bury it."

"Patch has been doing that, too?"

"What do you mean, *too*? None of the rest of the family is into burying things in the yard."

"I was under the impression that Kudos, your neighbor's dog, had tried to run off with a present."

"Oh, that's right. That has been the darnedest thing. I'd forgotten. Both dogs have a thing for the same present."

The darnedest thing, all right, I thought to myself, beginning to wish that I could just work with dogs and not their accompanying humans. I took the box with the earrings out of my pocket and showed it to Joan. "Was that particular present in this kind of wrapping paper?"

She glanced at it, smiled, and said, "Yes, as a matter of fact. And I recognize the signature wrapping paper. Jarrod got me a gift from Richards Jewelry Store."

"Do you know where it is now?"

She rose and said, "I've had to hide it in a cupboard out of Patch's reach. I'll go show it to you. It's pretty chewed up, frankly."

While Joan was out of the room, I called Patch to me and showed him my nearly identical box. He showed no interest.

"Take it, Patch," I said quietly.

He didn't respond at all. I tried setting it on the floor in front of him and urging him to take it. Again, no reaction.

"What are you doing?" Joan asked as she returned to the room.

"I was just testing."

"He doesn't seem nearly as enamored with your box as he is with mine," Joan said, showing me her second, longer box. "He's got his teeth marks all over it."

She held it out for me. In the blink of an eye, Patch raced over and snatched the box out of Joan's hand. "See what I mean, Allie?"

"He's acting as if there's something edible in the box," I said, thinking aloud. I retrieved my own jewelry box, which Patch had completely deserted. During the brief pause in which I did so, the dog had started tearing at the wrapping on Joan's necklace.

"Allie, for heaven's sake, stop him from doing that! He's going to ruin my present!"

The instant I'd retrieved the now-soggy box from Patch, Joan snatched it from me and said, "I just hope there's no damage to the . . ."

She had snapped open the velveteen-covered container

and was staring at its contents. I rushed over to stand beside her and shared in her surprise.

"Rawhide? A signature Richards Jewelry box contains rawhide chew treats?"

"That would explain why the dog was drawn to it. But not back when we were at my office and your husband showed me the necklace."

Jarrod rushed in through the back door and paled at the sight of the jewelry box and its contents in his wife's hands. "What's that? Where's the necklace I bought you?"

His surprise struck me as miles short of genuine. That made me realize I needed to collect the shreds of wrapping paper, which, having lost the rawhide strips, Patch was now attempting to ingest. I stuck the paper shreds in my pocket.

"Ben Richards!" Jarrod said derisively in the meantime as he took the rawhide strips from his wife. "I'll bet he did this! Him and his mutt! He must have trained that dog of his to come in here and . . . and get the box, then he swapped the contents!"

Joan was shaking her head and sobbing.

"I'm gonna get that bastard on the phone," Jarrod continued, maintaining his act. "Then I'm going to call the police and—"

"What did you put on the wrapping paper, Jarrod?" I asked.

He stared at me, his mouth agape, looking the soul of confusion, except for the slightest hint of desperation in his eyes. "What are you talking about?"

"If you're trying to pull off an insurance fraud, I'll turn the wrapping paper in to the police. They can analyze it. I would bet you scented it with hamburger, or something similar, before you came to my office a couple of days ago. There would have been no other reason for Patch to show such interest in the box, which, at that time, contained an expensive necklace. And I have a hunch that you've been using yellow food dye to fool your family into believing that you had an excuse to contact a dog psychologist. You set me up, didn't you?"

Joan had stopped crying and was now looking at her husband intently.

"I . . . did no such thing. It must have been . . . Ben could have put something on his wrapping paper when I wasn't looking. Something that attracted his dog to the box."

"That would have been possible, except you told me you got the box back before Kudos could escape with it. And your wife has had it hidden in a cabinet. If the box never left your house, only someone in the house could have swapped the necklace for the rawhide."

Jarrod's cheeks were now beet red, matching his hair, and he looked from me to his wife and back in desperation. Joan walked away from him and slumped down onto the couch.

He blinked a few times as if running new lines of defense through his head, then finally sat beside his wife, who refused to look at him. "I'm sorry, Joan. She's right. I did exactly what she said. I couldn't afford the necklace. I was going to report it missing on Christmas Eve and use Allida to verify that the dog went after the jewelry and probably buried it somewhere."

Joan was staring at him, aghast. "How could you do that!"

"We've . . . been losing some customers, and the business isn't doing too well right now. But I wanted you to have a nice Christmas and realize that I *did* get you that necklace you'd been eyeing; I just couldn't afford to give it to you right now, is all. I was hoping to 'find' where Patch had 'buried' it, once I could afford to give the money back to the insurance company. It's the thought that counts, after all."

"And Kudos taking the gift and trying to run out the dog door? Did that ever happen?" I asked.

Jarrod shrugged. "Yeah. Once I snatched him out

of Ben's yard and brought him over here. Couldn't even convince the stupid mutt to use the tunnel I dug. I just . . . used Kudos because the day after I bought that necklace, I went into Ben's store, and there was another identical one. The creep had been lying about his one-of-a-kind designs! I thought it'd serve him right if I could throw some suspicion his way."

"Where's my necklace now?" Joan asked, crying softly once again.

"I . . . had to sell it at a secondhand store for less than I bought it for. But I was going to buy it back, just as soon as business picked up. And I figured by reporting it missing instead of stolen, the insurance company wouldn't call in the police." He turned his gaze toward me. Suddenly he smiled and then laughed with relief. "I didn't do anything illegal, Allida. I didn't report the necklace as missing to our insurance company yet, so there's nothing you can do to me."

"This is the last straw, Jarrod!" Joan rose, lifting her chin defiantly despite the tears running down her face. "Maybe there isn't anything she can do, but I'm suing for divorce. I'm taking the house, the kids, and every nickel you've got left!"

"Let me know if you need a witness," I said to her. "I'd like to at least make sure you get custody of Patch."

"Thank you, Allie." She looked again at her soon-to-be ex-husband. "As for you, get out of my house. Now. Or I'm calling the police to escort you out."

He spread his hands and opened his mouth as if to protest his innocence, muttered, "But . . . but . . ." Then sighed and headed out the door, shaking his head.

I touched Joan's shoulder. "Are you going to be all right?"

She nodded. "Eventually. I should have thrown the bum out years ago."

We said our goodbyes, and I left. Snow had begun to fall. The first few soft flakes were whirling in the light breeze.

Jarrod was waiting for me beside my car. I steeled myself and grabbed my keys. I ignored him as I unlocked my car.

"Can't you say something to my wife on my behalf? I'm the one who hired you, not her!"

"You wouldn't want anyone to hear what I have to say about you." I got into my car, with Jarrod glowering at me. As I shut the door, I met his eyes and said, "By the way, Jarrod. You were right about one thing. The thought *does* count."

Yellow Snow

Jeffrey Marks

In addition to serving as editor of *Canine Crimes*, an earlier anthology of dog-related mysteries, JEFFREY MARKS is the author of numerous short stories that have won the Barnes and Noble Prize, Honorable Mention from *DreamWeaver* magazine, and a grant from Malice Domestic. His author profiles and scholarly essays on mystery authors have appeared in numerous national magazines. Mr. Marks wrote a biography of author Craig Rice (*Who Was That Lady?*) that to date has appeared only in French translation. Having been reared in the company of beagles and terriers (Bugular, Malady, Almanzo, and Busters 1–4), he now lives in Cincinnati with a Scottie named Ellery.

The adage to "beware of yellow snow" is never truer than when the dog demands an outside sojourn at five A.M. Norman had woken me from a wonderful dream about what I would find in my stocking in the morning. I'd donned a pair of plaid pajama bottoms as I stumbled to the entryway. Icicles nettled my chest before I'd even opened the door. Someone in a fur coat doesn't mind the cold as much as the naked apes.

A fine layer of powder had coated the front walk as my beagle slipped between my legs to sully the fresh snow. He sniffed around three separate bushes while I stared out over the landscape. Norman shuffled across the encrusted yard, occasionally breaking through the membrane into several inches of compacted snow and ice. Typically, Cincinnati has one bad snowstorm a year, enough to make the population glad they don't live farther north. The situation on the highways rapidly deteriorates from a winter wonderland to something from *Alice in Wonderland*: Tweedledum behind the steering wheel. This year's precipitation had paralyzed the city three days before Christmas. I'd closed the antique store for the duration and settled in for a long winter's break. Norman enjoyed the company and the opportunity to sniff his presents, the tree, the ornaments, and whatever else came in the path of his extended snout.

I rubbed my eyes twice, trying to comprehend the scene in my neighbor's yard. The Maxwells had selected a quasi-religious theme this year of angels heralding the arrival of Santa Claus. Sheep and oxen kept time with the eight tiny ice-covered reindeer. The delicate sleigh and Santa on their front lawn had an extra passenger. Drake Harrington slumped against jolly old plastic Saint Nick with a strand of Christmas lights wrapped around his neck. The man's dashing good looks had been abused by the weather. The wind had blown his ebony hair into his face; his normally rugged good looks had grown mottled. Though he was dressed in a shirt and jeans, he didn't look warm enough for a night like this.

Even from here, I could recognize death. The strand was pulled tight enough around his neck to have cut off the circulation of a dormouse, much less a full-grown man. The twinkle of red and green bulbs against his chalky skin made me certain that Drake wouldn't be home for Christmas.

I'm normally not the nosy neighbor type, but Jo-Ann Lemmen had stopped by on her annual fruitcake pilgrimage to deliver more than cement pastries. She spilled the entire story of the neighborhood doings. Apparently, Sarah Maxwell, my neighbor's daughter, had invited her longtime boyfriend, Ernie, to spend the holidays with her when they rendezvoused at Thanksgiving. That trivial detail hadn't stopped her from bringing Drake at Christmas after they started a rather torrid affair at Columbia University. Mrs. Lemmen had hinted at things that would have made Ken Starr blush. Ernie, usually as constant as gray skies on a Cincinnati December day, hadn't learned of this turn of events until he'd shown up yesterday. Granted that behind his tiny wire rims, Ernie wasn't much to look at: hair that looked like it hadn't been combed since the last holiday season, freckled face. But how attractive must you be in order to be treated with respect? Being a local boy, I'd expected Ernie to turn tail and run, but he'd decided to stand his ground against romantic Visigoths.

So the trio had trekked back to the Maxwell abode to celebrate the holidays in what could politely be defined as a tense atmosphere. I heard shouting from the house next door, mostly the two men jousting over Sarah. Frankly, I couldn't understand Sarah's fatal attraction. At best, I would have dubbed her cute; at worst, self-absorbed. No Helen of Troy in the Cincinnati suburbs. She stood a head shorter than her suitors, with limp blonde hair and brown eyes that expressed a lack of interest in the outcome of this situation. I'd known many men to mistake indifference as hard-to-get and get hurt in the process. As I saw Drake's body, I wondered again what had possessed her to make such decisions.

The whole family had suffered the consequences. Ross Maxwell, Sarah's younger brother, had come home from college as well, but alone, without a menagerie of romance. Both Maxwell children attended the same school, showing some semblance of family despite their circumstances. Ross had the same blond hair as his sister, styled in what was politely called a bowl cut. Bangs hung down in front of his eyes, and wispy strands of gold collected behind his ears. He towered over his sister with a six-foot frame and upper torso that told he'd spent more time at the gym than the library since he'd been at school.

He had not been coming home until three or four in the morning. Norman was thoughtful enough to announce the neighbors' timetable with a plaintive wail.

My beagle had deigned to share my bed for the duration of this cold snap. His love of showers (which he shared with his namesake, Mr. Bates) waned with the advent of icy tile. His sleeping rearrangements left me painfully aware of the Maxwell children's every move.

Mrs. Lemmen couldn't have asked for more details about the menagerie next door than Norman cared to provide with his nightly alarms. Mrs. Maxwell had passed away before the family had moved in next to me, and I'd only met the father and two children. James Maxwell, the patriarch, seemed to live for these visits from his rapidly maturing children. He'd been spending inordinate amounts of time adjusting the outside lights and the plastic figures, which combined a crèche and Santa and his sleigh. My single electric candle in the window felt Grinchlike in comparison.

Now Norman had decided to conduct his own investigation of this Christmas crime scene. He'd finished his business and made a cautious path over to the red plastic sleigh. Several sets of footprints made their way to the decorations, including two pairs circling each other like a double helix. All the tracks led from the Maxwell house. Not a surprise, since the neighbors on either side of us had left town for the season.

Norman didn't bother with these late night ruminations. He put two paws up on the side of the sleigh to have a peek, and he'd summarily slid down the side of the plastic faster than Santa down a greased chimney. I made cautious negotiations to retrieve my dog and learned why he'd had so much trouble in maintaining his perch. The ground surrounding the sleigh was solid ice. It appeared as if the warmer temperatures had thawed the ground enough to refreeze the water when the mercury dropped again. The plastic runners on the sleigh had sunk into the block of ice and wouldn't budge. Nothing like winter in the Midwest. The wind must have swept the dusting of snow away because the area was slippery enough for a Tonya Harding sighting.

I tried not to disturb the footsteps in the snow; rubber-soled prints crunched toes deep into the powder. A few steps made their way back to the Maxwell home.

Norman made another attempt at the sleigh, but ice repelled his advances. I hooked a finger under his collar and crunched back toward the house to call 911.

Twenty minutes later, the front yard shone with red lights and yellow police tape, the closest I would get to lawn ornaments for the holidays. The police tramped around the sleigh, taking pictures and measurements before they removed the unfortunate houseguest.

The Maxwell clan huddled around the activity. Sarah, for her part, looked genuinely aggrieved. I wasn't sure if it was because Drake was dead or because there would be no more squabbling over her this holiday season. Her father stood next to her, trying to coddle her with a ratty discolored blanket that had seen too many holidays. He hovered over her like the star from the East. For her part, Sarah pushed him away, standing alone and weeping.

I couldn't read Ernie's face from this distance, but he either grimaced at the cold or sneered at the elimination of the competition. Ross stood behind the group, visible only from the neck up. I tried to contain my curiosity, but it tugged at me like a gift under the tree. I wanted to know what had transpired in their house to produce this drastic turn of events.

I put a pan of milk on the stove and cocoa powder in some mugs. As I filled the cups, the marshmallows barely breached the brownish surface of the liquid. I wasn't sure about police protocol, but hot chocolate seemed appropriate to serve at a winter murder investigation. Martha Stewart would approve.

With dispensation from the police, the Maxwells trudged inside my home for a cordial grilling. Ross and Sarah didn't disturb the ice-crusted ground covering as they walked, but Ernie and James had to take high steps to extricate their feet from the snow. Neither man wore boots. Norman pranced around them, thrilled at the prospect of additional hands to feed him. He performed figure eights through their legs as they stomped Nature's gift from their feet.

I settled them in the living room, served them hot chocolate, and sat down to pry. Under the incandescent lights, Sarah looked every bit the coed, a stretch from the holiday spoiling vixen. She wore only an oversized Columbia University T-shirt and a light cotton robe, which did little to expose the reason for the perpetual bickering next door. Her eyes were red, chapped around the corners. She huddled over her mug in my armchair and tried not to make eye contact with anyone in the room.

Ross broke the silence. He'd worn his own version of his sister's outfit, a T-shirt from the University of Cincinnati and jeans. His slippers didn't look sturdy enough to make the footprints outside. "Man, this is just like TV. I keep expecting Drake to stand up and join us. Too weird."

His words were sufficient to break the ice. Sarah began to sob, heaving with a force that made her put down the mug and cover her face. Tears streamed through her ring-spangled fingers. She wiped her eyes on the sleeve of her robe. "I can't believe he's gone. I can't understand why this happened."

James tried to comfort her again, but she'd selected an overstuffed armchair which accentuated her loneliness. Norman circled her feet a few times but realized he wouldn't be the center of attention near a crying woman. He shuffled off to his food dish to crunch dry kibble.

Ernie sipped his chocolate and coughed politely. "You shouldn't make such a production. It's not like you knew him that long. You'll get over it."

Sarah sniffed loud enough for me to take the hint and fetch a tissue. By the time I returned, James had already found a box and set it next to his daughter. She was talking between sniffles. "I doubt it. We were married last week."

A hush fell over the room, more awkward than if Santa had passed gas. James fell off the arm of the chair and spoke from the floor. "Sarah, when were you going to tell us this? I-I didn't even get him a present."

"Christmas Day. Drake and I wanted it to be a surprise."

"I would have been surprised all right. I would have felt like an ass." Ernie had stood up. From the color of his face, I surmised that his circulation was doing fine, despite the cold. His neck had reddened to the shade of a poinsettia. Ernie shifted, and Ross clapped a sympathetic hand on his shoulder.

Sarah looked up at the men. Her eyes looked as cold as the gales outside. "Get over it, Ernie. I told you last night we were finished. Get it through your head. Why can't you just accept that?"

James looked at me with eyes begging that this situation go unreported to the neighbors. I could see the mortification in his face as his mouth drooped. "Sarah, I thought you and Ernie were going to—"

"You thought wrong." Sarah picked up a pillow and cradled it against her chest. "Drake was incredible. We were going to stay in New York after graduation. You just didn't take the chance to get to know him and now y-y-you never will." She began to wail as she rocked back and forth.

I cleared my throat. "Did anything happen last night to give you an idea that this was going to occur?"

James furrowed his brow. "What indications tell you that one of your houseguests is going to be murdered?"

Sarah stared at her father. "Drake and I sat downstairs talking for a long time last night. Alone. He wanted to tell everyone about our marriage and not wait until Christmas day."

"Why was that?"

Sarah shot a glance to Ernie and then looked down at

her hands. "He said Ernie was giving him the creeps. He wanted him to know we were married, so he'd leave me alone."

"What time did you go to bed?" Norman stuck his snout between my legs so he could observe the proceedings and make sure I wasn't going anywhere without his august company.

Sarah shrugged. "About two, maybe two-thirty. It was late."

Ernie bristled for his turn to speak. "How could I be giving him the creeps? I wasn't even around last night. Ross and I played video games until about three A.M. and then I went to bed."

Ross nodded in agreement, making his bowl cut jiggle. He squeezed Ernie's shoulder with the hand that had never left the man's side. "We did. Ernie and Drake were both sleeping in my room, so I can tell you he was there."

"What time did Drake come upstairs?"

Ross shrugged. "He never did. I just figured he was downstairs letting Sarah unwrap his gift."

James bit his lip at that last statement. "I came downstairs about four to get some milk and no one was around. Somewhat of a stumper, eh? Why didn't Drake go to bed?"

Ross stood up and took a seat near Sarah's feet. Norman stalked over to see the person who sat at his eye level. The boy absentmindedly rubbed my dog's long ears as he looked at his sister. He probably would have scratched his sister's ears if he'd thought it would help. "Don't worry, sis. The police will solve this case in no time."

"It still doesn't bring him back."

Ernie sneered at Ross. "Don't be too sure. In case you didn't notice, there weren't footprints near the body. Those fools aren't going to be able to solve this crime without a gift from Santa and a star overhead to point them in the right direction. Without physical evidence, anyone could have done it and no one could have."

James looked at the young man. All traces of compassion had disappeared faster than wrapping paper on Christmas morning. "What are you saying?"

"Just that we shouldn't expect the police to solve this."

I cleared my throat and spoke. "There was ice all around the sleigh. That's why there aren't any tracks. I did find one set of boot tracks."

Ross looked at me as though I wasn't the host. "Hello, it's winter."

Sarah nodded. "We kept an extra pair of boots by the door for running outside in this weather. Anyone could have worn those outside with Drake. Or Drake could have worn them himself."

Norman whimpered by the door, and I let him outside as the winter winds invaded the room. "But he didn't strangle himself, so someone went outside with Drake."

I kept an eye on the police as they cordoned off part of the street. Santa would have to resort to desperate measures to call on my house tonight. The snow around the sleigh had been flattened in some places by their boots. I could still see the shine of the block of ice from the moon's glow, though soon no one would be able to trace the footprints to the Maxwells'.

Norman started to do his business on the sidewalk, but I shooed him to the bank of snow just beyond the hedge. I didn't want any yellow ice on my walk to slip and fall on in the morning. Just the thing to be sued for—a neighbor slipping on your dog's pee. Norman jaundiced the front lawn and trotted back to the front door through my legs. He didn't want to miss a moment of drama.

He curled up on the kitchen floor as I slipped him a treat. I returned to my guests and laid a hand on James's shoulder. "How are you holding up?"

The blanket was wet and clammy. I wiped my hand on the back of the sofa and sat down again, facing the group of people. I figured since their Christmas was already ruined that I didn't have to worry too much about tact. "You know it just seems very convenient about the sleigh being frozen in ice. Most of the rest of the yard is still snow."

Ross shrugged and went back to pulling the marshmallows from his hot chocolate. Ernie continued his vigil of Sarah, as she wept for her dead husband. James seemed to be the only one paying attention to my soliloquy.

"If we thought the ice might not be an accident, it might explain a few things which have been puzzling me. Like Norman's reaction to the murder."

Ross looked up at me. "Do you have cable?"

I squinted my eyes at him to make sure he was human. "Yeah, I do. In the living room. As I was saying, Norman didn't bark when the killer took Drake out to the sleigh. I was confused about that for a while. He'd been barking at Ross, and he wouldn't really know Sarah or Ernie, so they would get the four tone treatment."

Sarah looked up. "Maybe he just slept through the whole thing."

"I don't see how. He knows when Ross gets home and that can't be noisier than carrying someone out to a plastic sleigh and murdering him. Norman doesn't miss much."

Sarah shivered and I knew it had nothing to do with the freezing temperatures outside.

"The lack of footprints bothered me. At first, I thought that it indicated that someone too light to make tracks had committed the crime, but the ice made me wonder. The killer would want the ice if he planned to use the sleigh to hold the body. That plastic will slide easily in all the snow."

Ernie stood up. "What exactly are you trying to say?"

"Just that the killer would have to put the body in the sleigh and that the weight of the body and his weight would make the sleigh wobbly, taking time and perhaps making a lot of noise. Ice would make the sleigh stay put."

"So the killer froze the sleigh into the ice how?"

"Water, maybe a hose or a bucket. Which was it, James?"

The man looked up, eyes vacant. "The hose actually. I made sure the water seeped into the snow."

"Then you knocked out Drake and took him out to the sleigh to strangle him. You used your blanket to drag him outside so that you wouldn't make prints with his body. The cloth is still wet from where it absorbed the snow."

Sarah broke into sobs. "Why?"

"I couldn't bear to see you leave town. You're my only daughter. I didn't realize that you'd gone and married him. I wanted to see you with Ernie so you could have lived in Cincinnati. I'm so sorry."

Ross's mouth hung open as Ernie stood up. "Dad, how could you? What were you thinking?"

"You and Sarah were all I had since your mother died. I just wanted to make sure you were nearby. Ernie seemed to ensure that."

Ernie's face reddened again. "So you killed the other man so Sarah would be interested in me? Some prize that would be. Second place."

The doorbell rang and I went to open it. Outside, the bells of a nearby church chimed the start of the holiday celebration. We'd have a present for the police on Christmas morning.

O Little Hound
of Bethlehem

Taylor McCafferty

BARBARA TAYLOR McCAFFERTY has so many *noms de mystère* she confesses that she has no idea who she really is. As Taylor McCafferty, she is the author of the Haskell Blevins mystery series; as Tierney McClellan, she is the author of the Schuyler Ridgway novels. Moreover, with her twin sister, Beverly Taylor Herald, she has created a series about identical twin sisters Nan and Bert Tatum. "O Little Hound of Bethlehem" was written in memory of Taylor's dog, Ogilvy, who was her furry friend for seventeen years.

If I had not put up the Christmas tree the night before, I know I would've spotted him the second I walked in the door. There wasn't much in my sparsely furnished living room that a man as big as Harlan Campbell could hide behind. The seven-foot Scotch pine that I'd decorated with as many ornaments as I could buy at Wal-Mart for twenty dollars was, in fact, pretty much it.

It did cross my mind, as I closed the door behind me, to wonder why my dog Ogilvy wasn't standing there the way he always was—tongue lolling, quivering all over, waiting to give me his usual welcome-home licking. I got my answer as soon as I switched on the floor lamp next to my couch, and Harlan stepped out from behind my Christmas tree, moving quickly around the brightly wrapped presents encircling the tree's base. He came around all in a rush, as if he thought maybe I'd try to get away.

I just stood there and looked at him. My heart had started pounding, and my mouth had gone dry, but I would never give Harlan the satisfaction of running from him.

He'd have enjoyed the chase too much.

Not to mention, I'd tried to run from Harlan just once before—shortly after he and I started living together. What he'd done to me after he'd caught me was something that still made me shiver when I thought about it.

Ogilvy, the traitor, had apparently been keeping Harlan company behind the tree. It must've been a tight fit for both him and Harlan between the tree and the opposite wall. Ogilvy's mom had been a pedigreed Old English sheepdog, and his father a handsome German shepherd who evidently could jump six-foot chain-link fences. The eleven puppies that had resulted from their union had ended up with the shaggy coat and white/gray coloring of a sheepdog, and the erect ears and large frame of a shepherd.

Ogilvy's shaggy coat was quite a bit curlier than his brothers' and sisters'; he'd looked as if he'd just given himself an Ogilvie Home Permanent. I'd decided what his name would be the second I laid eyes on him.

As Ogilvy brushed past my Christmas tree to stand at Harlan's side, several branches shook so much a couple of glass ornaments dropped to the floor. When they hit the floor, they made little clinking sounds, but Ogilvy didn't even glance in that direction. He was too busy licking Harlan's hand.

What a guard dog.

"I think the damn dog remembers me, Beth," Harlan said. I hadn't seen Harlan in almost three years, and yet the man spoke as if he were simply continuing a conversation that had been interrupted.

Some interruption. Three years at the Kentucky State Reformatory for Women. Three long, long years.

Harlan reached out and scratched Ogilvy's head. "He sure does seem happy to see me again."

What could I say to that? Ogilvy has never been known for his discriminating tastes. If Ogilvy thought there was a chance that you'd pet him or feed him or scratch his ears, he was happy to see you. If Charles Manson had showed up with a dog biscuit in his hand, Ogilvy would've greeted him as if he were a long-lost relative.

I hadn't said a word so far, but Harlan didn't seem to notice. He just kept on scratching Ogilvy between his ears. The dog's tongue lolled happily. "I sure remember Ogilvy, too," Harlan went on.

The owners of Ogilvy's mother had not realized immediately that her new family was not purebred, so they'd bobbed all the puppies' tails. Poor Ogilvy has always seemed to realize that he'd been short-changed in the tail department. He'd apparently decided a long time ago to make up quantity with quality. Now, at the sound of his name, he wagged his stump with such vigor, his entire rear end wagged, too.

"Yep," Harlan said, smiling, "I recognized Ogilvy the second I saw his picture in the paper."

So that was how he'd found me. Not exactly a surprise. Ogilvy's photo had appeared on the front page of the Louisville *Courier-Journal* yesterday morning. I'd known, of course, that the picture was going to be in there. Fact is, I'd been worrying for a week, ever since a staff photographer from the *C-J* had shown up at my front door, asking who I was and what Ogilvy's name was.

I'd briefly considered refusing to tell the guy anything. And, even more important, refusing to give permission to print the picture. And yet, how could I do that without attracting even more attention? The reporter, no doubt, would have been curious as to why I was so publicity-shy. What's more, it wouldn't have taken much to dig up the whole story. I sure as hell had not wanted another story about the bank robbery showing up on the front page of the *Courier*.

I'd seen enough stories about that to last me a lifetime. The headlines back then had all but screamed at me: LOCAL WOMAN ARRESTED IN BANK HEIST! BANK ROBBER REFUSES TO NAME ACCOMPLICE! And let's not forget my personal favorite: ROBBER GETS TEN YEARS!

As it turned out, that last headline had been in error. I'd been paroled for good behavior after serving just a little over three years, after which I'd moved into this rental house in Valley Station, a suburb of Louisville. I'd gotten a new job working as a secretary; and I'd been more or less taking it one day at a time, trying to make up my mind what I wanted to do with the rest of my life. The last thing I needed was the *Courier* taking a walk down Memory Lane. Compared to that, just having a picture of my dog appear in the paper seemed like a cakewalk.

I hadn't counted on Ogilvy's photo being on the front page, though. Or that the damn thing would take up almost one quarter of the page. Or that it would give the address of the church beneath the picture. That's what made me mad. Because the second I'd seen the photo and, even more significant, the headline in big bold type over the photo, I'd realized that I should've expected this. I mean, how stupid could I be? It was the Christmas season, for God's sake.

It being the Christmas season, in fact, was what had started it all. The house I'd rented was right across the street from the Valley Station Baptist Church. Ever since the church had set up their Nativity scene the day after Thanksgiving, I'd been having trouble with Ogilvy. I couldn't keep him in the backyard. Having apparently inherited his father's remarkable talent, Ogilvy kept jumping the back fence and running across the street.

What was the attraction? Oddly enough, Ogilvy seemed to be convinced that the church, in its infinite generosity, had erected a doghouse just for him. That this doghouse only had three walls, that it had a glowing neon star attached to the roof, and that it sheltered weather-worn statues of Mary, Joseph, and the Holy Infant, did not matter in the least to Ogilvy. All Ogilvy wanted to do was curl up and go to sleep on the nice soft straw, his body curved around the sandaled feet of Joseph. I'd had to haul that dumb dog back home at least five times before one of my neighbors—or maybe somebody just driving by—had decided that Ogilvy was a photo opportunity and had phoned the paper.

After taking Ogilvy's photo, the reporter from the *Courier* had hurried across the street to find out whose dog this was. According to what he'd told me, he'd gone to my next-door neighbor's house first, and then had been directed to mine. And, of course, once he'd heard what my name was, he'd been beside himself. "Oh, this is great. This is terrific!" he kept saying.

My name, you see, is Beth Saunders. The Beth is short for—would you believe—Bethlehem. I know what you're thinking. Who in their right mind would name a baby Bethlehem? The answer to that one, of course, is: my mother. I'd heard from various relatives over the years that Mom had apparently found religion right about the time she met my father. I'm sure Dad's being a good-looking, Methodist minister was purely coincidental to Mom's sudden conversion.

Before meeting my dad, though, my mom had been pretty rowdy. Drinking and partying and carrying on with one guy after another. To make sure that the Almighty—and, not incidentally, my straitlaced dad—knew that she'd truly repented, Mom had named every one of her kids after some place with religious significance. My two younger brothers are Israel and Jericho (Jeri, for short).

I did ask Mom once, when I was in high school, why she didn't just give us the usual Biblical names—like

Ruth and Mark and Matthew—but Mom had sniffed, "Too ordinary." She'd also added, "You should be glad I didn't call you Gomorrah."

What could I say? She'd had a point.

With my name being what it was and it being the Christmas season, I should have known that a photograph of Ogilvy would not be buried on some back page of the *Courier*. Hell, the photographer had probably thought of the headline as soon as he heard my name: O LITTLE HOUND OF BETHLEHEM. Even though Ogilvy was not exactly little, and he was most certainly not a hound, it was a headline no journalist could pass up. No wonder the photographer's eyes were all but dancing as he left.

In the week that it had taken for the photo to finally appear, I'd told myself that maybe Harlan wasn't even in the area any more. Maybe he wouldn't even see the picture in the paper. Maybe he wouldn't even recognize Ogilvy. Harlan and I had only had the dog for a year or so before my life had taken an abrupt detour. After that, I'd had to give Ogilvy to my mother so that she could keep him for me until I served out my sentence.

"Yep, Ogilvy takes a real nice picture," Harlan was saying. "Real cute."

I still hadn't spoken. Did the man expect me to stand here and chat about dog pictures? Was he kidding? "How did you get in here, Harlan?" I said.

Harlan ran his hand through his blond hair. Was there ever a time when I'd thought him good-looking? In faded jeans, cowboy boots, and a scuffed brown leather jacket, Harlan has always been trying a little too hard to look like James Dean. I don't know now why I didn't see it right from the start. Maybe, like Ogilvy inheriting his jumping ability from his dad, I'd also inherited something from a parent. From my mom, I'd inherited a wild streak.

Harlan had been as wild as they come. I'd met him after work one night at a local bar, and for a while, he'd seemed to me to be the most exciting man I'd ever known. If he drank a little too much, and he gambled away his paycheck a little too often, I was so blind crazy about him that none of that seemed to matter. Harlan made the men I'd dated at General Electric, where I worked as an administrative assistant, suddenly seem boring and dull.

Harlan had already moved in with me when I found out about his temper. By that time, I'd been telling my parents and friends for months that they were wrong about Harlan, that all he needed was a good woman to straighten him out. My mom and dad had only lived two blocks down the road from my apartment, so I could have gone to them for help anytime. And yet, I'd been too proud to admit to anybody how often Harlan hit me, or how every day I grew a little more afraid of him.

When Harlan had lost his third job in a row, and yet never seemed to be short of cash, I'd asked him where all his money was coming from. His answer was to become a familiar refrain: *That's for me to know, and you to find out.* I half expected him to say it now. "How'd I get in here?" he drawled. "Well, Beth, it's the oddest thing—" He had the expression on his face that he always wore when he was lying: wide-eyed sincerity. "I don't know if you know it, hon—"

I couldn't help it. I winced when he called me *hon.*

Harlan frowned, but he let that one go. "—but your bathroom window is busted."

I didn't have to guess how that had happened.

"Since the window was already open and all," Harlan went smoothly on, "well, I just climbed in and waited for you," he said. He took a deep breath and looked me up and down. "It's good seeing you again, Beth." His eyes traveling over my body felt like insects. "You're looking damn good. Damn good."

My throat tightened. "You didn't come here just to tell me how good I looked, did you?"

Harlan smiled. "You're still mad, aren't you? But, Beth, sweetheart, I didn't have a choice. There wasn't any need in both of us getting caught. You understand that, don't you?"

Oh, I understood all right. I'd gone over it in my mind often enough. Every once in a while, even now, I still had nightmares about that day. Once again, I'd hear Harlan telling me, with that look of wide-eyed sincerity, that he was just going to stop by the bank, that's all. He was just going to make a quick withdrawal from his account. As it turned out, while I sat out front, Harlan went inside and made a quick withdrawal of every cent in the vault, the ATM machine, and the tellers' cash drawers. It had amounted to close to a quarter of a million dollars, according to the *Courier*. The exact amount was not known since the bank had just taken delivery of some payroll deposits which had not yet been counted.

Harlan had come running out, his eyes wild and excited, actually laughing as he tossed the bags of currency into the backseat of my car. Since he hadn't bothered to mention that I'd been recruited to drive the getaway car, I hadn't even left the engine running. I was so stunned, so totally unable to fathom what was happening, that Harlan had to yell at me three times before I had the presence of mind to start the car and pull into traffic.

The elderly bank guard inside was evidently not anywhere near as good as I was at following Harlan's instructions. The old guy had not lain down on the floor with the other bank employees; instead, he'd followed Harlan out, yelling. Harlan had shot at the guy twice, as I was screeching away from the curb.

Both shots had missed.

In my nightmares over the years, sometimes those shots didn't miss. I would awake, trembling, bathed in sweat, seeing again the fear in that old man's face. The fear, no doubt, mirrored in my own.

Halfway back to our apartment that day, I'd heard

the sirens. In my rearview mirror, I could see a police car, lights blazing, heading directly toward us. Beside me, Harlan turned around and looked out the rear window, his face white. "Okay, slow down, and let me out here," he said, pointing at the next street corner. His voice was shaking. "I-I'll meet you back at the apartment."

He'd run, leaving the money behind in my car. He was already a block away when the squad car had shot right by me. I never did know where it was going, but it had not been chasing me. I realize now that Harlan had been certain that I was about to be caught; he'd been turning over the money and me to the police in one nice, tidy package.

When the police car went by me, I'd sat there for a long moment, waiting for my heart to stop pounding, and half expecting Harlan to show up again. He was long gone, however. The police were at my apartment almost as soon as I got there—the old bank guard had given the police my license plate number, and they'd just run a trace on my address—but Harlan was still nowhere to be seen.

In the last three years, I hadn't heard a word from him. Until now.

"You understand I just wanted that money for you and me? So you and I could go away together—so we could go someplace on the beach where neither one of us would ever have to work again." Harlan reached down and scratched Ogilvy's head. "You and me and Ogilvy." Ogilvy's ears perked as he wagged his stump.

"You and me and Ogilvy," I repeated. I forced myself to smile. "You mean it, Harlan? You were just getting that money for us?"

Harlan grinned, his eyes confident now. "Sure, baby, sure," he said. He paused, looking down at Ogilvy, and then he said softly, "So where is it?"

I gave him a blank look. "Where's what?"

Harlan's eyes flashed with irritation, but he still smiled

at me. "The money, Beth. Where did you hide it?" He glanced toward the hall. "I've been looking around, and I have to hand it to you, Beth. You've hidden it real good."

I followed his glance. Even from where I was standing, I could see all the stuff littering the hall. Harlan had been looking all right, and he had not been neat about it. I noticed, too, now that I was looking, that the cushions on my sofa were a little uneven—as if someone had looked underneath them and then replaced them in a hurry. Harlan had left my living room intact, so I wouldn't know the second I'd opened my front door that something was wrong. He hadn't wanted to tip me off.

"Harlan," I said, "I don't have the money. The police took it."

Harlan gave up on trying to smile. "Beth, don't give me that. The *Courier* said the money was never recovered."

"I know what the paper said, but I'm telling you what happened. One of the cops took it out of my car."

Harlan just looked at me. "Oh, Beth," he said. His voice sounded infinitely sad. "I sure didn't want to have to do it this way." As he spoke, he pulled a gun out of his leather jacket.

I couldn't seem to drag my eyes away from the gun. The thing seemed to fill the room. "Harlan, I'm telling you the truth."

Harlan was shaking his head before I'd even finished speaking. "You know damn well I can't trust a word you say."

"You can't trust me?" I was incredulous. "Are you kidding? I did three years, Harlan. Three years, and I never said a word. They offered me a deal, too—told me I could maybe just get probation—but I still kept my mouth shut. If that doesn't prove you can trust me, I don't know what does."

Harlan's eyes flashed in an expression of fury that was all too familiar. "All that proves is that you knew what I'd do to you if you didn't keep quiet." He cleared his throat. "Now I want that money," he said. His voice was so quiet, it was almost a whisper.

I didn't even blink. "I don't have it."

He took that one well. The words were barely out of my mouth when he'd slapped me across the face. Ogilvy, that watchdog of all watchdogs, cocked his head to one side, as if trying to decide what game Harlan and I were playing.

"I want the money," Harlan said again.

My jaw ached. I rubbed it as I said, "Harlan, the police got it out of the back of my car, and I never saw it again."

Harlan shook his head. "You expect me to believe that?" With that gun pointed at me, it was hard to think straight.

"You've never heard of this happening? Instead of turning in the evidence, the police keep it?"

Harlan was staring at me now, his eyes narrowing. I hurried on, trying to convince him. "The police kept on asking me about it, too, but I sure didn't have it anymore. They needed to be asking one of their own, Harlan. You need to go down to the police station and find out who was here when they made the arrest."

It did my heart good to see Harlan look so furious. "Let me get this straight," he said. "You really think I should go down to the station and have a nice long talk with the cops about the day they busted you for the robbery I committed? That's what you think I should do?"

I shrugged. "All I know is, one of the cops has the money. Not me." Harlan stared at me, studying my face. After a long moment, he said, "Okay, Beth, have it your way." He took a deep breath, and pointed the gun at Ogilvy. "If you don't tell me where you hid the money, I'm going to shoot your damn dog."

My breath caught in my throat. Harlan always did know how to home in on my weakest point. "Please, Harlan—you can't!"

His only answer was a crooked grin as he raised the gun again.

"You damn coward! Only a first-class chicken would hurt a harmless animal!" The words seemed to burst out of their own accord.

Ogilvy doesn't have a huge vocabulary, but those words he knows, he knows well. Other than his name, and the word *sit*, most all the words he recognizes could be listed under the broad category of food. Words like *biscuit*, *steak*, and *hot dog*. Now, at the sound of the word *chicken*, Ogilvy's ears perked. Totally ignoring the gun pointed at him, he glanced first at me and then over at Harlan. I knew, of course, what he was doing. He was waiting for one of us to produce one of his favorite treats: boneless chicken.

It was such an absurd moment, I felt almost lightheaded. Ogilvy was about to die, and yet, all the silly dog could think of was: *Where's my snack?*

I turned to glare at Harlan. "You heard me," I said, "you're a damn chicken!" I emphasized that last word.

Ogilvy's eyes darted expectantly from my face over to Harlan's. He was beginning to quiver all over.

Harlan's face was red with fury, but he turned the gun back on me. "I'm a chicken, am I? I'll show you who's a chicken," he said, taking a step toward me, raising his hand.

It was too much for Ogilvy. The second Harlan moved, Ogilvy jumped on him, trying to nuzzle his jacket pockets, looking for the snack that Harlan kept mentioning. If Harlan had expected it, he might've been able to brace himself, but as it was, Ogilvy nearly knocked him down. While Harlan was trying to regain his balance, I kicked the gun out of his hand, sending it skidding across the floor.

Since Harlan was busy with Ogilvy, I had no trouble at all beating him to the gun. In fact, if Harlan had stayed where he was, I would not have had to shoot him, but after flinging Ogilvy away from him, he lunged toward me. The sound of that gun going off was deafening. And, yes, most satisfying.

It was also most satisfying to phone the police and turn Harlan over to them. As it turned out, the bullet had only grazed his left leg. When the police were putting him on the stretcher, I went over to my Christmas tree and unwrapped one of the presents. Harlan actually moaned a little louder when he saw the neat stacks of twenties inside.

He'd been right, of course. I did have the money. I'd stopped on the way to my apartment on the day of the robbery, and I'd hidden the money up in the top of my parents' unlocked garage, in a box of my old toys. My mom and dad had both been at work; they hadn't even known I'd been there. The money had been waiting for me all the time I was in prison.

I'll admit it. Ever since I got out, I'd been thinking about whether I should keep all those lovely bags of currency. As a sort of payment for the years I'd had taken from me. Harlan showing up had made up my mind. I couldn't turn him over to the police without turning over the cash, too. Besides, if I'd kept all that cash, I'd have felt like I was the same as he was.

I watched the police take him away—watched them get in their cars, carrying every single package that had been under my tree—and I had to smile. When they were all out of sight, I went into the kitchen and got Ogilvy a snack. It wasn't chicken, but it was a hot dog—another one of his favorites. "Good boy, Ogilvy, good boy," I told him.

After that, I walked out to my car and opened the trunk. Inside was a single brightly wrapped present.

Like I said, if I'd kept all the cash, I would've felt as if I were just like Harlan. Now, though, I felt more like Santa.

Toy Pincher

H. Robert Perry

H. ROBERT PERRY is a Cincinnati-based author who works as a marketing coordinator for a textbook company. His short stories have appeared in *Mean Lizard*, *Tomorrow*, *Tense Moments*, and *The Stake*. Along with his wife and infant son, Spenser, Mr. Perry is owned by a Doberman named Shai.

I became involved with the toy thief because he made the news, the television news. Or, more precisely, because I could use the phone. I wouldn't have owned a television set except that my VCR and DVD player were hooked up to it. I didn't have cable, and I lived in a valley with no television reception, so the set was never on unless I was watching videos that would make Joe Bob Briggs cringe. My job involves hours of esoteric research, from strange pointless, plotless videos, to children's fads, to technology breakthroughs online and offline. I could be watching *My Dinner With André*, *Barney's Big Adventure*, or a DTS DVD on a fifty-thousand-dollar home theater system (provided by several local dealers and one large electronics corporation), trying to distinguish subtle aural differences that would keep a stereophile newsgroup arguing for years.

But for all the movies I watched, for all the time I spent in front of a monitor writing and searching online, I never seemed to watch television. The irony lay in the fact that I was often called upon to mention *Friends*, or *Seinfeld*, or *Star Trek* in its various incarnations, or *Xena* in an article, but I never made it through an entire episode of any of them. Online served as my Cliff Notes. As for my phone skills: I had fingers.

Last Christmas I received two things that changed my television viewing habits or at least those of my household: Hobbes and Nietzsche. Hobbes and Nietzsche are my two Dobermans, puppies rescued by a local pure breed shelter and then foisted off on me because I was too slow to say no. Upon reflection, Nielson households now seem more understandable.

I had done an article on animal abuse and had come across some numbers that baffled me. I was reading reports on dogs that cost anywhere from seven hundred low-end to a couple of thousand, or more, toward the other end, and people that pushed lit cigarettes into their skin, beat them to the point of broken bones or internal hemorrhaging, or just didn't care about them. Over half of the dogs at the rescue had been malnourished. About ninety percent were untrained. Many of the owners were the same people who had a summer house they hadn't seen in ten years, owned a Jaguar they kept in their garage to show business acquaintances, or had trophy spouses and children to boast about but never cared for any of them.

Some of the abusers were crack dealers who heard rottweilers or Dobermans or Staffordshire terriers or wolf crosses were tough. Some were blue-collar workers looking to make bucks on the side by selling so-called pure breeds. Abuse flowed across demographics.

Part of my research was conducted at pure breed rescues where the lucky victims wound up, and the closest one to me was a Doberman pinscher rescue. The woman who ran it, Donna Parks, gave me about two days of her time, showing me every aspect of her business, from court time to poop scooping. I mouthed the platitude: "Call me if you ever need anything."

Donna was a library of anecdotes. She had been a trainer and a breeder for nearly thirty-five years. The rescue was an afterthought, when some of the dogs she sold came back with burns and cuts on them. When she told me about the screening process her potential adopters had to go through, adopting a child sounded easy by comparison, and she still saw the occasional dog allowed into a bad home. Most of her contempt was heaped on "backyard breeders," the fast buck crowd who'd mate anything and skimp on every step of the process.

Months later she called me and a brief discussion ensued. The next day, my house had two new owners, and a new philosophy on what made a good living environment. Hobbes and Nietzsche did not like silence. They would whimper, cry, bark, lick themselves compulsively, have total anxiety attacks unless I was watching a movie. I discovered that and was on the phone to Warner cable within the same thirty-second time span, long enough only to check the soothing qualities of the radio. It had none. My guess is the asshole who owned them previously used to turn down the volume of the television before he beat them. I don't know. They can't talk, and the rescuers don't often get complete stories for the orphans they save.

Other than the minor neurosis, Hobbes and Nietzsche were intelligent and conscientious. Housebreaking took no time (Donna gets most of the credit for that), and all of our schedules seemed to merge without conflict. I would usually work in my study for five or six hours a day, eating breakfast with them, catching a lunch snack by myself. Then we would spend an hour or two at a park. Rain kept us inside, so I'd watch movies or the occasional nature program to keep the boys happy, even though they had been watching television since about eight in the morning.

Within months, I began noticing odd occurrences: the television remote would be moved and wet, the television was on a different channel than I had put it on, there was mud on the remote, nose prints on the television screen. I set up a video camera on top of the television. It wasn't that it was difficult to figure out; I just didn't believe it. The videotape showed Hobbes and Nietzsche (they took turns) taking the remote off of the entertainment center, carrying it across the room, then hitting buttons with their paws. They weren't real good at changing channels, but they did seem to find nature shows frequently.

Remotes for the visually impaired worked better. We went through several before we found one they were comfortable with. I started checking on their viewing habits after that. Animal Planet was a big hit. The Discovery Channel. Commercials were tolerated, or ignored while one or both went out to the kitchen for a drink. I considered teaching them to use a snack dispenser that would fill a bowl with potato chips, but I figured that might be extreme. I was the proud parent of two canine couch potatoes.

We went for walks, played in a nearby park, dined on medium rare New York Strips, green beans, and twice-baked potatoes for dinner. They ate whatever I ate, a mostly balanced diet. Hobbes hit eighty-nine pounds of solid muscle, standing about thirty inches at the shoulder. Nietzsche weighed four pounds less and was two inches shorter, but his chest was broader. Both were healthy, despite the vet's protest over their diet and my misgivings about their television addiction. Eventually the need for television abated but the desire for it remained strong. I could turn it off and no one complained, but an hour later the two of them would have on some program about wildlife in Madagascar.

Eleven months after my house was taken over by the two precocious curs, Christmastime was fast approaching. It was impossible to spend time at any of the local parks: Hobbes and Nietzsche had a personal comfort thermometer that ranged from sixty-eight to seventy-six degrees Fahrenheit. Thirty degrees and wet didn't cut it. Which meant I was inside with them more frequently when I wasn't working. We had a problem.

Television does not relax me. It irritates me. Too many

commercials, too much drivel, hyperkinetic editing: I'd rather read. If there was something on I wanted to watch, Hobbes would change the channel. If I moved the remote, Nietzsche would distract me, pressing his head against my leg, staring into my eyes mournfully, while Hobbes found the remote and moved it. We watched a lot of nature shows. Finally, I explained who was master: I gave them the remote and told them I would be in my study, reading. Occasionally, during commercials I assume, one of them would check up on me.

We made it to two weeks before Christmas with short walks, more television (including one viewing of the Grinch while the remote stayed under my cushion), and a little grumbling. I was caught up on my work and shopping, so I tried to spend more quality time with the boys, wrestling, reading, even watching television. Mostly I watched them watching television. Hobbes was a channel surfer. Nietzsche was more laid-back, watching whatever Hobbes picked, growling occasionally when the channels changed too frequently.

Since television and dogs were both new to me, an epiphany of sorts hit me on the way from my study to the bathroom: Petsmart is perfect. Maybe not their prices, I almost never buy anything there, but the store is a huge heated warehouse where you can walk your dogs for an hour. What could be better, from a dog's point of view, than a car trip, a long walk in a heated environment surrounded by wonderful smells, another car trip, and possibly a snack of some sort? The boys loved it, and we tried it a couple times a week when it was cold outside. Other dogs seemed to be steady customers also, and I recognized several faces, almost as well as my dogs recognized the scents of newly discovered friends. It was the kind of place that set tails wagging, butts wiggling, and nostrils flaring.

December fifteenth, someone stole all of the toys donated to Toys for Tots, a local charity that provided needy kids with a visit from Santa. Hobbes had put on

When Animals Attack or some such Roman entertainment, and the local Fox affiliate ran the story of the toy thief every one of the two hundred commercial breaks. Same story every time, same bad sketch, same pompous tones and practiced look of concern by the anchor. I was more worried about the possibility of media violence influencing animals than I was about the stolen toys, but I considered whether there might be a story possibility in the exploits of a real-life Grinch. If caught, maybe he could use the "heart three sizes too small" defense. The story eventually was replaced by bigger and better things, though it ran at least once an evening over the next couple of days.

Three times the week before Christmas, Hobbes and Nietzsche seemed ill at ease while at their favorite store. They growled. Hair raised from neck to tail, ears up, scare-the-piss-out-of-mail-carriers angry growls. Same dog each time. Same guy each time: black shoulder length hair, sort of thin, five o'clock shadow looking dark against pale skin, maybe six feet tall, gray sweatshirt. He was owned by a little brown haired German shepherd mix who hid behind worn blue jeans, peering out between his owner's calves. I made them sit, the first two times. The third time, I made them sit and asked them what exactly was wrong. The man never noticed.

Hobbes immediately stood and pulled me over to the row with Frisbees and balls and squeaky plastic hedgehogs. I was just dense, I guess. I asked him, "The dog took something?" Nietzsche cocked his head and Hobbes's head butted me in the groin.

"Damn. Sorry. Sit. Now something about the ball?"

The dogs were now giving me looks reserved for advertisements for Buddy's Carpet, the kind I reserve for people I interview over the phone who speak English as an alien language even though they seem to use the same words an English speaker might use. Hobbes and Nietzsche began nudging all of the items up and down the row.

"You want a toy?"

The bark as I said that word was one loud, piercing comment on my inability to understand effective communication.

"Toy?"

Hobbes barked.

The wheels began turning slowly. "That man has something to do with toys?"

Nietzsche ran over and licked my hand.

"Are the two of you trying to tell me that"—I lowered my voice—"that man is the toy thief?"

Both barked once, quietly, as we shared our group secret.

"I do not believe this." We made a final lap around the store, and I watched for the accused. They led me right to him, but I kept walking out the doors and toward our car. I was sure that 911 does not like anonymous tips from people who say "my dogs told me...," so we waited inside my Toyota Tacoma extended cab, watching for the Grinch.

Ten minutes passed, ten hot, smelly minutes with panting dogs steaming up the windows and passing gas in their excitement. I wondered vaguely how 911 would respond to an emergency call with a man passed out in his car due to canine flatulence. My head cleared a little when the dogs pushed their heads against the passenger windows and I eased mine down a crack; then Hobbes turned and grabbed my arm. I backed the truck out and drove behind the baby-poop-brown primered Camaro the suspect climbed into. Pulling up to the curb fifty feet past him, I jotted down his license number.

I'd like to relate the heroic story of following him home, catching him with the goods, and overpowering him with the help of my fearless canine companions. That didn't happen. We did follow him home. Upon driving past his Camaro and seeing hordes of Beanie Babies and Tickle Me Elmos tucked in the backseat, I figured the police were better equipped than we to handle the arrest.

The police caught him, from my tip, and his house had a smattering of the stolen toys, along with enough electronics to stock a Best Buy. So he went to jail, I wrote an article, and Hobbes and Nietzsche were awarded honorary badges, detective grade. I don't fuss at them as much anymore for watching television, and they occasionally let me pick the program. I'm thinking of teaching them music appreciation.

The Fencing Crib

Mark Graham

MARK GRAHAM was born in Philadelphia in 1970 and has spent most of his life in the Lehigh Valley of Pennsylvania. He is the great-great-great-grandson of a Philadelphia policeman, and he briefly served as constable in Lehigh County. Moreover, he is a medieval and religious studies scholar. His novels (featuring Philadelphia police detective Wilton McCleary) include *The Killing Breed* and *The Resurrectionist*.

Christmas was not a good time for a policeman. The holiday season of 1870 was no exception. The festive mood manifested itself less in a spirit of giving than in a spirit of drinking. Philadelphia was perhaps less rowdy than some other cities, but there were always gangs of mangy-looking belznickels and mummers, invariably intoxicated, who roamed the streets at night. They did little but drink and beg, but they were a nuisance. I'd already had to walk one back to the station house that night.

I was glad for the respite. The streets were slick with ice, and the mercury was low enough to numb my limbs.

It was only three days before Christmas Eve. I would spend that night, like this one, on the beat.

It could have been worse. There weren't many folks out on the streets in this weather. The citizens weren't particularly rowdy either. These folks didn't have much to celebrate. It was five years after the war and they still weren't able to vote in a city election. Or hold a job other than the most menial sort.

This was the Seventh Ward, the colored section of the city. And the most dangerous beat any copper could have. I'd gotten my assignment courtesy of Sergeant Walter Duffy. It was my punishment for refusing to collect the usual bribes for him from the bawdy houses and blind pigs on my previous beat.

But tonight I didn't mind the Seventh Ward. It was mighty quiet. Even the black and tan bawdy houses had their red lights doused.

The only thing in the street with me was a stray dog. The two of us were fairly well acquainted. The dog and I saw each other practically every night, usually just before dawn. Perhaps he had his own regular beat, just like I did. Now he was poking his dirty nose in an even dirtier pile of rotten meat.

I looked up and down the street. The brick row houses were like giant pickets of a fence that stretched from one river to the other. I felt like the dog and I were in the same pen, just rooting for different garbage.

He was a vicious-looking cur—a gnarled, filthy mutt. His hide was covered with scars from numerous scraps. He seemed as old as the street itself, his viciousness honed through years of hunger and deprivation. Not too unlike the two-legged creatures occupying the same street.

As soon as he saw me, he shambled across the cobbles and headed toward me.

I had a piece of mutton ready for him, just in case. The dog was friendly enough for a stray. Over the past few weeks he'd gotten used to me. But he never took any food I gave him, even if I threw it in his direction.

The stray began to follow me, like he usually did. There was an air of perpetual hunger around him. I wasn't sure if he fancied the mutton in my hand or the hand itself.

Tossing the mutton in the gutter, I turned around to see if he took the bait.

He didn't. Like all the other nights, he ignored the

morsel I offered. Instead he followed me. As I proceeded I could hear his claws scrape against the icy pavement.

Frustrated, I said over my shoulder, "Get lost, you." I was almost ready to club the thing. If it was too stupid to take my handouts, the hell with it.

Then I heard a sound coming from a half square away. It was a human sound. I could hear crinoline swishing even at that distance. That told me it was a woman.

She had a bundle slung over her shoulder and was walking hurriedly. I had the feeling something was a little queer about it. Our handbook's fifty-first rule said: *Question anyone carrying bundles at night.* Especially when they're white women wandering through the lowest negro district in town.

Ladies didn't go out for a stroll at that dead hour. Not any I'd ever met. But some other kinds of women did.

I didn't figure her for a sneak thief. Not in this neighborhood. The people didn't have much worth stealing. But I was bored and I hadn't made a good pinch in a few days. I followed her.

Whenever she came to an alley or a cul-de-sac she stopped for a moment and peered into the shadows there, like she was looking for a certain spot. Once she halted like that and stood very still. Quickly, I ducked behind a broken dray that rested against the curb. My unfriendly companion was still wandering around the street, sniffing the gutter beside me. I wondered why he stuck with me. After a pause, the woman began walking again.

A few squares away from the colored cemetery, just at the limits of my beat, I saw her dart between two ramshackle wooden hovels. The buildings were like the ancient trees you see in bone orchards—hoary and bloated from feeding on the dead.

I stayed where I was, trying to decide what to do next. I looked east, toward the Delaware, and saw the first intimations of dawn peer through the sky like those purple blossoms you see hiding in the grass. It was a pretty scene. I got so caught up in it that I forgot for just a moment where I was. Then I pictured that bundle and my curiosity got the better of me.

Taking care to mind the ice, I made my way over to the alley, the cur in tow.

At the mouth of the alley, I could see the woman placing her bundle on the frost-covered earth.

Then she saw me.

In that moment I got a good look at her face, as well as the rest of her. Her eyes widened at the sight of me, like I was as ugly as the cur standing behind me. Or maybe it was my harness—the blue coat and the star—that was ugly to her.

Then she pulled something from out of her coat. We were close enough to each other that I could tell it was a single-shot derringer.

It was aimed at my head.

Before I could open my mouth, several things happened in quick succession.

The stray inexplicably began to snarl at the woman. Then, to my astonishment, he darted between my legs to attack her. Surprised, I took a step back, a little too quickly, and slid on the ice.

That was when the derringer went off. I heard a loud noise, but I wasn't sure if it was the shot or my head cracking against the pavement.

It seemed to me like I was stunned for just a few seconds. But it could've been minutes. When I got to my feet the woman was gone. The sound of the shot must've scared the dog off. He was nowhere to be seen.

I owed the cur a whole carcass of mutton. He'd saved my life.

Rubbing my head, I took a peek around the corner. A door slammed in the distance. There was a hack, two squares away. Its horse was starting off down South Street. I shouted for the driver to stop, but he probably couldn't hear me with all the racket from the wheels and hooves. Just as it turned a corner I caught its number on the side: 56.

As I replaced my cap on my throbbing head, I noticed a nearby pile of hay. It was slumped against a set of stable doors. There was something sticking halfway out of the mound.

The woman's bundle.

My hands closed around the cloth. There was something inside, something soft. I pulled it out, laid it on the dirty cobblestones, and unwrapped the contents.

An infant's face stared at me without seeing me. I tried to close the eyes but the lids were stiff. I touched its cheeks and patted its head. It was a girl. Had been. She was dead now.

As soon as I got to the station house I wrote a report about the murdered child. There was no question in my mind that the woman killed her. I hadn't seen any bruises around her throat. The child was probably smothered.

Sergeant Duffy told me he'd forward it on to the dicks. But I knew what that meant. It was destined for the circular file. This was not the only infant that had been dumped. I'd found more than my share thrown in lots or tossed down privies. Unwanted bastards, nuisances to be removed like so much trash. No one much cared if colored folks, like the ones on my beat, killed their children off.

This case was different. The woman wasn't colored. She'd been dressed a little too fancy for the Seventh Ward.

And the baby wasn't colored either.

When I got home that night I was still thinking on these things. I lay in bed without lighting the lamp. I watched the fires of the oil works from my window and sniffed the kerosene fumes that floated past my thin curtains. My eyes stayed open. If I closed them I saw the child staring at me. I tried to look into the girl's eyes to see the image of her killer. I read somewhere that was possible. The only face I saw there was my own.

Then I pictured the woman's face. White, plain, haggard. Forty-five, fifty years of age. A mole on her left cheek. Gray hair underneath a black bonnet, tied under her chin with a bow of crepe. There had been crepe trim on her dress, too. I smelled that stuff from where I'd been standing. Crepe has a strong odor to it. Not a pleasant one. It usually isn't worn unless someone has died. That and the black gloves and lusterless black skirts she'd worn spelled mourning to me. For what or for whom I didn't know.

The woman's face was leering at me now, taunting me just like the child was begging my help.

Sometimes the child seemed to speak to me. Not with words really. Ideas popped into my head from somewhere else.

Why me? How come you let her get away? Are you going to forget about me?

I felt my fingers on her eyelids, tried to close them again, but they wouldn't go down. The stare was merciless. There was so much fear in it, the fear of being forgotten.

Find that woman, the child was saying. *Find her for me.*

I kept my eyes open and watched the petroleum flames leap into the sky.

On the twenty-third of December I spotted hack number fifty-six at the Market Street terminus. The hackman had his back turned to me. He was adjusting the halter on his mare. I tapped him on the shoulder. The way he whirled around made me think he was going to slug me.

His face was swollen with too much lager beer. Burnside whiskers made his jowls look even bigger than they were. A frowzy, broad-brimmed hat was tilted back to reveal a forehead damp with sweat. Dust coated his vest and pantaloons.

"Now what?" he asked truculently.

"You the driver of this hack?"

"That's right."

"Name?"

"What is this, anyway? I ain't done nothin'. I ain't been overchargin'! That old hag make a complaint? Listen, I took her a total of twenty-six squares and I took the straightest route. That's over two miles so I got every right to charge the extra fifty cents! She don't like it let her ride the streetcars."

"Cool it. I wanna ask you about something else."

He squinted, shifting his gaze from left to right. Then he said, "Hey, look. Can we take this somewheres else? It ain't good for business to have a copper breathin' down my neck."

We nearly got run over by an omnibus as we crossed the street. The market sheds provided a little relief from the chill winds. I planted myself on the edge of a grocer's table and said again to the driver, "What's your name?"

My club was in my hand. He swished some tobacco juice in his mouth.

"Cowles. Bill."

"Bill, a few nights ago you picked up a fare at the corner of Eighth and South. Early in the morning. Sunup. A woman in mourning. You remember her don't you?"

"What would I be doin' in darkyville at that hour?"

"I'm asking you."

"I don't know what you're talkin' about." His finger crept into his mouth and picked at his teeth. "Listen, I gotta get back to my hack."

He started to walk away. Before he could make another move I poked my club in his face. I left it there propping up a couple of his chins.

"I think you know damn well what I'm talking about. I was there."

"Please, officer. Please. I ain't done nothin' wrong."

"I don't wanna have to hurt you, Bill." I was telling the truth.

"I done what they told me to do! I don't unnerstand . . ."

"What? What did they tell you to do?"

He took a gulp. Down went his tobacco juice.

"They, they . . ." His eyes darted back and forth, like someone was watching him.

I took my fingers, stuck them in his nostrils, and yanked up. He gave a yip and jumped backward. My fingers dug into his flaccid chest.

"They told me not to say nothin'. About her, about where I took her."

"You know her then?"

"No, no. I just took her where she told me."

"Where?"

"Up Eighth. I let her off on Chestnut. I didn't see where she went."

"Don't give me that."

"Don't hit me! I ain't done nothin'. They didn't want me seein' where she lived. They told me to keep my trap shut if anybody came askin' around. They told me if I didn't, I'd take a dip in the river."

Without wasting a breath I asked him, "Who's they?"

His eyes popped out. Sweat trickled through his whiskers.

"C'mon, Bill. I don't wanna have to take you to the sweatbox."

"All right, all right. I'll tell ya. Just don't hurt me anymore."

I waited for him to pull himself together.

"A copper told me. I don't know what his name was. But I think he was a dick."

Now it was my turn to sweat.

"What did he look like, Bill?"

"Kinda big fella. Mustache like yours, but oiled. Salt-and-pepper it was. And, uh, I noticed one of his eyes looked at me while the other one didn't, like maybe it was fake or something."

"Dandruff on his jacket?"

"What's that?"

"Flakes of skin, from his hair?"

"Yeah! He didn't have much hair though."

"You're doing fine, Bill. Now, how much did he pay you to keep quiet?"

Cowles looked at the ground and said, "You ain't gonna make me give it back are ya?"

"Not if you tell me the truth. How much was it?"

"Ten cans."

"That sounds about right." I took my nightstick out of his face.

"Now get back to your hack. And you never spoke to me, understand?"

He nodded and got out of there.

I still didn't know where the woman lived. Chestnut was the busiest street, day and night. She could have gone anywhere from there. But there was someone who could point me in the right direction.

From the hackman's description I twigged that the copper who'd paid him his graft was Michael "Evil Eye" Seibert. He wasn't a dick like Cowles thought. Just a special officer, which was close enough. I knew him from my ward. He and I worked together busting up the Schuylkill River gangs the year before. Seibert had been a coward and a drunkard back then and he still was. After nearly two years as a roundsman he decided to buy himself a promotion. He was related by marriage to the cousin of a fellow in the Gas Ring. The special officer badge had been a bargain at five hundred. As a special officer he was about standard. It didn't take much gumption to round out buzzers from a depot or recover stolen property from warehouses that you partially owned.

* * *

I found Special Officer Michael Seibert with his back teeth afloat in a lager beer saloon near the central station house. It was the afternoon of the Sabbath, when all saloons were supposed to be closed for business. But you wouldn't see the police enforcing that law here.

This particular establishment was a "good" saloon, according to the blue bellies. If they called it "good," that meant they could get free drinks from the owner. That made them overlook things like faro tables in the back, or opening on a Sunday in violation of the excise laws.

The German beer slinger didn't take me for a copper. I was in civilian clothes.

"Nickel," the German said without looking at me.

"I'm not drinking."

I had a bottle of rye stuffed in my coat. When I got to Seibert's table I put it on the top and said, "Crack a bottle with me, Mike?"

One eye glanced at a space a few inches from my head while the other stared right at me. Both of them were glazed with drink. His large head rolled from side to side like it had an ocean inside it. Tiny flakes settled on his shoulders. Some of the free soup that came with the drinks had gotten stuck in his mustache.

"Who the hell are you, friend?"

"You don't recognize me, Mike? I'm miffed. I really am. Tell me you don't remember our night together underneath the Chestnut Street bridge last year. With the Rangers. The night you jumped into the Schuylkill and left me alone to hold off those plug-ugly pieces of shit. I can still feel that broken arm I got when it rains."

He leaned over the table like he was going to be sick.

"Hiya, McCleary."

It came out like a groan.

"I see you do remember, Mikey. Took me almost half an hour to polish those Rangers off. And you remember what happened after that? How I didn't tell the captain you turned coward and left me to take your whacks for you? How I even told him what a great job you'd done, clubbing 'em left and right? I think you got a commendation for that one."

"Yeah, I remember, you paddy son of a bitch."

"Now, now, Mikey. Don't get personal."

"Why'd ya do it, huh? Why din't ya blow the whistle on me?"

The words were slurred, mumbled.

"Here, Mikey. Have one on me. Have a barrel full."

I poured the rye into his beer stein, filling a good part of it. I pretended to take a swig from it myself saying, "Here's at you!"

After he slurped it up, he bit down on his lip and inhaled. "That's mighty fine stuff, Mack. Mighty fine."

"Have another."

He was good and soused after ten minutes. The rye must have mixed well with the laudanum I put in it. Seibert started chuckling at things: me, the cig between his fingers, the room.

"How's the detective business, Mikey? I hear you've been a bad boy. Threatening cabmen and the like. Is that any way for an officer of the law to behave?"

"What you talkin' 'bout?"

"I'm talkin' about the fella who picked up some old mab on Eighth and South after she left a dead baby sticking out of a hay pile."

"I don't know nothin' 'bout it."

"Sure you don't. You're a good detective."

"S'right. I do what they tell me to do."

"Sure you do. They tell you to lean on the cabman, make sure he doesn't say anything about her . . . what's her name again?"

"Lena."

"Lena, that's right. They tell you to make sure he

doesn't say anything about Lena and you do like they say, right?"

"S'right. Sergeant Duffy don't want no trouble. She pays her dues."

Seibert's head slumped onto the table. Drool trickled from his mouth.

I yanked both ends of his mustache. He turned to look at me, one cheek still pressed against the table.

"She paid me good. So did the sergeant."

"That so? Lena and Duffy are pals?"

"Nah, nah. She just pays him rent, that's all. I used to do the collections before November."

"I know, I know. That's why I came to talk to you. Sergeant Duffy wanted me to bring her something."

"He got you doin' the collections this month?"

"Yeah, and you know what? I forgot where her crib was! You wouldn't happen to remember where she . . . ?"

"I just been there last night! Duffy wanted me . . . keep a man there. Told me some copper was nosin' around with that cabman. One o' them square ones."

"Guess there are one or two of them still around."

Seibert snorted and said, "I'll hafta take . . . care of him. When I find out who he is."

"Have another one, Mikey. You got a man over there now?"

"Yeah . . . but he'll let you in to get the . . . rent."

"Well, can you tell me where to find her?"

"Sure, Mack. She's right on . . . corner of Seventh and Sansom. You give her my regards."

"I will do just that, Mikey."

His face was resting on the tabletop as I took my leave.

Walking my beat that night gave me time to think.

I had never heard of this Lena but she had to be pulling in the pieces, whatever her game was. Sergeant Walter Duffy didn't take graft from ragpickers. Big money was involved. They would kill me if I got in the way. I was a copper, but business was business. I would have to fly low.

The cabman must have peached on me. The scare I put in him had been just enough to keep his description of me vague. Otherwise Seibert would have been wise to me. I wondered if Cowles had seen the girl looking out of my head. Maybe he heard her saying, *He's going to get her. No matter what.*

I didn't like the idea of a bull guarding her house. It wasn't that I was afraid of a brawl. I just didn't want him to get a good look at my mug. There would be trouble then, from people bigger than he was.

I tried to take my mind off all my trouble by unwrapping the bone I'd brought. I hadn't seen the stray since we'd first met Lena in the alleyway.

Or maybe I had seen him, but just hadn't noticed, because I hadn't bothered to really look.

I thought on how many strays I'd seen in my five years as a copper, and how many mad ones I'd shot dead. Starved, ragged creatures—a whole society of them coursing through the streets and back alleys. You saw the miserable things so often you tended to ignore them. They became invisible, shadows flitting on the edge of the city.

It was easy to ignore creatures like them. They merely had to be contained, in a place like the Seventh Ward, a prison of sorts. I knew what it was like to be imprisoned for being nothing more than what I was. I'd been a prisoner of war in Andersonville. I became acquainted with misery there. And evil. And the bitter sting of knowing that the rest of the world didn't care if we lived or died.

The irony of my position now was not lost on me. Here I was in the Seventh Ward, sent by the city not so much to protect the population there as to contain them. My club was supposed to be like the pine walls of Andersonville, hedging them in, where they couldn't hurt respectable society. Let the swells prey on them in any way they could, but the moment they returned the favor, they were dealt with mercilessly.

That was the way our modern, nineteenth-century world worked. But I still took notice of the strays, just the same. I didn't feel the need to pretend they were invisible.

As dawn broke across the sky, I spotted the dog. He was curled up beneath a parked wagon. When he saw me, he got stiffly to his feet and clambered over. For a few moments we stared at each other. I held the bone out to him, urging him to take it in my gentlest, most soothing voice.

The dog thrust his tail between his legs and backed away from me.

Annoyed at being rejected by the stupid beast yet again, I threw the bone at him, aiming for his snout. It hit him dead-on.

Then the stray did a curious thing. Instead of fleeing from me, he stood his ground. With his eyes on me the whole time, he took the bone into his mouth, gingerly, and went back under the wagon. His eyes followed me as I walked away.

The next day, Christmas Eve, I went for her. On my way over there the murdered child's face was staring at me from the storefront windows.

Get her. Get Lena. That was what she was telling me to do. There was only one way to get her voice out of my head.

The Chestnut/Walnut car left me off at Eighth. I walked the rest of the way to Sansom, probably retracing Lena's own route.

The house was a three-story, redbrick row house with a dormer poking out of the slate shingled roof.

It had to be that one. A blue belly across the street had his gleems on it. He hadn't seen me yet. He looked like a reserve officer, one of Sergeant Duffy's thugs.

Circling the square, out of the guard's sight, I came to a rear court in back of the house.

The back door was locked, of course. Ash barrels and milk bottles were piled up around it, like a barrier. Some crates were thrown beside the neighboring door. I stood very still for a moment. No noise came from the house that I could hear.

The handle of my revolver broke a pane of glass right above the doorknob. I reached in and unfastened the lock.

I took a deep breath, hoping she wasn't at home.

Inside, there were smells of chicken broth. I was in the kitchen. Milk bottles were piled everywhere. The stovepipe leaked a little smoke. It hung in the air like mist on a pond.

The place seemed empty.

I went through the hall and into the parlor. It was furnished tastefully but not extravagantly. Yellowed lace curtains trailed to some threadbare Turkish carpets scattered on the floor. A few prints from Currier and Ives hung framed, all on the same level. Above a mirror was a motto. It said: "Safe in the arms of Jesus." A crude figure cuddled an infant in one arm and held a shepherd's staff in the other. I almost laughed at the irony. It made a good impression on her callers, I suppose.

A clock ticked on a false mantel draped with a dusty valance. The parlor's center table was decorated with a miniature cedar tree. Interspersed in the branches were tiny wax candles, resting in tin holders to prevent them from igniting the tree. Dangling from the branches were pieces of colored glass in the shapes of stars, fruits, and flowers. At the base of the table were a number of boxes, wrapped in white paper.

It looked like a typical Christmas scene. The only thing needed to top it off would be a warm, glowing hearth. As it was, the fireplace was cold and drafty.

She had certainly outdone herself in making her parlor cheery and festive. But there was something artificial about the whole scene. As if everything were arranged out of a sense of habit, almost perfunctorily.

Picking up one of the presents, I shook the box. There was nothing in it. It was the same with all the others. They were empty decorations.

Through the curtains I could see the copper across the street with his eyes on the front door. Nobody was coming yet.

For a moment I thought of walking out the way I came. What was I going to do to her anyway? How could I possibly prove that she killed the infant? She certainly wouldn't confess to me.

But if she were paying "rent" to the police that meant she was dirty, somehow. All I needed to do was find out what her game was.

I took another peep out the window. A figure walked past the copper on the other side of the street, crossed, and headed for the front door. A veil covered her face. Her body was draped in layers of dull black crinoline. Lena was coming home.

As I turned back to the parlor, wondering what I should do, where I should go, I heard a baby crying. It sounded like it came from upstairs.

By the time I heard the key turn in the lock I'd made it to the second floor. The narrow hallway had one door closed at the end.

From behind it, I heard wailing from many infants.

There were sounds from downstairs, kitchen noises. Lena was making her luncheon.

I got closer to the door, moving quietly. I opened it.

The room inside was a little larger than a closet, but not much. Paint was peeling off the walls. On the wooden floor were piles of mouse droppings. There was barely any light. Heavy drapes covered the small window. It was frigidly cold inside.

The draft did nothing to alleviate the putrid stench.

In that room were six cribs, with a total of nine infants in them. All of the babies were naked. A few were crying. Eight of them were white. The other looked mulatto. Two seemed asleep. I nudged them just to make sure. The first one swiped at my finger with her tiny hand. The other one right next to her didn't move. His chest rose slowly, as if he were struggling for breath. I rocked him back and forth on the soiled linen. The child's flesh was covered with bedsores.

It reminded me of the kennel at the pound, where they toss strays for a while until they kill them all to make room for the next batch.

I'd heard about these places, knew they existed. But respectable people didn't talk about things like this. It was better to ignore them.

A baby farm.

To me, it seemed more like a fencing crib, where sneak thieves go to get rid of the goods they've stolen.

Here the daughters of society got rid of their mistakes and saved themselves from shame. Instead of giving them cash like a fence would, Lena gave them the chance to be respectable again.

If a young lady got in trouble, she could solve that trouble here. First the mother-to-be suddenly got sick. She was quarantined until she delivered. Then they dumped the newborn at a place like this. The masher or parent paid for the child's upkeep for a few months, just long enough to assuage the conscience. Once they were gone, the children could be easily forgotten, left to rot in their own peculiar prison. When the weekly payments of three dollars stopped, the child got sick and died. There was no sense in keeping it when it was worth nothing.

The baby farm was a nice game. I figured these bastard children were sons and daughters of some of Philadelphia's biggest bugs, the ones with reputations that couldn't be tarnished, theirs or their daughters'. That would explain why the police were in on it. I bet Lena was pulling in the pieces.

The door opened behind me.

I turned to meet Lena's gaze.

"You!"

She remembered me.

"How'd you get in here? How'd you get past . . ."

"Not important now, Lena. What you should be asking is how are you going to get out of this fix you're in."

You could barely hear us over the noise from the cribs.

"I done nothing wrong. I swear."

"Sure you have. You smothered a little girl to death and stuck her in a hay pile. You're letting another one die right here. Didn't the girl's father pay up last week?"

"You can't prove nothin'."

Her sallow face was twitching now. A tear glistened on her cheek. I wasn't moved.

I took a look at the nine bawling infants, half-buried in their own filth. All of them became the little one in the bundle, staring at me. They were saying: *Get her.*

"That's murder, Lena. Infanticide. Not to mention popping your derringer off at me. You're gonna love Cherry Hill. You might get a cage all to yourself."

Then she held back her head and laughed.

"All right! Go ahead. Take me to the station house. See what happens."

"I'll do just that, you heartless bitch."

I was aching to put a blue pill right through her neck. I settled for prodding her out the door, the revolver trained on her back. I planned on sending someone back to take care of the children once we got to the station house.

We walked right out the front door, past the reserve thug across the street. I was careful to stroke my mustache, making sure my hand obscured my face. He must have wondered how I got in the house without him seeing me. He must have thought about it for a good ten seconds before his brain got overtaxed. A square away I saw him still standing there.

Lena was a good girl. She walked by me nice and steady, like she was my lady and we were out for a stroll.

I decided to take her on the streetcar to the central station house. We walked back up Eighth toward the stop. Before we reached it, she said to me, "You don't know who I am, do you?"

"A killer."

She snorted and said, "A lady in business. And I got some friends. You'd be surprised, the friends I got."

"I'm sure I would be."

"You think they're gonna let you put me in the hatch? Uh-uh. 'Cause I'm not going down without taking them with me. They know that. They don't want the names of their little girls in the paper. They'd do just about anything to stop that from happening. That means keeping me out of the chokey."

"Back home at your fencing crib? Getting rid of the goods?"

"I provide a service, that's all. For which I am paid. When payment ceases, so does the service."

We were on Chestnut, two squares from the stop. I could see the horses pulling the green streetcar through the slush. They were just turning the corner. For a moment, we halted.

"What's the point of taking me in? You know I'll get off. You know the captain's one of my friends. And others above him. They can step on you like a roach. And they will. I hope I'm there to watch."

The car was getting closer. I could hear the gong ringing for the stop. The harness jingled against the horses' hide.

She was right. There was no point in it. They would see to it that she wasn't charged. Too many reputations were at stake. No one cared about bastard children. Children died all the time. I was the only witness. They could rig it to swing her way. I'd seen them do it before.

I felt weak and small. I felt like nothing.

I closed my eyes and saw the little child's face, staring at me.

I heard the horses' hooves clattering, just a couple rods away.

Then I opened my eyes. I looked to the left. Lena was smirking at me. I looked to the right. The streetcar was about to rush by.

A crowd of people were running to catch it. They ran around us, shielding us from view for a brief second. I could hear the prattle of the passengers, the horses snorting.

I did what I did.

Lena fell out into the street, right in the path of the on-coming car. She was pulled under the horses and whiffle-tree and dragged for a square until the brakes kicked in. By the time the car came to a stop there wasn't much of her left intact.

People screamed in horror. Someone shouted for the police as I went off in the opposite direction.

I wasn't worried about what would happen to me. I have friends, too. You'd be surprised, the friends I have.

On the beat that night I met up with the stray again. I heard him before I saw him. When I turned around he was there, poised on the pavement, waiting expectantly.

He accepted a steak I'd purchased for him. But this time I didn't have to toss it into the street. The dog walked over to me slowly and snatched the meat from my hand.

As he devoured his Christmas feast, I ran my hand over his back, feeling the gangly bones underneath. His hunger was palpable. Now I understood the varieties of that hunger. He craved my touch as much as the steak. The stray's tail started flitting back and forth.

While the dog licked his chops, I patted his mangled ears and thanked him for saving my life. My words were meant for something beyond him and myself.

That night I watched the fires at the oil works again. I sniffed the kerosene fumes and they were like perfume to me. When I closed my eyes I saw darkness. Just darkness.

Red Shirt and
Black Jacket

Virginia Lanier

VIRGINIA LANIER lives in southeast Georgia with her husband, Hoss. Her first novel, *Death in Bloodhound Red* (marking the debut of Jo Beth Sidden), was nominated for an Agatha and a Macavity—and won the Anthony. Ms. Lanier has completed another novel about Jo Beth and her bloodhounds—and she is planning a new series.

I stepped from the van into a penetrating cold wind. It was an unseasonably chilly day in southeast Georgia. We usually had a few days like this in late January and early February, but not a week before Christmas with carols reverberating in our ears and a Santa in every mall. A northeaster was blowing between eighteen and twenty-five mph.

I had donned my bright Day-Glo orange-colored rescue suit and was fully protected from the cold and wind. I attached the long leads to Caesar's harness, then Mark Anthony's, stepped aside, and watched them bail out of their cages with unrestrained enthusiasm. They are two highly trained, man-trailing bloodhounds from my kennel. I tucked items into my zippered pockets and attached a quart water bottle. Jasmine Jones parked her van behind mine.

I watched her unload. We wore identical suits. My hair is a mousy brown. Her black tresses artfully hugged her scalp and complemented her long regal neck. She is African-American with skin one shade lighter than milk chocolate. I'm pale, never tan, and look like the girl next door after a bad night.

I hired and trained her in man-trailing, search-and-rescue, and drug searches. She lives beside me in a garage apartment and we are close friends.

Jasmine unloaded Ashley and Miz Melanie and secured them to the van. She smiled and started toward me. I met her halfway.

"For right now we'll leave the backpacks here."

"Right. Aren't you taking your gun?" Her holster was fastened over her rescue suit.

"Never leave home without it." I patted my left breast. "Move yours inside your suit. The dispatcher mentioned shots were fired. We're out in front if we man-trail. I don't want the perps to know we're carrying, might keep us from being used as target practice."

"What do you know so far?" She was placing items in the pockets of her suit.

I glanced across the empty parking lot and saw Sheriff Philip Scroggins emerge from the double door of the Suwannee Swifty convenience store. He spotted us and waved.

"Have you ever met Sheriff Scroggins?" I asked.

"Last June, when the Shop 'n' Go was hit. You were busy with the seminar."

"Right, I'd forgotten. Brace yourself. Here he comes."

"Oh, dis ol' gal don't have to fret 'bout being bear-hugged," she drawled, parodying southern mush-mouth. "I be duh wrong color for dat!"

I examined her guileless countenance and saw a hint of a smile on her lips.

"It's getting to where I can't take you out in public," I complained. "Behave yourself."

We lifted the sagging yellow crime scene tape and ducked under.

Sheriff Philip Scroggins was sixty-five, bald, and almost as wide as he was tall. He was five feet four and weighed over two hundred pounds. He had been my father's friend and was now mine. His booming voice was always a shock to the senses.

"Jo Beth, darlin', how are you?" he bellowed, grabbing me around my waist and lifting me a foot off the ground.

"Not breathing," I grunted. "Put me down . . . please?"

He complied, then grabbed Jasmine.

"Jasmine, my beauty! I'm so glad to see you!" He held her aloft and turned two complete circles before releasing her.

The shocked expression on her face made me start giggling, which I tried to cover with a fake fit of coughing.

He thundered an apology. "Me carrying on like this, while a good woman was murdered in there a little over an hour ago. I'm ashamed of myself."

He contemplated the building and turned back to face us.

"Who died?" I asked.

We were in Collins, the county seat of Gilsford County. It was only twenty miles to Balsa City, my hometown, and I knew a lot of people here.

"Mrs. Walter Pearson, only fifty-seven years old. A nice widow woman with two grown sons." He looked pensive. "Who expects to die during a robbery on Main Street at nine in the morning?" He sighed. "Sergeant Lyons is driving the sons home now. He'll be back shortly."

I didn't know her. "Any witnesses?"

"I think we're gonna get lucky on this one, Jo Beth. I hope we have a credible witness and one of the perps lost his cap inside the store."

My pulse quickened. We had a chance.

"The cap was bagged and not handled by anyone?" I inquired, trying to mask my anxiety.

Some deputies and bystanders will finger a scent item, searching for a name—or worse, pass it around like a collection plate. This contaminates the scent article with other people's scent.

"Rest easy honey, Lyons was the first officer on the scene. He found the witness and bagged the cap before the ambulance attendants arrived. Your scene isn't too contaminated either. The only ones who went inside were me, Lyons, and the ambulance attendants."

Deputy Sergeant Tom Lyons and I were smiling enemies. He hates my smart mouth and feminist ways, and I despise the way he talks about women and mistreats his prisoners.

"Where's the witness?" I was anxious to get started.

"He's sitting in my squad car. Come on over and I'll introduce you."

The three of us walked over to his car. Scroggins opened the door and nodded at me. I leaned down and saw a small black boy who was huddled in the far corner of the backseat. He was wrapped in a blanket and was clutching its folds under his chin. His eyes were showing too much white and his small hands were shaking. He stared at me.

"Hi," I said awkwardly. "I'll be right back."

I straightened, closed the door gently, and glared at Scroggins.

"Where's his mother? He should be taken home!"

"I agree," he said quietly, "but so far he hasn't remembered his last name, and I'm certainly not going to let a pile of people line up and try to recognize him. How do I know that one of the perps isn't out there in the crowd standing around watching? Just a look at his face would traumatize the kid and we'd never get anything.

"He spoke a few words to Lyons when he found him in the store, then he clammed up, and started shaking. There were two black perps, and one lost his cap. They both had guns. One fired a shot in his direction when he spotted him peeking around the ice-cream case. He's got a right to be shaken up. His name is Malahki, and he's nine years old. I think this calls for a woman's touch so I'll leave you to it."

Sheriff Scroggins squared his shoulders, marched off, and left it to us.

I huddled with Jasmine and spoke softly.

"Which dog do you prefer? I'm going to put two back in their cages. We're going to do this search by the book. No court appointed attorney is going to question the use of two dogs."

"I'll work Ashley, but why don't I put them back while you question the kid? It'll save time." She sensed the way the wind was blowing.

"Nope, Malahki is all yours. Cuddle and mother him. After he calms down, get all you can. I'll wait by the vans."

She looked askance at my suggestion.

"I've never cuddled a kid in my life," she stated succinctly, forcing the words through barely opened lips. "Why me, and not you?"

I used my best mush-mouth drawl.

" 'Cause Honey Chile, dis time *you* be the right color!"

I left her to it.

When I walked to the van I found both braces of bloodhounds with their leads twisted together. As I untangled them I decided to work Caesar. When I commanded Mark Anthony to load up, he sprang into his cage not knowing his day's outing was canceled. The same with Miz Melanie. When they discovered they were being left behind, they would moan and groan.

Bloodhounds love to trail. They enjoy searching for an illusive scent among many, many thousands of others. Every step we take we drop thousands of tiny skin particles, lint, and dust; all impregnated with our body odor which is unique. No two people smell the same. When a bloodhound is presented with an article that has been worn by one person they can lock onto the scent and follow.

However, the present strong wind had me worried.

The ideal scent trailing is on a damp windless day with high humidity. The odor drops to the ground and hovers nearby. On days such as this, we could be searching over twenty to fifty feet away from the actual route the perp took. Hell, it could be blown into the next county by now, who knew?

Our sense of smell is infinitesimal compared to a bloodhound's. Many experts claim it can be a million or more times greater. So we humans train them, teach them manners and to follow orders, then let them drag us around. We can only hope that they are following the right scent. We certainly can't tell.

I taught myself from books several years ago, trained the hounds, then other handlers. I mostly used a brace of bloodhounds, meaning two. I have strong shoulders, and both of my arms are probably slightly longer than they should be. Controlling two dogs weighing over a hundred pounds apiece is not for the fainthearted, believe me.

Bloodhounds are the only breed of dogs whose testimony is considered in a court of law. I know, I know, times are changin', and soon other breeds will be allowed if they can pass the test of having the right criteria. Still, bloodhound owners point to this law that has been on the books for over a hundred years with great pride. The upstarts may claim the ability, but they can never match our long history in court cases.

The rules for bloodhound testimony are very specific. Each owner has to prove his or her man-trailer is AKC registered and has had successful experience in actual man-trailing. Their finds have to be documented and proven. The dog also has to be reliable and there must be supporting evidence. Every defense attorney picks at these threads and tries to unravel their evidential worth.

As of this day and as far as I know, the laws of Georgia do not exclude the evidence if one handler works two bloodhounds. The new proposed procedure would be one bloodhound and one human trainer. Seventeen other states now have passed this new provision into law. I know an ACLU lawyer upstate who is working to get the new law passed, as I stand here. I have no reservations about this one-on-one, especially for beginners, either human or canine. I would also like to note that the aforementioned lawyer lost a previous major case because a good ol' boy did everything right with three bloodhounds and fried his ass in court.

I couldn't take the chance in a murder investigation, so Jasmine and I would work one-on-one. The law might have already passed without my knowledge and ignorance of the law is no excuse.

"Well, Sweet Thang, how's tricks? Getting any lately?"

I'd recognize that voice on the dark side of the moon.

"Deputy Sergeant Lyons, I'll make this statement only once." I enunciated each word slowly. "My name is Jo Beth Sidden. You may call me Jo Beth, Ms. Sidden, or hey you, but one more use of my name as slop or sexist drivel, I'll kick your balls into your rib cage."

"Jo Beth, hon— listen, I'm mortified you're in such a sour mood. Pardon me all to hell and back. You've got a foul mouth just like me. How come you can call me names and I can't rib you a little? Answer me that!"

"Only friends can rib me, and you don't qualify. Also, we have a law that works to protect both you and me. We're equals, remember?"

"When hell freezes over," he said sardonically.

I saw Sheriff Scroggins approaching with Jasmine by his side.

"May the bluebird of happiness shit on your pillow each morning," I whispered.

Lyons opened his mouth to retaliate, then shot a foot in the air when the sheriff's voice boomed a greeting directly behind him.

I laughed and Lyons looked murderous. Even Scroggins could sense the testosterone wafting on the breeze.

"What?" Scroggins barked, looking from me to Lyons.

"We were discussing birds," I explained.

Lyons flushed but remained silent. I turned to Jasmine.
"What did you get from Malahki?"

"His last name is Fenmore. There were two men; he doesn't remember any facial hair. Both were in jeans. The one who lost the cap had a red shirt, and the other had a black bomber jacket. Both fired one round at the clerk, and black jacket shot at Malahki. They heard or saw a car drive up. When they went out the door they turned right. Malahki didn't move from hiding until the customer came in and discovered the clerk's body. He wants to go home."

"You did great," I said. "I don't blame the kid. Did he tell you what he was doing in the store at nine? Shouldn't he have been in school?"

Jasmine hadn't looked my way since she arrived. She was p.o'd about having to do the questioning.

"He has a friend with a new computer game. He was killing time till the friend's mother left for work. They were gonna ditch and play games all day. He wants a policeman to take him home and explain why he isn't in school. He's afraid of getting a lickin'."

"Sounds like he's recovered to me," Scroggins commented with a grin. "Tom?"

Lyons reached inside his tunic and handed me the plastic Ziploc with the perp's cap. With my back to the sheriff I pretended to wet my index finger, and drew an imaginary line in the air for a one, meaning I had won the first skirmish. He flushed but remained mute, and left to find an officer to take the kid home. God, I was acting childishly, but it felt so good to pull his macho chain.

Jasmine and I silently unhooked the dogs, held up the sagging tape, and started across the parking lot.

"I'll stay outside," boomed the sheriff. I gave him a backhanded wave and glanced at Jasmine.

"Thanks. I was right you know."

Her expression softened and she gave me a ghost of a smile.

"Say you're sorry," she demanded.

"I can do that."

"Well?"

We were at the door of the store.

"Later," I said with a grin, holding the door open.

I was the last one in. No sooner than the door closed, both dogs stopped, began an eerie whining, and tried to go through me in their haste to reach the door. Jasmine was struggling to pull Ashley back, and Caesar bulled his way between my legs, toenails scrabbling on the waxed tile floor, and wrapping his lead around my right leg.

"Go outside," I yelled to Jasmine over the dogs' frantic baying, straining to grab Caesar's harness and remain upright.

I went down hard on my tailbone and saw stars floating in my blurred vision. The pain was intense.

"Are you all right?" Jasmine screamed. She was braced against the open door, holding on to Ashley for dear life. At the far limit of his lead, Ashley was pulling backward, trying to free himself.

I quickly hit my left shoulder twice with my left fist. It was a silent command to get the hell out. My head was throbbing in rhythm with my tailbone, and the dogs' howling was an added assault. I didn't feel like yelling. I had Caesar's harness clutched in my right hand and was trying to keep him out of my face. He was squirming on my legs trying to hide his head in my stomach. He weighs one hundred pounds. I had my hands full.

Regaining my feet and choking up on his lead, I pulled him outside. In the open air they both stopped making their terrified sounds and stood hassling for breath. I limped over to the low curb of the sidewalk, rubbing my tailbone. I sat down gingerly and Jasmine joined me. We were also panting and trying to regain our breath.

"What happened?" She sounded awed by what she'd seen.

"Blood," I said shortly, gazing out at the people milling around behind the tape. Sheriff Scroggins and Tom were on their way toward us. I'd have to explain again to them, so I was waiting for them to arrive.

Sheriff Scroggins squatted, so we were more or less eye to eye. He looked concerned. Tom remained standing slightly behind the sheriff.

"Blood," I began. "So much blood. I could even smell it and the dogs got their large muzzles full of the scent. The heat in there just intensified the odor. They went bananas. They smelled death, or maybe they know that so much blood means death. They are very sensitive to human suffering."

While I was speaking I happened to glance at Tom. He was sporting a smirk, making a movement in the air that signaled he had also chalked up a score. It only took me seconds to remember. He had been by my side more than two years ago when two of my bloodhounds had refused to enter a car where a man had died from his throat being cut. When I had opened the car door, they had leaped back nervously from the blood smell and bolted. The bastard remembered and let us go in there uninformed.

My ire was so great I felt like I was choking. I had to move.

"The dogs need water," I said in a strangled voice to Jasmine.

She followed after me, trying to keep up with my angry stride.

"What gives?" she asked quietly when we arrived at the van. She could see I was very angry.

"Tom sent us into the store deliberately, knowing the dogs would be spooked. He saw the same thing happen sometime back. Never fear, he'll pay dearly for that rotten trick."

"Good," she agreed.

"Let's put away Ashley and Caesar. They've had it for

today. Luckily we held back Mark Anthony and Miz Melanie."

We returned to the front of the store where the sheriff and Lyons were standing.

"Sheriff Scroggins, I'll need four men. Two with me, and two to go with Jasmine.

"Jasmine, start Miz Melanie at the door. We have a fifty-fifty chance she'll pick up black jacket's scent. I'll use red shirt's cap."

Lyons came trotting back across the tarmac with three deputies in tow. One was plump with salt-and-pepper hair. He had to be fifty. I pointed at the two young deputies and told them to stay with Jasmine.

"You other two come with me," I said, not using Tom's name or rank.

"One drives and the other stays at least ten yards behind us, in case the dogs have to double back. That way you won't contaminate the trail."

I was praying that some scent was left on the ground; the wind was picking up. I put the opened Ziploc under Mark Anthony's nose. He buried his muzzle inside the bag, taking deep sniffs of the cap. I pulled out two pieces of deer jerky and held them under his nose. He gobbled them down.

"Seek, Mark Anthony, seek!"

He bent his head and started working. Nose down, he ranged eight feet or more in a loose figure eight, trying to locate the odor that he was seeking. A bloodhound's long flapping ears are important tools. They are natural funnels that scoop up the scent around him and send it to his nose.

Suddenly, Mark Anthony's tail became a metronome, swinging back and forth with his own personal rhythm. He tugged on the lead, urging me to give him slack. I followed along behind, wanting to believe that he had picked up the scent so quickly, but I was doubtful. He had never been fast on the scent.

He hurried around the store and turned right on brown

dried grass that crunched with each step. Discarded litter lay scattered among the weeds. The verge was twelve feet wide between the convenience store's south side and the wall of a hardware store. It ran back about forty feet where two large trash Dumpsters sat side by side facing the alley.

Mark Anthony turned left into the alley. We walked several feet down the road before I glanced back. Miz Melanie appeared and turned *right*, stopping in front of one of the Dumpsters. Both lids were thrown back and they were overflowing with trash.

Miz Melanie stood on her hind legs scratching her front toenails against the metal, trying to climb its vertical surface.

I pulled Mark Anthony off the scent trail and went back to watch. Jasmine shortened the lead by coiling it several times and waved a deputy forward. He started past her to peer in the Dumpster, but she called him back sharply, handing him the lead.

"Place the loop over your wrist and wrap it three times. Don't, under any condition, turn it loose."

She watched carefully as he followed her instructions. She caught the top of the Dumpster and pulled herself up until her body was balanced against the Dumpster, near her pelvis. Balancing there on her left hand, she reached into a pocket with her right and pulled out a baggie. She drew up her right knee and leaned precariously over the messy contents. I held my breath. If she tumbled in she would have to be fumigated, the garbage smelled ripe. She held up the gun carefully with two covered fingers on the very end of the barrel.

"Yes!" I cried, giving her a pumped fist salute. I hurried over and helped by removing the gun from her lowered hand. She then slid down gracefully. Her two deputies gave a few halfhearted ragged-spaced claps that sounded derisive. She did a graceful curtsy in rebuttal.

It was a cheap knockoff, a Saturday night special.

Cradling it in the plastic, I carefully broke open the cylinder. Two rounds were missing. Jasmine and I were grinning with delight. Our fifty-fifty chance just jumped to the max. She had Black Jacket's scent.

Jasmine retrieved the lead and dropped to her knees, crooning into Miz Melanie's ear while she hugged her neck.

"My big baby is so smart. Good girl, good girl!"

She fumbled in her pocket and produced a generous handful of jerky.

Lyons walked up, acting as if he wanted to snatch the gun from my grasp. It's a good thing he didn't try. I would've probably shot him with it. I walked over to the youngest deputy who looked as if he just started shaving and laid it gently in his hands.

"Take this back to Sheriff Scroggins. Tell him to send two units back to follow behind us. You drive for Jasmine and ask the older deputy to come with me. Lyons will drive behind me."

"Hold it, Pete. Give me the gun." Lyons couldn't hold still for this, his ego was smarting.

The deputy glanced at me.

I gave Lyons a cool smile and verbally pounced.

"Tell him to do as I said or Jasmine and I load the dogs and go home. Now!" I put a nice little snap in my voice.

He reluctantly nodded his head to Pete. He looked ready to chew nails.

"Remember to stay at least ten yards behind me where you belong," I snarled. "Have you forgotten we have two murderers to catch?"

I strode away without looking back. I led Mark Anthony back to where I had pulled him off the scent trail. I patiently let him smell the cap, fed him jerky, and again gave him the command to seek. It took him a while before he seemed to lock onto the scent.

This gave me time to glance back to make sure that everyone was set to go. The deputy with the salt-and-pepper-colored hair was trudging a few yards behind me, and Lyons was creeping along behind in his wake. The trail had split and Jasmine was trailing in the opposite direction with her escort. It was time for a radio check.

When Jasmine and I trailed together we turned to a seldom-used channel and kept the transmissions very short. We used the regular channels to converse with the lawmen. We also choose cutesy names to further confuse. A lot of people in this neck of the woods carefully monitor all channels: pot growers, DEA, moonshiners, ATF, retirees living in the boonies, hunters (and hunters' wives that want to make sure the hubby is out there training that bluetick hound that cost an arm and a leg and not off somewhere boozing or floozying).

"Trouble to Double. Over."

She had lowered the pitch of her voice. Over the tinny speaker, it was hard to tell she was female.

"Double here. Be careful. Don't be a hero. Call on contact. Over." I made my voice rough and husky.

"Same back at you. Over and out."

Mark Anthony was having trouble with the trail of scent. He ran sideways from the structure straight across the alley. It was the wind. It had scattered the scent all to hell and gone. This search just might end with a whimper, not a bang. Bad analogy to think bang. Success maybe, or roar; never bang. My perp up to this point still had his gun.

When I checked, and Salt-and-Pepper was still walking behind me, I motioned him forward and introduced myself. He told me his name was Donald Augustine. He was older than I had guessed. Hearing better diction than I expected, I asked him if he was local.

He hailed from Tallahassee, Florida. His wife was born and raised here. After he had put in twenty years on the police force and taken retirement with a nothing pension, his wife wanted to move back to her hometown. After six months of idleness and finding that he couldn't live on the small check, and gaining twenty pounds from his altered routine, he became a deputy here two years ago. Told me with a chuckle that he had to hurry up and get killed while on duty because compulsory retirement was fifty-five, which was six months away.

I liked him. He hadn't lost the twenty pounds, but with Sheriff Scroggins in charge he didn't have to worry about his weight for another six months. We talked as Mark Anthony whined in frustration at frequently losing the scent.

Suddenly he tugged forward, impatient with being tethered and wanting to hustle. I waved Deputy Augustine back with a smile and we took off again.

I checked out the houses, small businesses, and alleys we were passing. Gilsford County had 16,000 residents. Collins had 13,000 within the city limits. So the other three thousand in the county were the people who lived on the edge of Okefenokee Swamp or in isolated homes scattered among the hundreds of thousands of acres of planted pines. Lots of pine trees and only a few people.

Mark Anthony turned off the alley into small backyards and weedy empty lots. After going through the first yard, Lyons's unit was staying a street over or one behind, trying to keep track of our progress. When the people on the small roads, faces peeking from windows and bodies standing and sitting on porches, became predominately black, I motioned for Augustine to join me.

"Blacks don't appreciate whites chasing black men through their yards. Have you noticed how quiet the streets have become and no one is yelling greetings? Stay alert. Unsnap your holster and if we have to enter a house, you go in with your gun in your hand and stay in *front* of the dog and me. Keep your voice down. Sound does funny things in this kind of wind. Some places we won't be able to hear each other from six feet away. In others, they can hear us for several blocks. The bloodhound's name is Mark Anthony. If something happens to me, grab his lead and don't let go. Running free, he would be dead in five minutes. I hold you personally responsible for his safety. I'll return from the grave to get you, if he dies."

"Shades of Julius Caesar," he whispered.

"Nope," I returned softly. "That's the name of the other dog I worked with earlier."

"I swear to protect you and your noble beast until death," he vowed, hand on his badge, and a smile hovering on his lips.

"Now you're talking!"

We were walking within a six-foot gap between two brick buildings. The wind was screaming around the corners like a banshee wailing of impending death. Here I go again, referring to death. I had to quit relying on ancient history, wives' tales, and southern adages in my thoughts, but what was left?

No windows marred the three-storied symmetrical layers of old crumbling bricks. I felt the clutch of claustrophobia. It was close in here, and old crumbling bricks have a bad habit of falling down eventually. Could be today, right about now. I guess the lower scent was out of the wind because Mark Anthony picked up speed, and I pounded along matching his progress. I couldn't get out of these confining walls fast enough. We left Augustine in the shade.

We burst out into an open alley and Mark Anthony stopped on a dime. I guessed he had lost the scent. I glanced around to scope out the landscape. A tall building was directly in front of us with boarded up windows and nothing on either side but weeds. Even the parking lot had weeds in the potholes and cracks in the tarmac.

A short brick fence about fifty feet in length was a foot off the easement for the alley and directly in front of the building's front door. I turned back to see if Augustine had cleared the alley, just as Mark Anthony threw back his head and poured forth a loud baying. Red shirt was very near. Mark Anthony was celebrating!

Bloodhounds run mute. Only when they are almost on their target do they unleash that loud mournful bay, so beautiful to a man-trailer's ears.

I was mesmerized with Mark Anthony's vocal announcement of his accomplishment. At the edge of my vision I saw half a brick pop off into space. It came from the side of the building we had just run past. In that same instant I heard the shot.

"Run!" I screamed to Mark Anthony.

I was jerking him mightily, almost losing my balance. He was slow to react. It took a few seconds for him to process the rarely used command through his large skull and remember its meaning; but it seemed to take eons before he moved the way I was trying to pull him. He was still baying when I dove the last six feet and ended up with him standing over me dripping slobber.

Ignoring the numbing pain in my funny bone where I had rapped my elbow on the low wall, I grabbed him by his harness and jerked his right front leg out from under him, flopping him prone. I lay above him whispering frantically into his ear.

"Hush, hush, low, low, no, no." It was the command for silent trailing and not baying over his joyous victory. I wanted him to lie still and shut the hell up. I was also giving him the signal for silence, by pushing down firmly on his large head with my aching right arm. He finally got my message.

Panting, I lay close to the low barrier, running my memory film of the earlier scan of the building that now was directly in front of me a few feet away. I hadn't counted floors and wasn't about to lift my head to do so.

If Red Shirt had fired from the third floor or higher, we were dead meat. His first shot was high and wide. *If* his gun was the same as Black Jacket's, it wouldn't be accurate from that distance. He also had at least four rounds or more, and with enough altitude, he could see us easily and pick us off at his leisure. Considering the several factors, I was scared silly but not formulating immediate plans to travel. I hugged my big dog and cogitated.

I heard a noise over the wind and watched aghast as Deputy Augustine bobbed and weaved while awkwardly crouched, gun in hand, trying to cross the gulf of thirty feet. He was moving in slow motion, and graceful he wasn't. Not only was the damn fool gonna die while he was on duty, it was going to be right about now with me watching.

He slumped in front of me with his face less than a foot away from Mark Anthony's and mine. He hadn't been pierced with a bullet or even shot at; but I was feeling the urge to do that very thing, myself, this minute.

"Are you out of your cotton-pickin' mind?" I asked, in greeting.

"Best chance I've had in the past two years, and the sucker wouldn't cooperate," he complained.

His face was the color of chalk, his breathing was labored, and sweat on a day as cold as this one meant fear.

"You may wish to commit suicide, but not here, and not today. Am I getting through to you?"

"Yes'm," he replied, trying to grin.

He was wiping the moisture from his face with a handkerchief.

"And furthermore," I added icily, "I will repeat your conversation verbatim to Sheriff Scroggins. He doesn't need or deserve a loose cannon on his force."

"Don't," he said, grabbing my wrist for emphasis. "She's in a wheelchair with MS. I blabbed to you because I was shook up. I should have kept quiet," he muttered, disgusted with himself. "She needs the widow's pension and the medical coverage. Don't blow me out of the water. I don't fear dying, only that I'll bungle it, and need care myself . . . Please."

I gazed at him appalled, Red Shirt and immediate peril forgotten. I swallowed and tried to sound calm and in control.

"Have you checked out all the *other* possible solutions thoroughly?"

"As best as I can, under the circumstances." He added dryly, "I can't come right out with it, to Social Services. The counselor would remember after the deed was done, so to speak."

"Let me try," I said in earnest. "I'm in a different county and they'd never connect the two of us. I'll pretend I'm worried about a favorite uncle with similar circumstances. Give me thirty days for research to find a better solution. If I can't find one, you have my word that I'll come to your services and keep silent. But believe this: If you jump the gun before the thirty days are up, I'll be so pissed that you didn't wait for my learned advice, I'll scream your scheme from the rooftops and force them to believe me. Do we have a deal?"

"Give up this golden opportunity?"

He was being sarcastic and cast his eyes upward. He returned his gaze to mine in consternation.

"Did you know that I can see two upper floors and the roof from this position? *If I* can see them and if he's still up there, *he can see us!*"

"No shit Sherlock," I uttered waspishly. "About the time you were making your suicidal dash I kinda got distracted. Did you happen to use your radio to call in our location to the dispatcher before taking off on the 'Death Defying Thirty'?"

He looked embarrassed.

"I reported shots fired, but I didn't hold down the transmitting button during the last half of me describing our present location. Sorry."

"And you turned off your radio?"

I wanted to make certain before I started screaming.

"Sergeant Lyons can't be far away and people must have heard the shot. They'll direct him. Besides, I didn't want the ambulance to get here too fast."

"If asked, the locals will direct him in the wrong direction. Do you see a concerned citizen? Do you hear any sirens, by chance?"

I jerked out my radio and turned from the private channel where Jasmine could reach me and was repositioning the channel when I heard the faint wail above the wind.

Ten seconds later, Lyons roared around the corner, screeching to a halt at an angle where he could open his passenger side door and talk without leaving the protection of the vehicle.

"Dispatcher loused up, sent me two blocks west instead of east, or I'd been here sooner. Is he up there?"

I carefully refrained from looking at Augustine. I was afraid I'd brain him with the radio. I put it back in my pocket, and turned to Jasmine's channel.

"We think so unless he went out the back door," I said. Lyons answered quickly.

"There is no back door. I was in there last month with the fire inspector. Both back doors are nailed shut and boarded up. We have to go get him."

"What do you mean by *we*, paleface?" I retorted.

I tossed a thumb over my shoulder. "He's in there, and my participation in this exercise is over. Deputy Augustine isn't going anywhere. He's staying right here to protect me."

"You're the last one in this county that needs protection!" he yelled.

I smiled when I heard the Cavalry arriving. Every law-enforcement car that would run was on its way. Big happening in a small town.

Within minutes the narrow street was bumper-to-bumper with yellow and tan county vehicles, pale blue for the city police, black government units for the initials: DEA and ATF, assorted colors for personal cars of the SWAT team, and a large white boxy ambulance. The Georgia Highway Patrol colors weren't present. They must be out with their unit having coffee. There was even a green and yellow truck representing the Georgia Department of Fish and Game. If Red Shirt was still up there, he had multiple choices of targets.

Sheriff Scroggins had duck-waddled from around his vehicle and hunched by my side.

"I know I look damn ridiculous so quit holding back those snickers. This crouch is hard on an old fat man's knees. What happened?"

"Sheriff, Red Shirt fired one round after Mark Anthony started baying. He panicked. You know how some men fear bloodhounds. I'd say fifty percent still warn their wives and children to stand way back, that the dog is vicious. It's erroneous knowledge. You and I know they are gentle and don't attack. Some men would rather face a machine gun than a large charging dog."

I continued. "I think I have a good chance to get him out of there without anyone getting hurt. Will you let me try?"

"You want to try to talk him out?" Scroggins looked doubtful.

"No, I want to threaten that I'll turn the dog loose in the building."

Scroggins laughed. "That'll be the day. He'd lick him to death."

I laughed with him. "We know Mark Anthony is a pussycat, but Red Shirt doesn't. Can't hurt."

"Go to it. My knees are killing me. Keep your head down."

· He duckwalked back to his foam-cushioned seat in his cruiser.

I made a hand motion for Lyons to toss me his mike.

He glared daggers at me but threw it and flipped on the loudspeaker.

"I'm speaking to the man in the red shirt in the boarded up building."

My voice boomed on the brisk breeze, vibrating in my ears.

"This is the attack dog handler. I have been ordered

to release the dog. This is your one and only chance to come out without getting mauled. If you are on an upper floor, start down immediately. You have less than five minutes to follow my instructions. At the front door toss out your weapon. Remove your shirt and jacket. Empty your pockets and turn them out so I can see the white. Walk out slowly with your hands on your head. Three steps from the door, lie down spread-eagled on the tarmac. Keep your head down and don't move a muscle. If you do everything right, you won't be hurt. I will repeat this message because of the wind."

I tossed the mike back to Lyons. My mouth was dry. I drank from my water bottle and offered it to Augustine. He took it and drank. I pulled back my glove and saw that time was almost up. I moved fast to keep from thinking. Did I really want to do this?

I stood, jerked up a comfortable bloodhound from his snooze, and was striding around the barrier before anyone noticed. I began yelling at Mark Anthony.

"Where's your man! Find your man! Find your man!"

I held the cap down by my leg. He raised his head and started his raucous baying while he moved to the far end of his lead, straining mightily to go after his guy.

I ignored the shouts behind me. Maybe, just maybe, they wouldn't try to out-hero me by charging to the rescue. To the uninitiated, Mark Anthony would be deemed a hound from hell. His strident cry was his desire to let the world know where Red Shirt could be found. He was doing everything but jumping up and down and pointing at the door.

I kept a jaundiced eye on the large metal entrance. A mantra wouldn't hurt.

I will not be shot, he's gonna fold, I will not be shot, he's gonna fold. Amen.

A dark gap appeared and widened teasingly slowly, and an object sailed on the breeze before landing on the pitted tarmac. It was a gun. A figure appeared in the doorway, then advanced and slowly moved forward.

Stripped to the waist with pockets turned out and his hands locked on his head.

He was saying something but the wind wasn't bringing me the message. Mark Anthony was doing his jiggle dance trying to reach him. I began to haul back on the lead when I could understand the man's message.

"Don't turn him loose! I'm down, I'm down!"

He was indeed down and several feet from the gun.

Figures flew by me falling on the suspect as if each one wanted to be the one to cuff him. Someone produced leg irons. When they stood him up, I released my tight resistance on the lead and Mark Anthony surged forward to claim his victory. I let him have his moment. He deserved it. He nuzzled and licked the prisoner, whining for joy. He wanted to be hugged and petted, but the man cringed and didn't have a way to touch him nor the desire, I suspected. Mark Anthony did everything but hug him.

Later that evening over a pepperoni and cheese pizza, wine for her and beer for me, Jasmine told me about her search.

"Deputy Benifield had his gun drawn as he pounded on the door. I was trying to restrain Miz Melanie on a shortened lead and hold the screen door open, and she was baying her head off. Black Jacket's mother opened the door shouting and praying, and a small child started screaming at her first sight of a huge dog straining to enter. You couldn't hear yourself think. I wasn't expecting a pint of ground black pepper scattered on the front threshold. On the back sill certainly, but not the front. Miz Melanie began sneezing and baying, slipping and sliding . . ." She paused for another sip of wine.

"To make a long story short, she entangled us in her lead entrapping our legs and took us all down like bowling pins with the exception of the little girl. She ran back to tell Black Jacket what was going on. He was hiding under his mama's bed doing some screaming of his own. His mama had taken his gun, put it in the oven and turned it on so he wouldn't be tempted to shoot us.

"It took us a long time to pull Black Jacket, his sister, and Miz Melanie, out from under the bed. When the sister told Deputy Pete the gun was in a lit oven, he grabbed Bomber Jacket and his mama and I had the kid and Miz Melanie. We all ran outside and hid behind the house next door.

"The second deputy finally arrived with the fire department. They turned off the propane gas at the tank and were waiting for the oven to cool down when we left. They said it was a miracle that the ammunition hadn't begun exploding, sending rounds and flames all over. You know what mama said when she heard him say it?"

I gave a negative headshake.

"I wasn't born yesterday young man. I only turned the knob to *warm*, not bake!"

The day before Christmas Eve I met with Patricia Ann Newton, a recently acquired friend who had more money than Midas. That afternoon I met Deputy Donald Augustine in the city park. I explained to him that an anonymous donor had added his name to a living trust that would furnish him ample funds upon his retirement to enable him to care for his wife comfortably and would continue if he died first.

He was embarrassed for having to use his handkerchief to wipe the pine tree pollen away that was making his eyes water. It also bothered mine as I wished him merry Christmas.

The Village Vampire
and the Yuletide Yorkie

Dean James

In collaboration with Jean Swanson, DEAN JAMES is the author of the Agatha Award– and Macavity Award–winning reference book, *By a Woman's Hand: A Guide to Mystery Fiction by Women*. With Jan Grape and Ellen Nehr, he edited the Edgar Award–nominated *Deadly Women: The Woman Mystery Reader's Indispensable Companion*. Mr. James's latest work of nonfiction is *Killer Books: A Guide to the Popular World of Mystery and Suspense*. His story "Best Served Cold" appeared in *Canine Crimes*. In addition to two cats, the author has a poodle named Candy, who anxiously awaits her appearance in a future story.

Even the dead like Christmas.

Though you might think it odd that a vampire like me would want to celebrate such a holiday, truth be told I'm not so far removed from my formerly human existence that I can resist the lure of tinsel and packages, stockings and strains of carols in the air. This was, moreover, my first Christmas in England, and the devout Anglophile in me reveled in the notion that I'd be spending it at a stately home, observing a traditional English Christmas firsthand. I had kept myself amused, during the drive down from Bedfordshire to Kent, with speculating on just what delightful English customs I'd witness during the coming week.

Knocking me out of my reverie, my companion at last pulled the Land Rover to a halt in front of Wiggleton Priory and threw out her hand in a flourish. "Here we are, Simon," she said unnecessarily. "Imagine, Christmas at one of the celebrated stately homes of England." She smiled in delight. "I'm so thrilled that you managed to get me invited along."

"My dear Hilda Mae," I responded, "I couldn't leave you to spend Christmas all by yourself in my cottage." *Because,* I added silently, *I certainly didn't want you snooping through my things while I was away.* Hilda Mae Herlihy was nosiness personified.

A former colleague of mine from Houston days, Hilda Mae had been in England on sabbatical since the beginning of the fall semester. I had been rather surprised to hear her voice on the phone just before Thanksgiving. "Glad I tracked you down, Sammy boy," her voice trilled over the wires.

I winced at the relic of my former—and human—existence. "Simon, if you please, my dear Hilda Mae," I said in my most prim tone.

She giggled. "Whatever! Though I can't imagine what you're trying to live down. Unless it's man trouble, as usual."

"Your point in calling?" I prodded her, none too gently.

"Why, to say a big ol' *howdy*! What'd you think?" She giggled into the phone again, reminding me why small doses of her girlish charm usually sufficed. The woman had a first-class mind and was a linguist of no mean ability, but she had the appearance and the manner of a runway bimbo.

"Well, howdy back at you!" I sighed and settled down for a long one. Conversations with Hilda Mae were never short.

Somehow, during the ensuing hour, I had persuaded myself that I couldn't let poor Hilda Mae spend Christmas in England by herself. Or maybe I didn't want to be alone myself at that time of year. For whatever reason, I heard myself inviting her to spend a week at Christmas at my cottage in the quiet Bedfordshire village of Snupperton Mumsley.

A week later I received an answer to a letter I had posted two months earlier. The letter was postmarked somewhere in Zimbabwe, which might explain the delay in response time. From the expensive, beautifully engraved paper and nearly illegible crabbed handwriting, I learned that Lady Antonia Pinchley-Fyggis would be delighted to let me examine her family's copy of a medieval chronicle I had been hoping to consult. Moreover, I would be more than welcome to come the week of Christmas, when Lady Antonia would again be in residence at Wiggleton Priory.

Lady Antonia graciously assented to the inclusion of Hilda Mae in her invitation, once I had carefully explained that Hilda Mae was also a scholar of some repute and would be of great assistance to me. I was a bit surprised, frankly, that Lady Antonia, daughter of the seventeenth earl of Wiggleton, had been so willing to open her home to strangers at this time of year. Far be it from me to look a gift aristocrat in the mouth, however.

From the Land Rover, I stared up at the impressive facade of Wiggleton Priory. Once the site of a Benedictine nunnery, the priory had been transformed, thanks to the Dissolution and countless pounds of Pinchley-Fyggis money over the ensuing centuries, into a vast pile of a stately home of no discernible, single architectural style. How anyone—besides Bill Gates, that is—could possibly maintain a house this large in this day and age astonished me.

Hilda Mae had already hopped out of the car, and I followed her up the steps to the front door, where she rang the bell. Scant moments later, the huge door opened, and the butler cast an inquiring gaze over us. "Dr. Simon Kirby-Jones and Dr. Hilda Mae Herlihy to see Lady Antonia Pinchley-Fyggis," she announced in her breezy fashion, stepping forward over the threshold and forcing the butler to step backward. The cavernous hall inside was, if anything, several degrees colder than the winter chill outside.

"This way, please, madam, sir," the butler intoned, after introducing himself as Foxwell. He moved surprisingly well for someone who looked ready to totter into the grave at any moment.

We followed him down an overly ornate hallway to a large door on the south side of the house. From what I could see, there was no attempt to decorate for the holidays. No swathes of greenery, no bright bunting, nothing even faintly reminiscent of the season. Rather disappointed, I tramped on behind Foxwell and Hilda Mae.

Sweeping open the door, the butler marched through, announcing us as he went. Hilda Mae paused to hand the keys to the car to him, and I continued forward to present myself to our hostess.

Ensconced in a large armchair before a crackling fire sat a broomstick with pouting red lips and a fright wig. I blinked. The broomstick changed into an excessively thin old woman with skin the texture of dry leather, wearing makeup and hair appropriate to a woman less than half her age. Not to mention one used to earning her living on her back. How frail she appeared. Impossible to tell her age—she might be anywhere from sixty to ninety. I leaned forward to offer her my hand, sensed a blur of movement, and snatched it back just in time.

Normally, dogs are afraid of vampires. Few of them would dare try to bite me. But there are exceptions, like the pugnacious little Yorkie now standing to attention in Lady Antonia's lap.

"Do be quiet, Percival," Lady Antonia cawed, fondly stroking her miniature defender. "These are our guests, and you must behave, pweshus." Percival subsided, but the glare he offered promised that I hadn't seen the last of his sharp little teeth.

"Dr. Kirby-Jones," Lady Antonia continued in her peculiar voice, "we are delighted you could join us during this festive time of year." She extended a languid claw, which I grasped carefully in my hand.

"May I introduce my colleague, Dr. Hilda Mae Herlihy." Hilda Mae stepped forward, attempted a curtsy, changed her mind at the last moment, and dipped her head instead. Her teeth flashed in a smugly satisfied smile as she surveyed the richly appointed room.

Lady Antonia suddenly chortled with glee. "Looks like I should have had Foxwell prepare only one bedroom, eh? Not two. Save a bit of tripping to and fro during the night, what? Tasty bit of crumpet you've got there, Kirby-Jones. Some assistant, eh?"

"Mother!" came the outraged cry from a woman sitting in a nearby chair.

"Oh, do hush, Rosamond," Lady Antonia said, waving a claw airily. "Dr. Kirby-Jones is a man of the world and *far* more sophisticated than a lump like you could ever be." She sniffed. "May I present my daughter, Rosamond Anniston, and her husband, Piers."

Lump was rather an unfortunate, if accurate, word to describe Rosamond. Whatever avoirdupois shed by her mother, Rosamond seemed to have gained or at least shared with her husband Piers. Two round faces glared accusingly at Lady Antonia, and the male half of the duo struggled to shift his massive bottom out of his chair in order to shake hands with Hilda and me. Tweedledum and Tweedledee to the life. And playing attendance upon Jackleen Sprat, no less.

"Two bedrooms are quite sufficient," I informed Lady Antonia with a hint of frost in my voice. Now was hardly the time to announce that I was of an entirely different persuasion. I could feel the wave of embarrassment around the room beginning to subside. Vampires are sensitive to strong emotion, you see, and Lady Antonia and Percival were the only two living creatures in the room who hadn't been awash in it moments before.

"Whatever you say." Lady Antonia dismissed my polite rebuff. Then her attention centered upon someone behind us, and an unpleasantly calculating expression settled on her face. "Algernon, do come in and meet *your* guests properly."

Hilda Mae and I turned. Approaching us was one of the most homely young men I had ever seen. None of his facial features were quite in proportion. His nose was small, his chin jutted commandingly, and his ears might catch a stray tailwind at any moment and send him flying out the window. His hair, an exceedingly odd shade of red, zigged and zagged all over his head. For all that, however, he did have a pleasant smile and a striking physique.

"At last," Lady Antonia chirped, "my nephew, Algernon Pinchley-Fyggis, the eighteenth Earl of Wiggleton." She finished the introductions, and we shook hands with the earl, who had a strong, firm grip. He seemed reluctant to release Hilda Mae's hand. She is rather attractive, if you like petite, dark women with beautiful smiles, that is. I'd have to tease her later about her new conquest.

"Welcome to Wiggleton Priory," the earl said warmly. "And do call me Algernon. No need to muck about with the title and all that." His voice was deep and well modulated.

He really was rather short—but he was still a couple of inches taller than Hilda Mae.

"I am most grateful for your hospitality, and for your allowing me access to your copy of the Selsey chronicle."

"Not at all, Simon," Algernon replied smoothly, casting his aunt a pointed glance. "I'm quite delighted to be of assistance to scholars such as yourselves. Now," he said briskly, shoving his hands into the pockets of his expensively tailored suit, "let me show you to your rooms. No doubt you would like to see where you'll be staying for the coming week."

Hilda Mae and I inclined our heads in the direction of Lady Antonia, Rosamond, and Piers. Before we could get out of the room, Lady Antonia announced to Piers that it was his turn to take Percival out for his "walkies."

As we followed the earl upstairs, I heard Piers whispering to Percival on their way out the front door, "You just try to bite me again, you little shit, and I'll kick your arse to next Sunday. No matter what my sainted mother-in-law says!" I looked back down in time to see Piers jerk the leash and drag the resistant dog out the front door. Neither Hilda Mae nor the earl seemed to have noticed, so wrapped up in their vigorous flirtation were they. A vampire's hearing, you see, is much more acute than that of a human, even when they aren't billing and cooing.

Putting aside for the moment Piers's dislike of the poor Yorkie, I speculated instead on something else. Why did the earl so dislike his aunt?

While dressing for dinner that first evening at Wiggleton Priory, I reconsidered the events of the afternoon. After showing us to our second-floor rooms, two very well-appointed apartments with a connecting door, the earl had given us a tour of his home. I trailed along behind the earl and Hilda Mae, and it became obvious to me that the earl had little concern for my presence. Hilda Mae fluttered her eyelashes, gushed in her best Southern-belle voice, and pressed his arm at regular intervals. If I had to speculate, I'd say that Hilda Mae had her sights set on being the next Countess of Wiggleton. I shuddered.

The only real item of interest to me during the tour was the priory's library, where the family kept its copy of the Selsey chronicle. The earl pointed out the case where it was kept, handed me a key, and offered a few brief instructions for the chronicle's use. After that, he went back to forgetting I was there.

There was a knock at the connecting door, ending my recollections, and I called for Hilda Mae to enter. "Have you finished ordering the wedding invitations yet?" I asked her acidly.

She giggled. "Now, Simon, don't be jealous!" Her lips pouted at me. She knows better, but with her it's completely automatic.

"I must say, my dear," I told her honestly as I took stock of her appearance, "you do look stunning. The earl will ravish you right there on the dining table, if you're not careful." Hilda Mae's impressively compact figure had been squeezed into some sort of emerald green satin confection that lit up her eyes and showed off her dark hair and complexion to great advantage. Though Hilda Mae is a mere associate professor, Daddy Herlihy owns some huge conglomeration of chicken farms. Thus his little girl wants for nothing expensive.

She giggled again. "Not until after dessert, Simon, at the very least! Then we'll see."

I fussed with the alignment of my jacket, and Hilda Mae made herself comfortable in a nearby chair, watching with a critical eye.

"Rather an interesting family, don't you think?" I said, continuing to fiddle.

"Fraught with all sorts of undercurrents, that's for sure." Hilda Mae turned off the dithery act. "I looked them up, you know, after you told me I could come along on this little jaunt."

"What little tidbits did you dig up?" I prompted her, leaning back against a desk, abandoning my fussiness with my clothes.

"The earldom goes back nearly to the Conquest—a notion that impresses the heck out of my little Southern heart, let me tell you!" She showed me her dimple, and I waved for her to continue.

"The seventeenth earl died in a hunting accident about five years ago, having been predeceased by his son, the present earl's father, who died in a plane crash ten years ago. Lady Antonia is the elder sister of the seventeenth earl, and thus the great-aunt of the present earl. Her late husband, one Robert Dinglebury, father of Rosamond, was persuaded to take Lady Antonia's name, it being so much more august than his own."

"I had wondered about that," I said, stroking my beard. "Does Lady Antonia control the purse strings, by any chance? There doesn't seem to be much love lost between her and the present earl."

"I believe so," Hilda Mae said. "Rumor has it that the male line is pretty profligate with money, so the old earl, Lady Antonia's father, tied up the estate leaving her in control of most everything. At least until the present earl reaches the tender age of forty, or Lady Antonia dies before that day."

"Where*ever* did you get all this?" I asked, astonished.

She smiled enigmatically. "I have my sources."

"You and your feminine wiles." I laughed.

"Let's go down to dinner, Simon," she said, standing up and grinning mischievously. "Let's see what the earl is going to have for dinner."

Said meal, presided over by the lugubrious Foxwell and his minions, was an odd affair. Lady Antonia, garish in crimson velvet with a superabundance of lace and furbelows, dominated the conversation. With a fervor worthy of Mrs. Jellyby herself, she explained to me her interest in various good works, many of them having to do with unfortunates in Africa. I wondered wildly if, on our way downstairs, we had wandered by mistake into Bleak House. At first, I was laboring under the mistaken notion that these "unfortunates" were human, but, no, Lady Antonia expended her energies and her monies in the service of the starving animals of Africa. That explained the letter from Zimbabwe.

Hilda Mae, seated on the earl's right, had no trouble keeping the earl amused. The one member of the family party we had not previously met, the earl's betrothed, seated on his left, was not in the least diverted by the situation, however.

The Right Honorable Miss Ottoline Chance, a "charmin' gell" in Lady Antonia's parlance, seemed intent on relating to Hilda Mae every moment of her romance with the earl. Neither the earl nor Hilda Mae paid much attention. Miss Chance batted her heavily mascaraed eyelashes in the earl's direction at such a rapid pace I feared she would soon lift herself out of her chair. Which in itself would have been wondrous to behold, for Miss Chance must have stood six foot three in her stockinged feet, with a physique to match. She dwarfed the earl whenever she stood remotely near him.

Tossing her mane of glossy raven hair over one shoulder in a manner reminiscent of the slightly cockeyed horse she most nearly resembled, Miss Chance erupted into laughter at some witticism of the earl's. Directed, of course, at Hilda Mae, not at her. With one ear, I listened to the droning of Lady Antonia; with the other, I kept tabs on the other end of the table. Frankly, I wasn't that keen on hearing all the intimate details of the earl's first weekend with Ottoline at Lyme Regis, nor did I care to hear anything more about her horse, Sultan. Miss Chance babbled on, while the earl and Hilda Mae feasted on each other with their eyes.

Thankfully, Lady Antonia reclaimed my attention with yet another anecdote of her good works among the benighted quadrupeds in Africa. Oblivious to it all, Rosamond and Piers plowed through their meal with rarely a pause for breath—or mastication. Having had only this rather brief experience of dinner at Wiggleton Priory, I quite understood their taking refuge in massive quantities of food.

A determined yip interrupted the flow of Lady Antonia's harrowing tale of abused gazelles and starving wildebeests. Her Yorkie, Percival, reclined near her on a small stool upholstered in a velvet matching her dinner gown. From time to time during dinner Lady Antonia would feed Percival with choice morsels from her own plate, but she had become so caught up in her horror stories that she had been neglecting her dog.

"Oh, my widdle pweshus man, Mummy will feed you. After all, *you* are the one dearest to Mummy's heart in all the world." She held out a bit of beef Wellington, and Percival nearly took off her fingernail in grabbing the meat.

Lady Antonia turned to beam at me with pride in her darling's healthy appetite, while I did my best not to return my dinner to its plate in a rather disgusting manner. (By the way, vampires these days do eat and drink, lightly, of course. It's all thanks to these wonderful little pills we take. No more nasty bloodsucking for us, thank you very much. We can even go outside in the sunlight, but in moderation. It's all very civilized these days. The wonders of modern science!)

But I digress. Lady Antonia might be enchanted with her *widdle pweshus*—I hoped to be able at some point to expunge those words warbled in that voice from my aural memory banks—but various members of the party cast a baleful glance in the Yorkie's direction every time Lady Antonia broke off conversation to attend to her pet.

Over the dessert course, Lady Antonia cleared her throat, bringing the conversation between Hilda Mae and the earl finally and mercifully to a halt. While Ottoline glowered on, and Rosamond and Piers chewed, Lady Antonia announced, excitement bringing a near squeak to her voice, "As you know, my dears, in two days' time, it will be Christmas Eve. And, as is the tradition in this family, I will have some very important gifts to bestow upon the family after dinner that evening. I trust that our two distinguished guests will feel welcome to take part in our festivities, though you are of course not obliged to have brought presents for the family." Her eyelashes fluttered in my direction.

"We would be delighted, and most honored, dear lady," I said. "Your generosity in allowing us to partake of your hospitality at this time of year is most gracious, and we will do our best not to impinge upon you and your family traditions."

I detected such a wave of anger at that moment that I nearly dropped my wineglass. There was no doubt about the source of the anger. The earl trembled with the effort to hold back his temper. But at whom was it directed? Lady Antonia seemed the most obvious target.

The earl stood suddenly, almost sending his chair crashing back onto the floor. "You have not intruded in the least, Simon," the earl said, biting off the words. "I'm delighted to extend hospitality to a scholar of your stature. As my dear aunt stated, you are most welcome to be a part of our holiday festivities. Now, if you will excuse me, there is some urgent estate business to which I must attend. Have Foxwell bring you port or brandy, cigars, whatever you wish."

He stalked out, totally ignoring a crestfallen Hilda Mae and a thoroughly dispirited Ottoline, while Lady Antonia filled the strained silence with more nauseating baby talk to Percival, anxiously awaiting more tidbits from the table. I looked across the table at Hilda Mae. *What have we gotten ourselves into?* I wondered. Hilda Mae wiggled her nose up and down a couple of times, and I was hard put not to laugh. This week would prove most interesting, one way or another.

The next morning, the admonitions of Lady Antonia notwithstanding, I consulted Hilda Mae, who volunteered to drive to the nearest village to find gifts of some sort for the various members of the family. I walked with her out to the garage, and we discussed suitable items. Hoping that Hilda Mae wouldn't spend all her time lost in a roundabout, I detoured through the gardens on my way back to the house to enjoy the crisp, cold air of this gloriously cloudy morning. Vampires, as you might guess, thoroughly enjoy cold weather.

Pausing behind a concealing arbor of evergreens, I heard Rosamond approaching with a whining Percival. "Boiling in oil isn't good enough for you, you little rat! 'Take Percival for his walkies, Rosamond!' " Her imitation of her mother was savage in its accuracy. "I'd like to take you to the lake, tie a stone around your neck, and throw you in, that's what *I'd* like to do. To think that I was the one who gave you to Mother in the first place, two Christmases ago."

Rosamond's litany of complaints continued as she and Percival passed by the other side of my hiding place. The poor Yorkie looked to be in no immediate danger, or I would have assayed a rescue. Instead, thinking over what I had heard, I made my way into the house and to the library where I settled down to the work for which I had come here.

Hilda Mae returned from the village about two hours later, and I waved away her suggestion that I should inspect her choices. "Later, my dear, later." I pointed her toward the other end of the table at which I labored. "You have work to do here. Time to earn your keep."

Hilda Mae groaned. "Sit!" I said sternly. "I know you'd rather be flirting with the earl, but you did promise to help me with this, if you came along." She stuck out her tongue but set to work.

We had been working steadily for nearly two hours when the earl sauntered in. "I do beg your pardon, Simon," he began quietly. I had been so engrossed in a story of how the nuns of Selsey had managed to defend certain properties against the depredations of a local landholder that I quite started in my chair. "Oh, I do say, Simon, I hadn't meant to startle you," the earl apologized.

"Not at all, Algernon, not at all," I said, relaxing in my chair. "I was rather engrossed in my work, that's all."

"I thought you might like to know that there is a light

luncheon laid on in the dining room," the earl said. His words were directed at me, but his eyes could see only Hilda Mae.

I smothered a sigh. I sincerely hoped the situation wouldn't get out of hand before the end of our week here. Ottoline wouldn't take kindly at being nudged aside in the matrimonial stakes.

"*There* you are, Algie *darling*," boomed the hearty tones of Ottoline Chance, right on cue. We all looked around to see the earl's fiancée clumping into the room, Percival clutched tenderly in her arms. The earl tried desperately to control an involuntary shudder at the sound of her voice.

"Good afternoon, Simon, Hannah Mae." She beamed at us. Hilda Mae rolled her eyes at the deliberate mistake with her name.

Ottoline hovered, staring goofily at the earl, while he in turn gazed at Hilda Mae. They stood, backs to me, mooning at their objects of desire. I rolled my eyes back at Hilda Mae; she saw me and had to suppress a smile.

Percival barked. Miss Chance rubbed his head soothingly. "Yes, sweetums, Auntie Ottoline knows you're ready for your walkies." She held him up and rubbed her nose to his, then she kissed him tenderly on the nose. "You little darling!

"Isn't he just the most precious thing you ever saw?" She beamed at us again. "*Dear* Algie, I do so *hate* to tear you away, but Lady Antonia asked me to find you, so that you could take Percival for his walkies." She thrust the dog at the earl. "I *must* go back and help her draft an appeal on behalf of the gnus."

Dear Algie accepted the cowering creature with ill grace. Percival looked back piteously at Ottoline Chance, but, evidently assured in her notion that her betrothed adored the little dog as much as she did, she paid no attention to Percival's subdued whimpering as she departed.

"Damn and blast!" I heard the earl mutter under his breath. I watched, and it seemed to me that his right hand curled rather too tightly around Percival's neck. I was beginning to suspect that Percival's days in this world were numbered.

The earl having departed to attend to Percival's needs, Hilda Mae and I put away our work and went to find some lunch.

The rest of that day and much of the following, Christmas Eve, Hilda Mae and I spent at work in the library. I had no need to translate the entire Selsey chronicle, or we would have been guests of the earl for some time to come. Instead we skimmed through, searching for key words and phrases, and thus the work progressed swiftly enough. I was optimistic that I should have the material I needed by the time our week was done.

I dressed for dinner that evening with particular care. Neither Lady Antonia nor the earl had given us much hint of what to expect tonight, but I forecast a certain amount of fireworks, given the tension that seemed to exist between Algernon and his aunt. I surveyed my reflection in the mirror (sorry to shatter an illusion; it's those little pills, you know), quite pleased. The black of my evening wear suited me well (no pun intended), matching the black of my hair and closely trimmed beard.

"Vanity, thy name is Simon," Hilda Mae said from the doorway connecting our two rooms. "Stop admiring yourself, and let's go downstairs and see what Christmas Eve at Wiggleton Priory portends." She wore another stunning dress, this time in ice-blue satin which left few of her curves to the imagination.

I forebore to comment and followed her downstairs.

Dinner that night was much the same as it had been the previous two nights. Lady Antonia prosed on and on about good works, and her munificent support of them; Percival whined for food; Rosamond and Piers ate steadily without saying much of anything; Ottoline nattered on and on at Hilda Mae, confiding even more inappropriate things about her and the earl, alternating occasionally with stories about her favorite horse; and the earl slowly simmered into another rage. If Santa Claus showed up this evening, they were likely to dismember him and feed him to Piers and Rosamond. Was this the typical aristocratic English family Christmas I had so longed to see?

When the meal had mercifully ended with Foxwell's removal of the dessert course, Lady Antonia rapped her spoon against the delicate porcelain of her coffee cup. What desultory conversation had been going on abruptly ended.

Lady Antonia stood. Tonight's attempt at haute couture was a hideous shade of pumpkin orange, trimmed with black. She looked like a jack-o'-lantern had vomited all over her. I shuddered and looked away. Whoever said money couldn't buy taste had obviously met Lady Antonia.

Lady Antonia announced perkily, "It's that very special time of year again, my very favorite day of the entire year. The day I get to give *all* my dear ones their Christmas surprises."

As Lady Antonia beamed at the assembled company, I glanced around the table. Rosamond and Piers looked hopeful, Ottoline Chance utterly fascinated (evidently this was her first Christmas Eve at Wiggleton Priory), and the earl tense, though trying not to show it.

Lady Antonia sighed. "As you all know, I am getting on toward that time of life when one can only contemplate leaving this vale of tears. As I feel my life drawing to a close"—true, she had the appearance of a severely anorectic piece of string, but as far as I could tell, she stood nowhere near death's door—"I feel it incumbent upon me to make Final Arrangements for all those I hold dear. To that end, my solicitor, Nigel Farrington, will be motoring down to Wiggleton Priory early in the new year to draft a new will."

The earl tensed even further. I thought if I threw

something at him, he'd probably snap in two, he was stretched so taut in his chair.

Lady Antonia giggled. Trust me, it wasn't a pleasant sound. "I know," she said, "that I should have waited to tell you all this until after dear Nigel had visited, but I just *couldn't* wait." She clapped her hands girlishly.

"For my dear Rosamond and her beloved husband Piers"—Lady Antonia tried, but could not quite restrain the sniff in her voice when she pronounced Piers's name—"I wish a set of apartments set aside permanently at Wiggleton Priory for their use, as well as a sum of money to keep them fed in the style to which they have become accustomed." Piers tried unsuccessfully to suck in his gut. Rosamond turned bright pink.

"To dear Ottoline, who is shortly to become a most welcome member of our family, I bequeath my jewels. With your excessive height, my dear, I know you will show them to advantage in any light." Ottoline obviously didn't know whether she should be insulted or delighted. Or both.

"To my nephew, Algernon, I am leaving my cottage in the Algarve, the sum of one hundred thousand pounds, and my collection of snuffboxes. Dear Algie, since the house and its contents will be yours anyway, once I am upon that Higher Plain, I have little to add to your grandfather's legacy."

The earl sat deathly still. I caught Hilda Mae's eye, and she arched one eyebrow. If her research was correct, this might spell disaster for the earl. Lady Antonia allegedly controlled the family fortune, which was considerable, and its disposition. If she left the bulk of her money elsewhere, Algernon would be stuck with a white elephant of a stately home and nothing to pay for its upkeep. One hundred thousand pounds didn't go as far as it once did. Hilda Mae, the chicken farm heiress, had just moved up to first place in the contest to become the next Countess of Wiggleton.

Lady Antonia turned her beaming face upon Percival, who sat placidly on his stool, cleaning a part of his anatomy that no true gentleman would ever expose at the dinner table. "And to my pweshus liddle man, I leave the bulk of my estate for his care. Once he is deprived of his doting mother, I want him to have the very best care available. I know that you all will do your best for him, here at Wiggleton Priory, once I am gone."

The earl cleared his throat in the stunned silence that ensued this announcement. "Might I ask, Aunt, what happens to the money once Percival's time on this earth has come to a close?" With great admiration I noticed that he didn't sound as if he personally intended to make Percival's time on this earth as brief as possible.

Lady Antonia beamed even more. "It will go, in Percival's dear name, to the RSPCA, of course."

I had heard of batty peers of the realm, but Lady Antonia should be their poster child. I sat for a moment, feeling the rage emanating from nearly everyone in the room, with the exception of Hilda Mae (giving off waves of smug satisfaction), and I speculated that the idiot woman would be lucky to live to see her solicitor.

And, of course, I was correct. Hilda Mae and I escaped the fiasco of Christmas Eve dinner as quickly as possible, after presenting our gifts to them. Later, driven by my conscience, I found myself trying to explain to Lady Antonia the deadly potential of the powder keg she had ignited at dinner. Hilda Mae was of the opinion that Lady Antonia would think me stark raving mad.

Hilda Mae obviously knew her peers better than I, because that was exactly the reaction I got from Lady Antonia herself when I spoke to her later that evening. She laughed merrily when I tried to explain that I thought she was being rash in her plan to change her will and announce it publicly. "Nonsense," she said over and over again. I quickly gave up in disgust.

Sometimes sheer blind stupidity deserves what it gets. And thus it was, during my early morning walk, that

I found Lady Antonia, the back of her head bashed in, lying facedown in the ornamental pond in the gardens. Percival sat nearby, whining piteously.

Sighing, I picked up the dog, attempting to comfort him, but he finally seemed to have registered just what I was, and he struggled to be put down. I set him down gently on the ground and went back into the house to alert the family and call the police.

Three days later, Hilda Mae and I were driving back home to Bedfordshire, thankful to get away from Wiggleton Priory and the aftermath of Lady Antonia's murder. The police had arrived promptly, and I managed to pull the officer in charge aside and explain to him my conclusions about the case. Though he was not overtly appreciative of amateur assistance, he did pay attention. When I was proven correct, he bought me a pint at the pub in the village nearest the priory.

"Once you explained your reasoning that morning, Simon," Hilda Mae was commenting for the umpteenth time since the murderer had been taken away to be charged, "it all made perfect sense. Poor Percival was the essential clue, and he was the cause of the murder in the first place."

"Yes, the poor mite." Hearing us talk about him, Percival spoke up from his carrier in the backseat of the Land Rover. I turned in my seat to look at him. "Oh, do be a good boy and go back to sleep, Percival."

Hilda Mae laughed. "I can't believe you volunteered to take him, Simon. After all, he doesn't seem that keen on you."

I sighed. I certainly couldn't explain that one to her.

"We'll get used to each other. Eventually, I hope." I sighed again. "But I couldn't leave the poor little fellow there. He wouldn't have lasted a week."

Hilda Mae laughed again. "No, since the one person in that demented family—besides Lady Antonia, that is—who actually cared about him turned out to be the killer."

"Poor Ottoline. She had good intentions. Saving Lady Antonia's fortune for her beloved Algernon before the old bat could change her will. Not that it would have done her much good in the long run, even if she had gotten away with it."

I continued sourly, "I'm a bit surprised, actually, that you didn't want to stay behind and console the earl in his double loss."

Hilda Mae smiled. "Not to worry, Simon, my dear. Algie is meeting me in London after New Year's."

I groaned in mock despair. "So I guess you're going to give up the glamorous life of an assistant professor of medieval history to become the next Countess of Wiggleton."

"Now, Simon," Hilda Mae purred, "don't sound so censorious. Algie is rather adorable, after all."

"But my dear," I lamented, "those *ears*!"

She turned to flutter her eyelashes. "But Simon, don't forget! I have enough money for whatever plastic surgery it takes."

"Something that poor Ottoline couldn't offer," I commented wryly. "I must admit, I can't help but feel sorry for the poor dumb girl. If she'd been really clever, she would have bashed poor ol' Percy over the head with the same piece of wood she used on Lady Antonia. Then the choice of suspects would have been much bigger."

"Being a dog lover can be inconvenient, eh, Simon?" Hilda Mae shook her head. I had the feeling that, if Hilda Mae had been the murderer, there would have been two corpses and no regrets.

"The police officer wrapped it up very quickly. He listened well, but it didn't hurt that Ottoline acted guilty from the get go."

"Not to mention the fact that someone should have explained the concept of fingerprints to the poor girl."

Hilda Mae was at her bitchy best. "But since horses don't have them, it wouldn't have done much good."

"I suppose you didn't consider explaining that to her during your little chat after dinner on Christmas Eve?" And she probably thought I hadn't noticed.

Hilda Mae was not in the least disconcerted. "Why, Simon, it was just a little bit of girl talk. About weddings and such. You know the kind of thing I mean."

"Uh-huh," I said skeptically. "And Ottoline, who probably never had an original thought in her life, suddenly came up with the idea to do in Lady Antonia and thus save all the money for dear, dear Algie."

Hilda Mae grinned. "Now, Simon, even someone as dim as Ottoline can have the occasional flash of inspiration. However misguided it might be."

"And somehow be conveniently convinced that it was all her idea to begin with?" I observed.

Hilda Mae said nothing, merely smiled again, and I couldn't help but admire the ruthlessness of the woman driving my Land Rover. Probably a family trait.

As Percival complained yet again from the backseat, I said resignedly to Hilda Mae, "I think I'm going to find out just *how* inconvenient being kind to dumb animals can be."

"Merry Christmas to you, Simon!" Hilda Mae said, then talked about wedding gowns all the way to Bedfordshire. For the first time, I heartily regretted that I couldn't turn into a bat and fly home by myself.

Psycho Santa's Got a Brand-New Bag

Deborah Adams

Macavity Award–winning short story writer DEBORAH ADAMS agreed to a blind date with a man (who later became her husband) only because he had a Saint Bernard. She currently plays mom to Clifford, a shaggy black stray who wandered into her yard and forgot to leave; Data, an abused mongrel who was abandoned near the Adamses' home in Waverly, Tennessee; and an assortment of cats and tropical fish. One of her short stories, "Building Herbert," appears in the earlier *Canine Crimes* anthology.

Santa choke-slammed me to the mat and pinned me for a three count while Jericho chewed on my toes. Just another day at the Pole.

"I'll give you one more chance, Grady Elf!" the champ shouted. He grabbed my collar, hauled me to my feet, then prepared to execute a flying backflip off the top rope.

Unreasonable as it sounds, I went along with this daily ritual. You see, we've never unionized, and in this hard-core What You See Is What You Get world, there are damned few job opportunities for elves.

"Whatever you say, Boss," I agreed. "Just let me give Jericho his kibble first." I scooped the puppy into my arms and let him lick my face, reasonably certain that Santa wouldn't attack me and chance hurting Jericho.

The Big Guy was about to object when suddenly out

on the lawn there arose such a clatter ... no, wait. That's a different story. This time the distraction was caused by the arrival at ringside of an officious young elf named Hemmit.

"There's a breakdown on line three," Hemmit announced with a superior smile. "Would Mr. Claus care to have a look?"

Santa pulled his fire-engine red spandex tights over a belly that remained ample in spite of his rigorous training. "Are you completely helpless?" he screamed at Hemmit. "Can't you handle a little thing like that without interrupting my match? I'm defending my title here! Take some responsibility, why don'tcha?"

This was strategically unwise. I knew it. Hemmit knew it. Even Jericho started to squirm and whine. I tried to provide damage control. "Santa, perhaps you—"

"Always trying to undermine my authority, aren't you?" The once jolly old elf pounded the air with his fists and jumped up and down, rattling the loose boards under the mat. His face turned bright red, making a Christmasy contrast to the snow-white hair and beard. "I! Won't! Stand! For! It!"

Santa sputtered and spewed, continuing the sort of incoherent tirade that we were growing accustomed to at the Pole. Most of the elves in the audience watched nervously, prepared to dodge flying chairs if necessary. Hemmit, though, grinned with delight, knowing his side had scored another victory.

From somewhere in the crowd I heard an elf whisper, "The old guy's a psycho. The sooner he's gone, the better for us."

I sighed. Jericho buried his muzzle under my arm. Pro-Santa elves hung their heads; the others smacked their lips, tasting the sweet end to a vicious rivalry between Santa and Hemmit. Things did not look good for old Claus, or for those of us who tried in vain to defend his sanity and his job.

The revolution had started the day Mrs. Claus packed

her electric socks and ran away to St. Thomas, claiming she was fed up with dreary winters and housework. And with Santa, of course. She wanted a younger man, someone who would make her feel what she called "the zest of life" again.

Santa was stunned, then angry. Finally he pitched into a months' long depression that left the Pole essentially leaderless. After that it was a dizzying downward spiral laced with eggnog and coconut bourbon balls.

Changing standards in the Outer World only contributed to Santa's angst. Once upon a time, the good little boys and girls had been rewarded with dollies and red wagons, and the bad little boys and girls punished for their wickedness with lumps of coal. These days over-indulgent parents have assumed Santa's role, leniently providing an abundance of expensive toys for their offspring—regardless of behavior—instead of trusting in Santa Claus. It was no wonder The Boss felt useless and redundant.

That first Christmas after the breakup went down as the single most disastrous holiday on record. Santa drove the sleigh through power lines, causing blackouts in seven cities. He missed some homes altogether while leaving an abundance of dollies and tea sets under the tree of an elderly bachelor. Worst of all, the Claus gorged himself on cookies and milk in a home in Atlanta, then upchucked in a Minneapolis living room.

The following morning Santa staggered into the workshop looking as though he'd been trampled by a herd of reindeer. The fire in Rudolph's eyes suggested that possibility had been considered.

"Helluva night, boys!" Santa had said, and dropped his bag on the floor. "I'm ready for bed."

Kash Elf was horrified, as we all were. He hurried to retrieve the bag, then turned to me and whispered, "There's something in here."

Obviously Kash was mistaken. You see, Santa's bag is a magic bag. How else could all the toys we make fit into it? And how else could Santa pull out exactly the right toy for each child along his route?

This being the case, it stands to reason that there is never anything left in the bag because magic is meticulous and always provides exactly the right amount of itself.

"Nonsense, Kash Elf," I said. I took the bag from him and reached inside, only to grab a small handful of fur. "Gads! It's a dog!"

A puppy, to be more exact. It was largely brown with a few black markings on its face and a big red bow tied around its neck. This meant that somewhere in the world, a child had not gotten his Christmas puppy. Santa had broken a heart.

We had no way of rectifying the matter, since only Santa could keep track of millions of Christmas wishes and it goes without saying that he had no idea where the animal belonged.

And so Jericho joined our family. Born of the bag, he insisted on sleeping in it every night, as if returning to his mother's womb. This introduced us to an amazing property of the magic bag that we would never have discovered otherwise: each morning Jericho emerged from his sleep as if for the first time, reborn daily.

While Jericho brought a brightness and cheer to our lives that we'd never had before, there was still the overwhelming anxiety produced by Santa's mood. We elves walked on tiptoe throughout the village, always expecting the worst.

And then, after months of whining and moping, Santa had emerged one morning from the gloom of his TV room, pasty and bloated, but with a spark in his eye that we had almost forgotten. "Grady Elf!" he called when he saw me. "I need a trainer. You've got an athletic background, right?"

I tried to explain that my two-month stint as a reindeer jockey hardly counted, but once Santa gets an idea in his head, it's nearly impossible to dislodge it. Hence the many disastrous chimney incidents before that near-fatal one convinced him to change his MO.

I blamed myself. When Santa had argued against cable television, it was I who kept after him to have it installed. My reasons were purely selfish; I'd heard cable offered the sort of programming that could keep a lonely elf warm during long winter nights.

How could I have known that Santa would discover Pay-Per-View wrestling? Or that he would get it into his shaggy old head to earn the World Heavyweight Belt and surround himself with scantily-clad dancers in order to show his estranged wife that she had tossed away the best man she'd ever encounter?

And now Santa Claus, the professional wrestler wannabe, was throwing himself full-force into the ropes, threatening to destroy all comers. Since he had made good on the same promise several times before (not because he's a talented wrestler, but simply by virtue of his size), most of the elves exited our makeshift arena en masse.

Hemmit Elf lagged behind, his arms folded across his banty chest. He leaned casually against the doorframe and stopped me as I tried to escape the embarrassing spectacle in the ring.

"Well, Grady Elf," he said. "Do you still think he's capable of running this organization?"

I tried to shrug it off. "This is just part of the performance," I assured him, aiming for nonchalance. "It's entertainment."

Hemmit Elf snorted. "He's a lunatic! The revolution's almost over, and the dictator's about to topple."

At exactly that moment, Santa bounced off the ropes and pitched facedown onto the mat, sputtering, "Ho-ho-ho for life!"

The senior elves—Chabo, Kash, Malenky, and Bill—joined me in the executive dining room for a bachelor's lunch of sandwiches and grog. "I remember," Kash said, as he did every day, "when the Mrs. cooked up a hot lunch that—"

"Yes, Kash," I said sharply. "We all remember. But we've lingered too long in the past. After this morning's fiasco, Santa's job is hanging by a thread. We've got to make him see how his behavior jeopardizes the system. If he continues to neglect his duties—"

Jericho jumped into my lap and yapped for attention, unconcerned with our crumbling empire. I pulled a small rubber ball from my vest pocket and lobbed it at the wall. Jericho made a flying leap to catch and mangle the bouncing prey.

"Hemmit Elf has an unnatural ability to be in the right place at the worst possible time," I said.

"Worst time for *us*," Malenky Elf reminded me. "Perfect time for them."

By *them* he meant the rebels, the young elves led by Hemmit, who chafed at Santa's insistence on maintaining the status quo. Hemmit Elf wanted mechanization, computerized inventory, Humvees to replace the reindeer, and a cappuccino bar in the sleigh room. Santa wouldn't hear of it, of course. Neither would he trouble himself to offer other suggestions for updating the operation. Sometimes I wondered if he really wanted his job at all.

The rebels had begun to spread dissension among the crew, initiating sick-outs during the busiest season. They grabbed every opportunity to highlight Santa's apathy and bizarre behavior. And while I hesitated to point a finger, there had been several unfortunate illnesses that ran rampant among the reindeer.

Piled one atop the other, these minor annoyances had inflated the level of frustration among the workers. Where once we'd been a merry band of toy professionals, we were now a frustrated assemblage of blue elves.

"Maybe," Chabo Elf said, thoughtfully stroking his thinning beard, "it's time we surrendered to the inevitable."

Jericho's head snapped up. He stared at Chabo Elf as if he'd understood the words and was appalled by them.

"*Et tu,* Chabo?" Kash asked sadly.

Bill Elf grimaced and moaned, "Who's next?"

"Chabo Elf, you aren't serious!" I protested. "They're a small group of troublemakers. If we keep our heads, this nonsense will blow over."

"Will it?" Chabo Elf asked. "Christmas is only a week away. Our production is down eighteen percent. Rudolph isn't half-recovered from the stomach upset. The only thing that can save us is good old-fashioned Christmas magic, and the only person who can make that happen is a middle-aged, steroid-laden has-been who just issued a cage match challenge to Hulk Hogan."

"Look, Santa will snap out of it!" I was getting a bit testy myself. Truth was, I didn't know if Santa would ever be himself again, but elves of my generation are genetically inclined toward optimism. "It's a midlife crisis. These things happen."

"To Santa Claus?" Malenky Elf asked skeptically.

"Sure. Why not?" I nodded firmly. "We confront him—tactfully, of course—and lay it on the table. Once he understands—"

The dining room door blew open and in stalked Quiggle Elf, Hemmit's right-hand fiend. He was red-faced and shaking his fist in a perfect imitation of Santa's earlier performance in the ring. "You're all going down for this one!" he shouted. "Santa just attacked Hemmit and tried to kill him!"

We followed Quiggle at a run back to the workshop, with Jericho bringing up the rear. By the time we arrived, Hemmit's henchmen had him surrounded. Their sturdy little elf bodies formed a barricade around the leader, who sat cross-legged in the middle of the floor, an ice pack held to the back of his head.

Hemmit looked directly at me, smug even in his battered condition. His eyes didn't quite work in sync, but that hardly mattered. He could see the future clearly enough and it looked bright for him, indeed.

I sat on the floor beside Hemmit, feeling a smidgen of sympathy for the cockeyed villain. "Tell me exactly what happened," I said.

A lump stuck out on the back of Hemmit's head, already turning more colors than a string of Christmas lights. The skin had been broken, but the bleeding was light and had already stopped, leaving a reddish black crust in the center of the lump.

"Surely you can figure it out," Hemmit snapped. "Santa the psycho got caught up in his performance. He attacked me from behind. With that." Hemmit pointed to the Louisville Slugger lying on the floor behind him.

I scooted over for a closer look at the alleged weapon. A couple of hairs, Hemmit's length and color, remained on the bat and there was a small nick in the wood.

There was no denying that Hemmit had been hit with *something*, and the bat seemed the most likely blunt object. "But how do you know it was Santa?" I asked. "I mean, if you were attacked from behind . . ."

"Who else would've done it?" Hemmit's glazed eyes blazed with anger. "You heard the old freak threaten me just this morning!"

"The Boss doesn't usually walk the halls with a baseball bat at the ready," I said snidely.

"He got it from the bag!" Hemmit snapped back. He winced as he turned to point, indicating the low shelf where Santa's bag was stored throughout the year.

The bag was nowhere to be seen.

"Why would Santa conk you on the head just to get his bag?" I asked.

Hemmit's sly smile disgusted me. "Because," he said and flipped his hand airily, "he doesn't want *me* to have it. Childish of him, isn't it?"

"He's gone too far!" someone shouted, and the group concurred.

"Boot him out!"

"Hang him like a stocking!"

The other elves nodded agreement, and not just Hemmit's rebel crew; even among the loyal there were reluctant mutterings, or worse—silence.

Jericho paced the shelf, searching in vain for his bag. I thought I knew how he felt. The heart of our known world had disappeared; neither of us knew how to proceed so we told ourselves that persistence and diligence would make everything right again.

The shelf is empty, I admitted to myself, *and the Pole belongs to Hemmit now.*

A jingle of bells in the hallway told me the final battle in the war for Pole Control was about to erupt.

Santa bounded into the room, his cheeks red as cherries and his manner bright as tinsel. "Ho ho!" he boomed. "What's this? A party?"

"Keep him away from me!" Hemmit whined.

Instantly the front row of elves moved to surround their gutless leader. The Boss was temporarily confused; then he burst into jolly laughter. "Not to worry, Hemmit," he said. "I'm a ragin' madman in the ring, but just plain Claus out here."

I got to my feet and crossed the room to stand by Santa's side. Not a single elf joined me. Reaching up to tug at his beard, I whispered, "Santa, we have a problem."

The Big Guy listened quietly to my brief explanation, looked intently at the unforgiving faces of the elves around him, then turned and trudged back toward his living quarters. I watched him until he turned the corner at the end of the hall, but nothing in his demeanor answered the question on all our minds: Is Santa a homicidal maniac?

Chabo Elf quietly joined me in the doorway.

"There's no fight left in him," I said. This truth settled like a glacier on my chest.

"Hasn't been for a long time now," Chabo agreed.

"In that sense, this *is* his fault. It began to slip away when Santa lost his spirit."

I nodded. "Exactly right. Am I the last one to see it? Am I that naive?"

Chabo put a wrinkled old hand on my shoulder. "Not naive," he said mildly. "You have more faith than the rest of us. You *believe*."

"Yeah, well." I turned to look at the others. Elves formerly loyal to the Old Way were shuffling their feet, shamefacedly listening to Hemmit spout his detailed plans for revamping the system. "I have no belief in what's coming. I have no faith in Hemmit."

"Neither has anyone else," Chabo said, with a meaningful look.

I pondered this for several seconds before understanding dawned. "Without belief . . ."

Chabo Elf finished for me. "There is no Santa Claus."

It was a sleepless night in the village. The noise of celebration in Hemmit's quarters was almost as nerve-racking as the martial arts movie sound effects blaring from Santa's television. Even in a silent room, I'd have been wide-awake.

Jericho, too, roamed and whined, unable to sleep without his security bag. I cradled the puppy in my arms and laid my head on his. "There's a new world order," I told him. "It'll take a lot of getting used to, Jericho."

He cocked one ear as if he wanted to hear more, so I talked on. As the long night passed, I told Jericho the story of Santa Claus: that he stood for the magic of faith, that his miracles kept hope alive in a universe that sometimes tried to crush the souls of its children, and that, whatever happened, we should always remember Santa the way he had been in the beginning.

When the cuckoo called five A.M., I dragged myself out to meet the new day and the new regime. Jericho followed on my heels, probably afraid that I would disappear the way his security bag had done.

Passing Santa's door, I heard a ferocious burp from within and surmised that he'd been hitting the eggnog pretty heavily. *What does it matter?* I asked myself, and continued down the hall toward Chabo's room.

My knock was met by a grunt followed shortly by the slow, heavy steps of a downcast elf. Chabo opened the door a crack, peered at me through red and swollen eyes, then stepped back to allow me inside.

"Get any sleep?" I asked.

Chabo's room was a disaster, a hundred diverse items tossed into a pile on the floor. A small suitcase sat at the end of the bed.

"Change is inevitable, but I'd as soon go through it somewhere else." Chabo shook his head and sighed.

Jericho wiggled out of my arms and hit the floor running. I watched him scamper about, fighting through the pile of clutter as if the fate of the world depended on his victory. Satisfied that the pile posed no threat, Jericho stuck his fuzzy head under the bed, wiggled his tail, and disappeared. Presumably to battle evil dust bunnies.

"Want to share a sleigh to the bus station?" Chabo Elf offered. "Traveling is easier with a friend."

Leaving hadn't occurred to me until that moment. I'd never been away from the Pole, I realized. Never! The Outer World was as strange and new to me as each new day was to Jericho.

As I pondered the possibilities and pitfalls of starting a new life outside the Pole, Chabo waited patiently. The older generation is like that; we have learned patience through the centuries because without that virtue, we'd surely go mad. What is there to do at the Pole, after all, but wait for the year to pass and for Christmas to arrive?

"Yes, thanks," I said. "I'll start packing right aw—" My impulsive choice was interrupted by a noise coming from underneath Chabo Elf's bed. "What on earth is that?"

I leaned over for a look beneath the low cot. "It sounds like snoring," I muttered. "Poor Jericho must be worn-out."

Sure enough, the puppy was sleeping soundly—inside Santa's bag!

"Chabo?" I straightened and looked him in the eye. "How did Santa's bag get under your bed?"

Chabo stared right back at me, but he spoke not a word.

"You don't mean . . . *you* took the bag? It was you who clobbered Hemmit with the bat?"

This brought a mischievous grin to his face. "That's the most fun I've had in years."

I allowed myself a moment of vicarious satisfaction before expressing the appropriate moral outrage. "Don't you see what you've done? You've destroyed any hope of saving Santa's job. Chabo, you have to confess right away."

Chabo shrugged. "Oh, I'll confess, if you like. But that won't save Santa. Nothing will. I've tried"—he spread his hands to indicate the objects strewn about the floor—"to find an answer. All night I tried. This is the result."

I was confused and told him so. Frankly I suspected that Santa wasn't the only madman among us.

"That's why I took the bag," Chabo explained. "I knew nothing less than magic could set things right. It's gone too far, you know. Santa let it go too far. Sometimes changes take on a life of their own."

His desperation was understandable, but his methods were indefensible. "What did you expect to get from the bag?" I asked. "A time machine to take us back to the Good Old Days?"

"I didn't expect anything," Chabo said irritably. "That bag belongs to Claus. I was surprised it worked for me at all. As you can see, it produced junk. Just worthless junk."

I took a closer look at the objects on the floor: a set of Tinker Toys, a baseball glove, two Chatty Cathys . . . a collection of outdated toys from the bag of an outdated Claus.

Reaching underneath the bed, I slid the bag out gently so as not to disturb Jericho's long overdue nap. "Let's tell Santa," I said firmly. "We'll figure out the rest of it later."

Santa sat while Chabo related his sins. Santa *had* to sit; standing caused excruciating pain behind his eyes.

"For what it's worth," Chabo finished, "I thought I could help you. I'm sorry."

Santa rubbed his blotchy face with his hand then sighed heavily. "It was kindness, Chabo. I understand and I'm sorry I don't deserve it."

"Look, Santa." I still had Jericho and the bag in my arms. "Chabo will explain to all the elves that he assaulted Hemmit and then—"

The Boss held up a hand to stop me. "Let it go, Grady."

"But you can't—"

"Grady," Santa said sternly, "there comes a time when one must surrender to the demands of the majority. However imbecilic they may be."

Chabo hung his head, fully resigned to the demise of Santa's reign. I wanted to protest, to scream and shriek and by the very force of my heart bring back the wonderland of our youth. Instead I carefully pulled sleeping Jericho from his dark womb and held the bag out to the pathetic figure of a Claus before me.

Santa took it, running his stubby fingers over the soft, faded velvet. I could see memories etched on his wan face as he recalled the centuries of magic that he and the bag had shared. "Like a part of me," he said apologetically. "I wish I could set it all right again."

He closed his eyes and smiled a sad little smile, then reached inside. For a few seconds his hand lingered, reluctant to bring an end to the fantasy. Finally he withdrew a tightly clenched fist . . . but not an empty one.

"What's this?" Santa asked with surprise.

Chabo and I leaned in for a closer look. "Another bag?" Chabo suggested.

It was nearly identical to the bag in Santa's other hand, only newer and brighter, smelling of fresh snow and pine needles.

Jericho woke suddenly, no doubt disturbed by my gasp. The puppy wiggled free of my hold and confidently grabbed the old bag between his teeth. Santa watched as Jericho tugged the bag. "Here, pup. This one's all yours now. Hemmit can use the new one."

This arrangement suited Jericho just fine. He dragged his private sleeping quarters across the floor to a corner of Santa's room, pushed and pawed at it until the lumps were finely tuned, then curled up in the middle of the bag and fell asleep.

"Well," Santa said, "at least someone's happy."

I looked from Chabo to the Claus and back again. "Don't you get it? It's a new bag!"

"Yes," Chabo said, bewildered by my excitement. "What of it?"

"Santa pulled a new bag from his bag!" I spoke slowly, as if explaining a difficult concept to children. "When Santa Claus reaches into his magic bag, out comes exactly the right gift."

"But I wasn't trying to bring out a gift," Santa insisted.

"Weren't you? You said you wished you could set things right, and out came a new bag. With a fresh supply of Christmas magic. It's a second chance, Santa! You can take back your throne from Hemmit!"

"Oh, no." Santa folded the new bag over his arm, instinctively stroking it smooth. "The time has passed—"

I stuck my forefingers in my ears to block out his denial and chanted, "I believe, I believe, I believe."

After a few seconds Chabo followed suit and we chanted in unison. Then Jericho woke up and chimed in declaring, "Yip yipyip, yip yipyip."

The elves were assembled in the gym, curious to learn why they'd been called away from their work during the busiest season. A ladder stood in the middle of the ring, with the new Christmas bag suspended from the ceiling above it.

As Santa took center stage, a legal document in one hand and a microphone in the other, the room fell silent. Santa gazed out over the crowd, spotted Hemmit in the audience, and grinned at him.

"Hemmit Elf!" he screamed into the mike. "You got a big mouth! You been talking trash 'bout me, saying you can take my place. Well, I'm givin' you a chance to prove just how wrong you are!"

Hemmit and his gang snickered nervously.

"You think you can run the Pole? Huh?"

From the audience Hemmit answered with his usual arrogance. "Anything you can do, I can do better and twice as fast."

Santa feigned admiration. "Ooooh. A brave elf! Well, a talented upstart like yourself, you wouldn't be afraid to put that claim in writing. I've got a contract right here." Santa shook the paper at Hemmit. "You want a chance at the Pole? All you gotta do is sign this contract. Just agree to fight me in a ladder match. Whoever gets the bag"— Santa looked up at the prize— "gets the job. And the loser leaves the Pole forever."

"That's ridiculous," Hemmit muttered.

"Maybe," Santa allowed. "But it's the only way you'll get rid of me." Again he held up the contract, showed a mouthful of teeth to his nemesis, and hissed, "To be the Claus, you gotta beat the clause!"

I watched with satisfaction as Hemmit's face changed colors—red, magenta, purple. Santa had called him out, and if he didn't accept the challenge he'd show himself to be a cowardly blowhard. Quaking in his pointy shoes, Hemmit shuffled toward the ring.

Whatever the outcome, this would be a different sort of Christmas, the tone of which would be determined by the nature of the ruling Claus. There was no guarantee The Boss would be able to retain his title against a wily elf like Hemmit, of course. I was nervous, yes, but my optimism swelled as Hemmit climbed the steps to the ring.

I believe what happened next was an omen. Charged with excitement, Jericho dashed forward to meet Hemmit, who foolishly halted his ascent just long enough for the Christmas pup to prop a hind leg on the traitorous elf and . . .

Midnight Clear

Jane Haddam

JANE HADDAM is the author of sixteen Gregor De-
markian mysteries. (The most recent installment is *Skele-
ton Key*.) Married for thirteen years to three-time Edgar
Award winner, the late William L. DeAndrea, she lives
with her two sons in Litchfield County, Connecticut.

Once, when she was very young, Carolanne Tierney
had believed that she was changed. That was her First
Holy Communion, at Sacred Heart Church, on East
Main Street. In those days, East Main was a major thor-
oughfare, a street full of clothing shops and bakeries,
and the side streets that surrounded it were where good
people lived. Carolanne remembered the Murphys and
the Kellys and the Bohrs.

In those years before the subdivisions were built in
Bunker Hill and Robin's Wood, everybody lived in three-
decker houses with stacked porches and renters on the
top floor—except, of course, that Carolanne and her
mother *were* renters. That was because Carolanne's father had disappeared, nobody knew where. Carolanne's
mother said he was dead and went every week to light a
candle for the repose of his soul. At school, the nuns
taught Carolanne to say the rosary and make First Fri-
day devotions in honor of the Sacred Heart.

Even then, Carolanne knew that there was something
wrong in the way they lived. Nobody else's mother
locked herself in the hall closet for hours at a time, crying and praying at once. Nobody else's dinner came
down to nothing but bread and margarine at least two

151

days a week. There was more wrong there than that, but Carolanne had a hard time explaining it in words, even to herself.

There was something wrong with the way she was. Somehow, she never seemed to understand what people were talking about or when they were making jokes. Somehow, she could never be like the girls who walked down the steep hill to school with her. Years later, when all those people had moved away and there was nobody left on the street for her to talk to, Carolanne would be able to close her eyes and see just how very awful she had been. Fat. Slow. Stupid. Shabby. Maybe her soul had been transfigured, that First Holy Communion day. Her body had not been. In the elementary school pictures she still kept tucked into the top drawer of her bedroom dresser, she was the square, dark, ugly one, shoved into the back row with the boys. In the First Holy Communion picture she kept in a frame on top of her television set, she was barely visible at all.

It was visibility Carolanne was thinking of, that third day of December, when she saw Lucy Blackthorne for the first time in thirty years. Actually, she didn't see Lucy Blackthorne at all, not at the beginning. It was cold for that time of year in Waterbury, hard cold, as if the air itself had frozen into glass. Across the street, in the green and white house where the Kellys had once lived, the second floor tenants had put tinsel garlands all around their front porch. Downstairs, in Carolanne's own house, somebody was playing "Nasty As They Want to Be." One of the boys down there had a new tattoo and other boys from the street had come in to admire it. Every once in a while, there was the sound of breaking glass. Every once in a while—more rarely still—there was the sound of a toilet flushing. They took dope down there, and sold it, too, when anybody in the neighborhood had the money to buy it. Carolanne sometimes bought marijuana from them when she was feeling very bad.

That morning, she was thinking about Christmas decorations and what it would mean if she put some up. She had bought a silver tinsel garland and a string of red and blue lights. She wanted to wind them around the pillars on her porch and hang a tinsel flower at the center, to show people that she was one of the few people who still believed in God, who still went to church. The problem was that she was the only white woman left on the street. They talked about her already: about the way her coats always looked worn at the elbows and not the right size, about the way she went to work every day even though the job she had paid less than welfare, about the fact that she had nowhere to go for Christmas but the party that the parish gave. One or two of the older women had tried to befriend her. They'd come to her front door with casseroles in covered dishes and big loaves of bread. All Carolanne had been able to do was sit at her kitchen table with her hands folded, mute. It was the same kitchen table where she had eaten her breakfast on the day of her First Holy Communion. Nothing had changed, except that the kitchen now needed paint.

"You keep this up, you're going to end in the nuthouse," Mrs. Jackson had said, putting a tuna, noodle, and cream of mushroom soup dish in Carolanne's refrigerator. "A person needs someone to talk to. A person needs someone to love."

"I'm all right," Carolanne had told her.

"The people at that church of yours don't know how to behave," Mrs. Jackson had said. "The people of my church would never leave a body alone like this. They'd never let you live without even a telephone."

Downstairs, "Nasty As You Want to Be" changed to something else, to rap, a driving beat with no words behind it that Carolanne could make out. It was too hard to lift her arms when she was wearing her coat. She took her coat off and laid it down on the floor of the porch. There used to be a wicker chair out here, but it had disintegrated into twigs. She picked up the silver garland and went to the porch balustrade to begin to wind it around the column. Visibility, that was the problem here. How visible did she want to be?

She was putting Scotch tape on the end of the garland when she looked over the wall at the street and saw the dog, the most amazing dog in the universe, pure white and enormous. She stopped what she was doing and looked up and down the sidewalk. The dog was on a leash. No dogs in this neighborhood were ever on leashes. No dogs were ever pure white. If they started out that way, they got dirty, and nobody would clean them.

Carolanne looked at the other end of the leash. The woman holding on to it was tall and thin and dressed in a good camel's hair coat, the kind of coat women wore on the covers of fancy magazines like *Vogue* and *Town and Country*. Her hands kept going up to her face and rubbing it against the side. It was a gesture Carolanne had seen a thousand times, that meant that this woman was out of cocaine and needed not to be. *If she keeps it up, she'll smear her makeup,* Carolanne thought.

Then the woman turned her head and shook out her hair, and swivelled around on the backs of her stack-heeled boots. The sun came out from behind a curtain of clouds. The woman's large square-cut diamond and flat gold wedding rings gleamed in the light. Carolanne put her tinsel garland down and leaned over the porch balustrade to get a better look.

That was Lucy Blackthorne down there, who had the best veil in Carolanne's First Holy Communion class. That was Lucy Blackthorne down there, who had been the first to move away to a subdivision and the first to buy her clothes at Lord & Taylor and the first to announce that she was going away to college somewhere real, at Smith, which was too expensive a place for most of the people in Waterbury to go.

Carolanne picked up the garland again and threaded it through her hands. Any moment now, one of the boys on the street would notice this woman. He would see her rubbing the side of her face and know what she was looking for. Then Lucy would have her cocaine and she would take away her dog, and that would be the last Carolanne ever saw of either one of them.

The dog was leaping and prancing in the light, running in circles, barking happily. Every time it barked, Lucy Blackthorne seemed to wince.

It was one of the boys from the ground floor who came out to give Lucy Blackthorne what she wanted to buy. He was more cautious about it than she wanted to be, and drew her up on the ground floor porch in order to make the deal. Carolanne came out the front door to find them standing together, huddled, while Lucy counted out money. The dog was sitting still at Lucy's side, but looking as if it wanted to run. When the door opened, the two of them jumped. Then Miguel saw that it was only her and went back to what he was doing.

Lucy brushed hair off her face and blinked. "I know you," she said. "Don't I know you? It's Carol Something."

"Carolanne Tierney," Carolanne said. Her voice came out in a high squeak, she didn't know why. She leaned over and stroked the dog on its head. He seemed to like it.

Lucy took the clear plastic bag Miguel was holding out to her and stuffed it into her big leather shoulder bag. Carolanne knew what they called those shoulder bags, because they sold them in the mall and she had gone to look at them: Coach. Lucy had a pair of gloves that were made of leather, too, stuffed into the pockets of her coat. Carolanne stroked the dog again.

"You can come upstairs if you want," she said finally. "To lay out some lines, I mean. If you need to."

"Upstairs?"

"My apartment is upstairs. You've been there. When we were children."

Lucy swivelled around on the heels of her boots again. She took in the broken boards on the porch and the peeling paint on the porch ceiling and the people in the street. The men wore clothes that looked as if they had been dirty for years. The women wore bright colored Spandex everything, tight stretchy things in lemon yellow and lime green. Lucy rubbed the side of her face again and then started to bite her nails, viciously, as if she didn't care if she made herself bleed.

"You'd feel better if you did a few lines," Carolanne said. "It's just up the stairs. You could bring the dog."

"I don't understand how you can live like this," Lucy said. "White people aren't supposed to live like this."

Carolanne wanted to say that she knew a lot of white people who lived like this, but instead she stood back, and held open the door, and watched the dog. It was glad to be moving again, even if it was moving into a dark and claustrophobic house. Carolanne wondered why she had never noticed before how narrow the stairways were.

"Christ," Lucy said. "Were these houses this cramped when we were all growing up?"

The dog found a place on the couch as soon as they got into Carolanne's apartment. Lucy tried to make him get off and sit on the floor, but Carolanne stopped her. She liked the look of the dog where it was, comfortable and happy, in a way she couldn't remember anyone ever being comfortable and happy inside the walls of this apartment. She sat Lucy down at the table and got her best hand mirror out from the high shelf in the bathroom. She offered coffee or tea or Coca-Cola and was refused.

She doesn't want to drink out of any of my glasses, Carolanne thought, and then she sat down on the couch next to the dog to see what it would do. It pressed its nose into the palm of her hand and whimpered. It was even more beautiful close-up than it had been far away from her on the street. When she stroked it, it moved under her hand. When she put her face close to it, it felt as warm as the wall near the radiator when the heat was on.

Lucy had laid out her lines on the mirror. Her hands were shaking. Her whole body was tense. She looked through her big bag for a straw and came up with the stub of one. It was a good thing, because for cocaine you needed those thin cocktail straws, and Carolanne didn't have any.

"I can't believe I get like this," Lucy said. "It's all Dan's fault. Dan and his vacations. If there's someplace to score a little coke on Aruba, I didn't find it."

There was probably someplace to score a little coke on Aruba. Carolanne thought there was probably someplace to score a little coke in a convent, if you really wanted it badly enough. She wondered if Lucy's husband had been watching her, if everybody Lucy lived with knew she was like this. There was something about the idea that was very satisfying.

Lucy stuck the straw up her nose and inhaled. Then she stuck the straw up her other nostril and inhaled again. Almost instantly, she was both calmer and more hyper at the same time.

"Oh, thank God," she said. "I couldn't think straight. I've been going nuts all morning."

"I think you're supposed to watch it when it starts to make you nuts."

"Probably." Lucy had laid out one more line. She sucked half of it into each nostril and stood up. She now seemed not only alert but formidable, as if all her systems had suddenly switched on, as if she were a super robot in a late night science-fiction movie.

"Jesus," she said, walking around the kitchen.

Carolanne rubbed her hand into the dog's fur. It turned and shimmied at her touch.

"Is it a girl dog or a boy dog?" she asked Lucy.

"It's a boy dog. It's a Samoyed. We call him Sammy."

"Is Samoyed a breed?"

"Of course it's a breed."

"I didn't know," Carolanne said. "I don't know anything about dogs. I don't even know anybody who has a dog."

"It's a pain in the ass," Lucy said. "It's got to be brushed every day. And washed once a week. And it sheds everywhere. You have no idea."

"It's beautiful."

"It's useless as a guard dog. That's what I wanted him for. Today. Coming here. But they don't guard. They like people too much. Even bad people."

"Right," Carolanne said.

Lucy went back to the table and began to put away her cocaine things. She wet her finger and ran it over the surface of Carolanne's mirror, making sure to get the powder up. She checked twice that the clear plastic bag was securely closed, and then put it in her makeup bag just in case.

"I have to get out of here," she said. "Thank you for letting me use your kitchen. It really helped."

"You can use it any time. When you come back. You can bring the dog."

"I won't be back," Lucy said.

She heaved the big bag up on her shoulder and called to the dog. The dog leaped off the couch and ran to her, wagging its tail furiously, letting out little barks. *Sammy*, Carolanne thought, and then wondered why Lucy didn't seem to like him much. To Carolanne, he was a kind of miracle. She'd had no idea that animals like this existed in the real world.

Lucy went out into Carolanne's living room and to the front door. She went out the front door and into the hall. The hall was cramped and dark and smelled funny. The walls always seemed to be coated with some kind of grease.

"I wish I could buy enough to last me a year," Lucy said, "but you can't do that anymore. You can't have a ton of it. If you get caught they think you're trying to sell."

"Right," Carolanne said.

Lucy made her way down the stairs, very carefully, holding onto the walls. When they got to the first floor foyer she looked around again, at the rickety table where the junk mail was, at the strips torn out of the wallpaper over the mailboxes, at the narrow stained glass windows on either side of the front door. The door to the first floor apartment opened and Miguel came out. Lucy didn't look at him. She went out into the cold and down the front porch steps.

"Thanks again," she said, not quite over her shoulder, not quite looking back. She was headed down the hill toward East Main Street with the dog at her side, moving so fast she might have been running, except for the heels.

"I'd like to get that one at night," Miguel said. "What do you think?"

"I like the dog," Carolanne said.

"A dog for a dog," Miguel said. "You could keep the dog. Give me the woman. In the dark. Where I can do what I want and nobody would give a shit if she screamed her goddamned head off."

"You shouldn't swear at Christmastime," Carolanne said.

Miguel laughed a little. He turned around and went back into the house. Carolanne watched the dog going down the hill, and the glint that the sun made on Lucy Blackthorne's rings. It would be Lucy Blackthorne Somebody Else now. She would have a married name. Carolanne didn't know why that seemed to be important.

The first time Lucy came back it was a Saturday morning again, only a week later, and Carolanne wasn't even home. She had gone down the hill and across East Main to the new mall, which had been built right in the center of town, so that people could walk to it. She could walk to the place she worked, too—it was called the Quik Stop—but she never went there unless she had to be there. She liked the mall because there was a food court where she could get things like Burger King and Taco Bell, that didn't cost too much money. She liked it, too, because there were so many Christmas decorations up—tinsel and bells, crepe paper and Santa's elves made out of felt. Most of the rest of Waterbury seemed to be intent on pretending that Christmas wasn't happening at all.

Coming home, with the dark just starting, Carolanne stopped at Sacred Heart church and went inside. She knelt down in a pew in the back and said the three prayers she knew by heart, the Lord's Prayer, the Hail Mary, and the Act of Contrition. She told herself she should go to Confession, because it had been months, but there was no priest in the confessional and she didn't want to go anyway. She prayed that somebody would give her a big, white dog, a beautiful dog, as a Christmas present, and then knew that it wouldn't happen. The Christmas presents the parish gave were always the same. Middle-aged men got gloves. Middle-aged women got soap scented to smell like peaches.

Coming up the hill, it was the dog she saw first, again. Sammy was sitting on her own front porch, thumping his tail against the boards. He always looked as if he were smiling, this dog. Carolanne hadn't known that dogs could look as if they could smile.

When she got closer, she saw Lucy, standing on the porch with her hands in the pockets of her camel's hair coat.

"I'm just saying we should meet somewhere else," Lucy was saying. "Somewhere I could bring the car. I hate walking up this hill."

"Bring the car here. We got space on the street to park the car," Miguel told her.

Lucy let out a long stream of white air. It was cold enough to see your breath. Carolanne was shivering.

"I can't bring the car here," Lucy said. "I can't leave a Mercedes parked on this street. It would get stolen. You know it would."

"I bet you have insurance. Why do you care if it gets stolen?"

"I care about the report I'd have to make to the police. What do you think I would be able to tell my husband? That I came up here to shop?"

"Tell him you came up here to see Carolanne," Miguel said. "You and Carolanne are lifelong buddies."

Lucy turned on the step. She hadn't noticed that anybody was coming, although Sammy had. Sammy noticed everything and everyone. Lucy took her hands out of her coat.

"Oh, thank God," she said. "You're back. I knocked on your door and there wasn't any answer."

"I need two hundred fifty dollars," Miguel said.

Lucy reached into her bag and came out with an oversized wallet. It had a checkbook inside it as well as places for money and credit cards. There were a lot of credit cards. Carolanne couldn't imagine why anybody would need that many. Lucy handed the money over and took the clear plastic bag.

"I can't bring the car onto this street," she said again.

Then she went through the front door and up the stairs, toward Carolanne's apartment, without waiting to see if she would be asked.

"Stick her good," Miguel said in a half whisper, his lips right at Carolanne's ear. And then he laughed.

In Carolanne's apartment, the dog went straight to the couch and Lucy went straight to the kitchen table. This time she was angry more than she was jumpy. She was flying on hostility the way cokeheads sometimes got, and that meant she was already high. Carolanne got the mirror out and sat down on the couch next to the dog. The dog whimpered and nuzzled at her. It was insane how good that felt. She was an ugly woman, she knew that. She'd never had much in the way of physical contact of any kind, although she'd lost her virginity in high school, the way everybody did, because at that age you could always find somebody who wanted to do it. She remembered almost nothing about that incident, except that it had taken place under the bleachers on the football field in the chilly semi-frost of late fall, and the boy had been almost as fat as she was. That, and that his name was Jacky. Jacky had written her name up on the mirror in the boys' room when it was over, but nobody else had ever bothered to call.

Lucy sucked a line into her nose and then closed her eyes and leaned her head back. "I can't believe he really did it. I can't believe it," she said.

"Who did what?" Carolanne said.

"My husband. That's who. He took most of that bag I bought last week and put it down the garbage disposal. The garbage disposal, for Christ's sake."

"Why?"

"Because he's a pain in the ass," Lucy said. "Because he doesn't do anything and never did. Doesn't smoke. Doesn't drink. Doesn't snort. Doesn't do anything. Sometimes I want to burn down the house to see what he does when it's gone."

"Mostly I thought people like you didn't snort to begin with," Carolanne said, although as soon as she said it she knew it was a lie. Everybody did everything. You saw it every day. She put her head down into Sammy's belly and rubbed her face against his fur. He smelled like shampoo and violets.

"I can't focus when I don't have cocaine," Lucy said. "I never could. It used to drive me crazy. I could never get anything done."

"I wish I had a dog like this," Carolanne said.

Lucy got up and started putting things back into her bag. "I'm better with cocaine," she said. "I've always been better with cocaine. I'm even better in bed. You'd think he would appreciate it."

"You don't have to go right away," Carolanne said.

"Your friend downstairs is an asshole," Lucy said. "I can't bring the car into this neighborhood. If it got stolen I'd be stuck. I'd never be able to explain what I was doing here. He'd know in a shot."

"Miguel wants to jump you," Carolanne said. "Did you know that? Maybe you should bring the car. It could be a kind of insurance."

"I can't tell Dan I was coming here to see you," Lucy said. "He'd know it was a lie. Or he'd think you were dealing."

Sammy got up off the couch and headed for Carolanne's front door. Carolanne stayed on the couch this time, not wanting to see them both out. She could hear the edge of anger in Miguel's voice, even if Lucy couldn't. She knew what they were like down there, and what they wanted.

"You ought to watch yourself," she said to Lucy.

"I ought to find someplace else to buy cocaine," Lucy said. "I would find someplace else to buy cocaine if I got enough time to go looking. If Dan would stay the hell out of my things."

"You could come and visit and bring the dog," Carolanne said.

Lucy was already out the door and into the hall. Carolanne heard her steps on the stairs, and Sammy's steps, too. When Lucy got to the ground floor, the door to Miguel's apartment opened, and there was laughter. Carolanne could picture them there, watching Lucy in her coat and boots and rings, watching Lucy's dog.

Years ago, back when they were all growing up together, Lucy Blackthorne had started a club that girls could only belong to if they lived on the bottom floor. They were all about five years old at the time, and the rule kept out nobody on the street but Carolanne herself.

"I wish you wouldn't talk to me in the hall," Lucy

had said, when they were in junior high school together. "People will think that you and I are friends."

It was three days later when Carolanne saw the story in the *Waterbury Republican*, a small story with a big picture tucked into a corner on the page where the wedding announcements were. Carolanne almost never read the paper, but she had it that day, because she had needed it for cover. She had gone to the magazine rack at the Quik Stop and bought every magazine they had that was about dogs. She hadn't had time to look through them to make sure, and so she had taken them just in case. Then she had picked up the newspaper and put it on the top of the pile, to make it look as if she were just picking up a few things to read, to make it not so obvious that she cared about a dog.

It had been bad, really, since Lucy left this time. Carolanne hadn't been able to sleep for long, and when she did manage to knock off for a few minutes she dreamed too much. She dreamed of waking up and finding Sammy lying across her legs. She dreamed of Lucy dead on the sidewalk outside, her head smashed in, her body riddled with bullets, the trash left over when a drug deal went wrong. Then she would get up and go to the window and look out, willing the dog to come to her, willing him to want to be with her more than he wanted to be wherever Lucy was. He could come to work with her in the evenings and wait on the sidewalk outside until she was finished. She could take him farther up the hill to the little park where the policeman sat, twenty-four hours a day, seven days a week, to make sure nobody shot up.

The story in the *Waterbury Republican* was about a party given for a charity that Carolanne had never heard of. The picture showed Lucy with a tall, thin man in a tuxedo with a flower in his buttonhole. *Lucy Blackthorne Holt,* the caption read, *event cochair, with her husband, Dr. Daniel Holt.*

Carolanne held the picture up to the light, but there was nothing else to see. The dog was not with them. The people in the background were no one she had ever seen. She put the paper down on the table again. When they had all been in high school, there had been pictures like this one, in the school newspaper, of the people who ran the Valentine's dance and the prom.

The telephone book was under a blue plastic vase on one of the kitchen counters. Carolanne got it and opened it on the kitchen table. The names were set out under each separate town, instead of being all blended in together. She tried Waterbury and got nothing. She tried Watertown and got nothing still. She thought about Sammy stretched out on her couch while Lucy did lines and wished she had him here, now, where she could touch him with her hands, where he could move under them.

She found the listing finally under Woodbury, which made sense. It was the most expensive town this phone book covered. She passed over the listing for Holt, Dr. Daniel, and concentrated on the one that said Holt, L. Dr. Daniel would be a doctor's office. She got a piece of paper and wrote down the information: the number, the address. The address would be no use to her. She couldn't drive, and even if she could have driven she couldn't have afforded to buy a car. She read the number over four or five times, until she had it memorized, and then she got her coat.

It was very late now, nearly midnight, and so cold on the street that once she got outside she had trouble catching her breath. There were lights on in all the houses around her. There were parties going on everywhere. She checked her pocketbook one more time, to make sure she had enough change, and then headed down the hill.

"Sammy," she said, out loud, when she was far enough away from people so that nobody could hear her. The word echoed in the dark. The side streets seemed to buzz. Her coat was useless.

"I could keep him here with me," she said, out loud again, but by then it didn't matter. She was at East Main. The street was deserted. She turned right and headed toward the center of town, where the bars would be open, where there would be telephones.

She found a phone in a place called Happy Acres. It was a place with only one small window, and that taken up by a blinking sign for Pabst Blue Ribbon beer. The telephones were in the back, near the rest rooms. The rest rooms smelled of urine and something worse. The bar had nothing but men in it. They all looked older than they should have. Carolanne put the money in the slot and dialed the number she had memorized. If she got an answering machine, she thought she would die. She had started to shake, the way cokeheads shook. She was so tense, she felt as if every muscle in her body was locked tight.

If Lucy came back to the street—what? Carolanne had her eyes closed. Visions were dancing on the backs of her eyelids. Sammy was lying on the couch in her apartment, on the bed, under the kitchen table. She never went out of the apartment at all anymore. She had too much to do.

"Lucy," a man's voice said in her ear, making her jump. "You've got a breather. On your private line."

"Hang the hell up," Lucy said.

The phone went to dial tone in Carolanne's ear. She looked at it in her hand, feeling stupid. Then she put it back in its cradle and stood up.

If Lucy came back to the street, Miguel would jump her. If Lucy came back to the street, Sammy would bounce and bark on Carolanne's front porch. If Lucy came back to the street, the coke she bought would be too pure and too perfect and she would end up dead in Carolanne's kitchen, her body as stiff as the bodies of the victims in antidrug television commercials.

The Happy Acres was decorated to death for Christmas, with plastic Santa Claus heads hung in clusters of three and four on every wall, but Carolanne didn't see any of it.

After that, for a week, Carolanne called Lucy at home. She kept heavy knots of change in her purse and in the pockets of her coat. She stopped at pay phones all along her route to work and back. Sometimes the phone rang and rang and nobody picked it up. Sometimes there was an answering machine, with a man's voice on the tape that Carolanne didn't believe belonged to Daniel Holt. Sometimes Lucy picked up herself. When that happened, Carolanne would sit very still, holding her breath if she could, while Lucy sounded more and more annoyed. What Carolanne really wanted was the sound of Sammy barking, but she never got it. It was as if there was no dog on the other end of that line. It was as if Sammy had died.

By then, it was nearly Christmas Eve. Even Waterbury had begun to look crowded. Nights at the Quik Stop had begun to feel longer and longer. The Powerball jackpot was up and everybody wanted to buy tickets in time for the holiday, as if that would bring them luck. Carolanne worked through a thick fog of fear. What if Sammy really was dead? What if Lucy had finally gotten so tired of him that she had gotten rid of him, taken him to the pound, driven him out into the country and dumped him on a dirt road? There was so much that could happen to a dog, especially a dog like this one. If Daniel Holt liked Sammy as little as Lucy did, he might have had Sammy put to sleep.

On Christmas Eve, there was a van going around the city, blaring out Christmas carols through a loudspeaker on its roof. Going home, Carolanne heard "Deck the Halls" and "The First Noel." The doors of Sacred Heart Church were propped open. People were coming for midnight Mass. Carolanne thought about going up there to say a prayer for Sammy, but she was due to go to Mass at ten the next morning, with the rest of the people who would be at the parish party, and she didn't want to go now. She thought she should have done something about her apartment. She could have put up a small tree, if she had wanted to. She could have stenciled her windows to look as if they were filled with snowflakes.

She was just turning up the hill when the car pulled up to the curb beside her. She felt it coming in behind her and froze. Men offered her dope from cars, sometimes. Men offered her money for sex, too, because some men liked to have sex with heavy women. It made them feel they were having sex with their mothers.

Carolanne made herself think about Sammy and stare straight ahead. She tried to move faster, although the hill was steep and she always had a hard time climbing it. Then the door of the car opened and Lucy's voice said, "Carolanne. Carolanne, for Christ's sake. Help me out."

It was the Mercedes, the car that Miguel was so interested in. Sammy was inside it, in the backseat, sitting straight up, looking alert.

"Jesus Christ," Lucy said. She looked like she had been sweating for hours, maybe days. She was drenched and dark.

If Lucy came back to the street, she might die of withdrawal convulsions. If Lucy came back to the street, somebody might lure her into an alley. If Lucy came back to the street . . .

Carolanne clenched her fists in the pockets of her coat. She couldn't leap at the car. She couldn't take Sammy out of there just because she wanted to.

"Lucy," she said.

Lucy came up close. Her breathing was coming too fast and too hard. "He's been keeping me a goddamned prisoner, that's what he's been doing. He's insane. Did I tell you my husband was insane?"

"He took your stuff again," Carolanne said.

"He took my *money*. I don't have any goddamned *money*. He threw away my ATM card."

Sammy had started to move in the back of the car. He was up on his feet and pacing across the seat. He was wagging his tail.

"You ought to let the dog out," Carolanne said. "You're making him crazy."

Lucy rubbed her hands against her arms. Carolanne thought she hadn't heard, about the dog. Lucy didn't seem able to hear much of anything. The dog was nearly leaping now, moving as much as he could in that small space. Carolanne wanted to rescue him.

"Wait a minute," Lucy said.

She went to the car and opened the back door. Sammy came barreling out, barking in high-pitched squeals. Carolanne reached out for him and he came to her.

"I've got to get some coke," Lucy said. "I don't have any money and I've got to get some coke. Now. Right away."

If Lucy came back to the street, Carolanne thought again—and then it all seemed perfectly clear—what she had to do, what would have to happen. Sammy was nuzzling the palm of her hand with his nose. He was begging for her attention.

Far up on the hill, the parties were still going on. Miguel had had some friends in earlier in the evening. They would still be there, lying on the floor of his living room in the middle of ancient boxes from McDonald's and Burger King and Kentucky Fried Chicken. The Christmas lights were on on Carolanne's porch. She'd turned them on, hours ago, before she'd gone to work.

"All right," she said, turning away from Lucy. "Come up the hill."

"I've got to move the car," Lucy said.

Lucy went back to the car and got inside. Sammy stayed with Carolanne on the pavement. Maybe the easiest thing would be to run, right now, while Lucy was putting the car out of the way on a side street, with all the other cars parked so that people could go to Mass. That would be easier than a knife or a push off

the porch onto the pavement. The only problem was
that Lucy knew where she lived. Lucy could come after
her. People always wanted to keep what they owned,
even if they didn't like it very much.

Carolanne bent down and stroked Sammy's long back,
making him whimper. Lucy came back around the
corner, on foot now, without the car. She looked impossibly tall in her long coat. She looked impossibly fright-
ened. Carolanne imagined her dead, the way she had
for so many nights now, the way she had when they
were all back in high school. There had been times,
back then, when she had wanted to take Lucy Blackthorne's head and smash it into a wall, into a gutter,
into something hard and unyielding and final, so that it
would stay smashed forever.

The dog pranced to Lucy and back to Carolanne again.
Lucy said, "We've got to hurry."

In the end, they went to Carolanne's apartment, because she couldn't think of anyplace else for them to go.
They went past Miguel's front door and listened to the
noises coming from the living room. The stereo was
turned up high and pumping out some sort of music
that seemed to be all bass. Carolanne had fifty-five
dollars in the back of her wallet, saved up so that she
could buy a parka in the January sales, but she knew
she wasn't going to use it buying cocaine from Miguel
to cure Lucy's stress. The last thing she wanted was
Lucy cooled out and straightened out, Lucy able to
think. Sammy was prancing and pawing. He recognized
this place. He wanted to lie on the couch. Lucy's hair
was as thick with sweat as if she'd packed it with bacon fat.

"Sit here," Carolanne said, putting Lucy in the living room.

"I'd rather walk," Lucy said.

Carolanne shrugged and went into the bathroom. She
was going to have to think of something to do with the

body. She could push it over the porch, but that would be hard. It would be obvious, too. Everybody on the street would see it. The police would come. She got a small plastic bottle of Bufferin out of the medicine cabinet and took out six pills. She dumped out the contents of a Baggie full of cotton swabs and put the pills inside it. If you crushed Bufferin, it looked just like cocaine. Miguel and his friends did that sometimes to cut the stuff they had, or else they sold Bufferin straight, to idiots from the suburbs, when they were short of cash.

As soon as she got the Bufferin pulverized, she would have to think of what to use. She would have to find a knife in the kitchen, or a big heavy object, the cast-iron frying pan, a Dutch oven, to use instead. Suddenly, she felt as stressed as Lucy was. She could feel every pore in her body sweating. She thought of Lucy's head like an egg, with the shell cracked open. She thought of Lucy's face full of blood. She got a big heavy jar of Vaseline out of the medicine cabinet and started to pound the pills.

"What's going on in there?" Lucy said.

"Just a minute."

Sammy yipped. When Sammy yipped, Carolanne pounded harder. She had to do it in three towels stacked up against the carpet on the floor, so that Lucy couldn't hear what she was doing.

"I'm dying here," Lucy said.

Carolanne stood up and opened the plastic bag, fishing out the three big pieces she hadn't been able to reduce to powder. She wet her finger and tasted a little of what she had. It tasted terrible. She folded the bag and tucked it into the palm of her hand.

"I don't have very much," she said. "I might not have enough."

"Anything will be enough," Lucy said.

Carolanne came out of the bathroom. Sammy rushed up to her, nuzzling at her hand. Carolanne bent down to rub her face against his side. He was so soft and so clean, the softest and cleanest dog she had ever seen. The dogs on the street always seemed to smell of something.

"Let me have it," Lucy said.

Carolanne handed it over. Lucy looked at the bag, but not for long. She took the mirror Carolanne had brought with her and put it on the kitchen table. Carolanne knew this routine. Cokeheads were all the same. Once they started thinking about coke, they couldn't think about anything else.

Sammy was still prancing around the room, running in circles as if he had been cooped up all day. Carolanne drew him to her and into the kitchen. The Dutch oven was too awkward. She had a hard time moving it even when she only had to put it on the stove. The cast-iron frying pan was at least easy enough to pick up, even if it took both hands. She could use both hands. Lucy would be sitting at the table, bent over the mirror, laying out lines.

"I love you," Carolanne said to Sammy, into his ear, where it would tickle.

Then she picked up the frying pan and stood up, moving very carefully, getting leverage, thinking what it would be like when the pan came down on the back of Lucy's head and the blood started to spurt all over the kitchen, all over everywhere. She would have to keep it away from the dog.

She was still thinking about the dog, about blood on the dog, when she realized that Lucy was not at the kitchen table setting up lines. Lucy was right in front of her, standing so close that her breath was hot in the air between them. The gun was hot in the air between them, too, and small, so small it should have been a toy. Carolanne knew it wasn't a toy. She knew it as soon as she saw it.

"You asshole," Lucy said, "you called my *house*."

"What?" Carolanne said.

Really, Carolanne thought. It had been like this forever. It had been like this all her life. She was never fast

enough. She could never move when she was supposed
to. She could never think when she was supposed to.
Now she was standing in her own kitchen with a gun
pointed at her heart and she had no idea what to do, no
idea at all.

I'm going to die, she thought, and looked up into
Lucy Blackthorne Holt's furious, triumphant face, the
face of a cokehead on a full-fledged paranoid high, all
the stops pulled out and all the kickers working, pumping and pumping, pumping out hate. Lucy must have
been high when she came. She must have been faking
the shakes. She must have—planned it all.

Carolanne grabbed the dog's fur as it went by her,
grabbed it and held tight, making the dog stop, making
the world stop.

"You *asshole,*" Lucy said again.

And then she pulled the trigger, and the dog started
to howl.

Fowl Play

Patricia Guiver

PATRICIA GUIVER, of Huntington Beach, California, writes about British widow Delilah Doolittle, a pet detective who tracks missing animals. Ms. Guiver's most recent novel is *Delilah Doolittle and the Careless Coyote*.

If I'd answered the telephone that Christmas Eve—actually it was the early hours of Christmas morning, come to think of it—things might have worked out differently. As it was I turned over and went back to sleep.

I didn't think about the call again until many hours later, after I'd had my first cup of tea and Watson and I had exchanged gifts. I had bought her a fancy leather leash and collar. She gave me the pink cashmere sweater I'd had my eye on for weeks, which had gone on sale two days before Christmas. Of course, I'd had to loan her the money and wrap the gift myself. But it's the thought that counts.

I had adopted the big red Dobie from our local shelter. Her previous owners had turned her in after she'd twice disappointed them, failing first at motherhood, proving unable to produce the anticipated championship litter, then later flunking a security dog course, the trainers being unsuccessful in their efforts to instill in her the necessary aggressiveness. Though she didn't graduate, she had, I was to discover, retained some lessons from the experience that occasionally came in handy in my job as a pet detective.

"No work today," I told her, studiously ignoring the flashing light on the answering machine. "It's a holiday."

We would be going to friends for Christmas dinner later in the day, and there would be more gifts. But for now, the two opened packages and discarded wrapping beside the miniature Christmas tree on the coffee table looked a little forlorn, making me homesick for past Christmases with family and friends back home in England's west country.

I attempted to get into the spirit of the season by listening to carols on the radio. But it wasn't easy. Christmas in California is an almost surreal experience for one brought up in colder climes. No Jack Frost nipping at your nose on these Pacific shores. No chestnuts roasting by an open fire, either—unless at a beach barbecue.

By nine o'clock, the red light still blinking reproachfully, my curiosity could stand it no longer and I played back the midnight message.

I wasn't surprised that I didn't recognize the voice. As a pet detective I am frequently called upon by complete strangers for assistance in tracing their missing animals. Neither was it unexpected that the tape took a minute or so to rewind, people being particularly verbose when it comes to their pets, especially their pets' misfortunes.

I poured myself a second cup of tea and settled down to listen as a woman's voice, soft and hesitant, told her story.

"I'm on my way to San Diego from Bakersfield with all my stuff in my car, and my pets—my dog, Bear, my cat, Smudge, and Daisy and Tulip, my turkeys."

"What? No partridge in a pear tree?" I said in an aside to Watson.

She must have seen my ad in the yellow pages. I advertise throughout southern California: Delilah Doolittle, pet detective. Your best friend's ticket home. I liked that last bit. It sounded positive, and though I can't claim a hundred percent success rate, I do have my resources— good contacts with shelters throughout the region, a knowledge of animal behavior, and a vivid imagination that allows me to put myself, metaphorically speaking, in the animal's paw prints.

"Please help me," the caller continued. She sounded young and unsophisticated. I wondered why she was traveling alone on Christmas Eve, and to a place several hundred miles from home. And where did she think she would find accommodation for a dog and a cat, not to mention those turkeys? "Your ad says you're a pet detective. I can't go to the police ..." Here her voice broke, and it was a moment or two before she continued. "Oh, my name's Mindy Rogers, and I'm staying at the Motel Seven." The tape ran out and she hung up in what sounded like an outburst of tears.

"And which Motel Seven might that be, young lady?" I said, addressing the now-mute answering machine. "Great Scott, Watson, she didn't even say what city."

At that I was ready to forget the whole thing. Really, if people couldn't be more explicit, why should I disturb myself, especially on Christmas Day?

But wasn't that the point? It *was* Christmas Day, the season of goodwill to all, including young women traveling with turkeys. What else did I have to do for the next few hours? And wasn't the antidote for the Christmas blues supposed to be to go out of your way to help someone less fortunate? Fate had sent me this damsel in distress, all alone in a strange town—none stranger if she was, as I suspected, in the Greater Los Angeles area—and I had better respond if I wanted to keep my karma account in good standing. Besides, I needed to get out of the house if I was to avoid a plunge into nostalgia from which I would be unlikely to recover until well after New Year's.

I took out the telephone book and called the central reservation 800 number for the Motel Seven chain. A weary voice informed me that their computers were down, and it being a holiday, they were unlikely to be up for another twenty-four hours. I counted eighteen individual Motel Seven listings in southern California. I decided to call each in turn, in ever-widening circles radiating from my home, until I tired of the game. A point I had just about reached when, having inquired for the tenth time, "Do you have a Mindy Rogers staying there?" a man's voice answered, "Room 113. Hold on. I'll put you through."

I waited while the extension rang a dozen times or more, then hung up.

She was in Winona, about a thirty-minute drive from my home. "Come on," I said to Watson. "It's a nice day. Let's take a jaunt out there."

Always ready for an outing, Watson was on her feet as soon as I reached for my car keys, and we were soon driving south on Interstate 5 in my old Country Squire station wagon, the tools of the pet detective trade—assorted cages and carriers, humane traps, a come-along pole, leather gloves, spare leashes and collars—rattling in the back.

"Two turkeys on the loose. Sounds risky at this time of year," I said to Watson. "I wonder if they're the cause of Mindy's troubles."

Holiday traffic was light, and I pulled into the motel parking lot sooner than I had expected. Bypassing the office I drove straight to unit 113. There was no car parked outside or in front of any of the neighboring units. Mindy had not yet returned.

With Watson by my side, I approached her motel room, surprised to find the door slightly ajar. She must have left in a hurry. I knocked, calling, "Hello. Mindy? Anyone here?"

Hearing a slight noise coming from inside, I pushed the door open a little farther. As I stepped into the room a sudden mass of energy rushed toward me, pinning me by the shoulders against the door as it slammed back on the wall with a crash.

Stunned, I found myself looking into the bright brown eyes of a huge dog. Judging by the coarse shaggy coat of charcoal gray, I guessed it might have had Bouvier and Irish wolfhound in its ancestry.

Watson hovered uncertainly in the doorway. "It's okay, girl," I quickly reassured her. She was ready to attack if I insisted, but considering the size of this creature, I could tell she'd really rather not.

Its smelly dog breath and yellowed fangs notwithstanding, the dog did not appear menacing, just overly friendly. "Nice doggy," I said, lifting his paws off my shoulders and pushing him away from me. But even with all four feet on the floor he continued to lean heavily against my legs, keeping me off-balance, and looking at me with that expectant expression dogs have when they just know you have something nice for them—usually food.

"You must be Bear," I said to the dog as I made my way over to the bathroom. "Where's your mistress?"

A bowl of water and a paper plate, which looked like it might recently have held a hamburger, indicated that Mindy had taken the time to see to her dog's needs before she left. The door lock was broken and a piece of string dangling from the handle suggested she had attempted to keep Bear confined in her absence. Efforts he'd made short work of once he heard me call out.

Strewn across the unmade bed were several leaflets. They were all published by a farm animal rescue group and carried titles like *Save a life, adopt a turkey. Save a turkey, don't serve one.*

I closed the motel room door on Bear, being careful not to trigger the bolt in case I needed to get back in, and made my way to the office, Watson padding along beside me.

Around the office window a few puny Christmas lights blinked in feeble competition with the brilliant midday California sun.

A young man sat behind the counter, his attention fixed on a small television showing cartoons.

"Good afternoon," I said. "I'm a friend of Miss Rogers

in Room 113. She's not there. Do you know where she's gone?"

"None of my business where the guests go," the young man replied over his shoulder, not bothering to take his eyes from the television screen. "I just hand out the keys and take the money."

I hadn't come all this way to be put off by an impolite young oaf. "Did she ask directions?" I asked.

The television program switched to commercials, and he was able to give me his full attention.

"She said something about wanting to know where some turkey place is, a few miles north of here. Bunch of crackpots run it."

"Has anyone else asked about her?"

"Yeah. About twenty minutes ago. A guy. Said he was her boyfriend."

"Did you tell him where she went?"

"Yeah. Gave him the same directions."

"What was he driving?"

"Gray van. Old Dodge, I think it was. Look lady, do you want a room, or not?"

I opened my purse, took out a five-dollar bill, and waved it under his nose. "Could you give me the same directions?"

He scribbled something on a notepad and handed me the slip of paper.

"If you catch up with her, tell her she owes another night's rent if she wants to keep the room." He looked at his watch. "Checkout time's noon. She's missed that. If I need the room, I'll have to take her stuff out and put it in storage."

"What about the dog?"

"Pets ain't allowed. If she's got a dog in there, I'm calling the pound."

The commercials were over, and he turned back to the television.

Trusting I'd be successful in catching up with Mindy, I took a spare leash from the back of my station wagon, and returned to the room to collect Bear. He came along readily, probably happy to be released from the confinement of the tiny motel room. I trusted that he and Watson, being of opposite sexes, would get along all right. I hadn't had time to check whether Bear was neutered, but Watson was spayed, so I was assured there'd be no hanky-panky in the backseat.

Following the directions the young man had given me, I returned to the interstate, exiting at a pleasantly undulating county road which led past dairy farms and orange and avocado orchards on the lower slopes of the San Bernardino mountains.

I must have been distracted by Bear and Watson romping on the backseat because I missed the turkey ranch turnoff, and it wasn't until I saw a sign leading back to the freeway that I realized my mistake.

I pulled off to the side of the road to get my bearings. While I was consulting the directions again, a sheriff's deputy drove by, stopped a few feet ahead of me, and walked back to ask if I needed assistance.

He was an agreeable sort. "The Turkey Safe House, you mean," he said in answer to my inquiry. "Yes ma'am. I know it well. Look for a narrow ranch road, with a small sign. Drive slowly, or you'll miss it again. Tell Stella I'll be along later for that Christmas dinner she promised." He chuckled. "She tells me her turkey tofu recipe tastes just great, and I'll never be able to tell the difference between that and the real thing." He cocked his head toward his car. "Better not let her know I brought along a roast beef sandwich just in case."

I doubled back until I came to a turnoff marked by an arrow and a small wooden sign with the words TUR-KEY SAFE HOUSE. FARM ANIMAL HAVEN hand-painted in black. A few miles farther along the dusty unpaved road I found what I was looking for. It was just as the deputy had described: a farmhouse, a corral, and a big red barn situated at the top of a small rise. I parked in the shade of a large oak at the foot of the hill, alongside an old brown Pinto, its windshield covered with dust and bugs. A faded bumper sticker admonished, IF YOU LOVE ANIMALS DON'T EAT THEM. I had found Mindy.

Through the lowered front window I could see a cat carrier on the passenger seat. My "Hallo, Smudge," was answered with a plaintive meow, making me regret having disturbed him. A large metal crate was wedged onto the backseat, a few white feathers the only evidence that it might have contained the turkeys.

There was no sign of the boyfriend's Dodge van. Like me, he may have missed the turning, possibly driving even farther out of his way than I had.

As I walked up the grassy dandelion-spotted hill, the leashed dogs bounding along beside me, several turkeys came out to greet us, making sharp, shrill chirping noises. Other animals came into view—goats, chickens, a cow—but turkeys dominated the scene. The barnyard smell, enhanced by the warm sunshine, was not offensive, rather it was almost comforting, evocative as it was of a more peaceful, simpler way of life.

Sitting on the grass in front of the barn were two women, one probably in her twenties, the other a comfortable-looking mid-forties. Between them sat two plump, white turkeys.

My guess that I had found Mindy was quickly confirmed as Bear nearly pulled me off my feet in his effort to reach her.

She put out her arms for him. "Bear? How did you get here?" Her thin cotton dress looked out of place for the time of year, and the wrinkled yellow ribbon holding her short blond hair away from her face could have done with a good ironing.

"Mindy Rogers?" I asked.

She looked up from petting Bear, surprise on her face. I introduced myself. "Delilah Doolittle. You left a message on my machine. It's taken me a while to track you down."

"You never answered, and I got desperate." She had

obviously been unclear as to what exactly it is that a pet detective does. "I thought you were a real private detective who specialized in animal cases, but Stella here," she indicated the older woman, "has been telling me that you look for lost pets."

"Well, since I'm here," I said, sitting down alongside them, "why don't you tell me what the problem is. Maybe I can still help."

Stella offered some refreshment, and while she went back to the house Mindy recounted her story. She had been living with her boyfriend, Steve, on a small ranch they rented in the Bakersfield area. Unemployed and short of cash, he had gotten mixed up with a bad crowd and had started on a series of petty thefts. Beginning in a small way with shoplifting and stealing from unlocked cars, they gradually became bolder and turned to breaking and entering.

"I tried to get him to stop," Mindy said, her eyes filling with tears. "But he'd started to gamble, and there was no other way to pay his debts."

Eventually, looking for a bigger haul, Steve and his friends had broken into a jewelry store. They had disposed of most of the loot at a swap meet, but had been unable to find a ready buyer for some loose diamonds.

Stella returned carrying a tray with a pitcher of lemonade and three glasses. While she poured the drinks, Mindy continued her story.

"So Steve hid the diamonds in one of the feed bins in the turkey coop," said Mindy, wiping her tears with the back of her hand. "But when he went to get them later, all he could find was the torn cloth bag they'd been in.

"He was so mad. He said the turkeys must have swallowed them along with their food, and he threatened to kill them to get the diamonds out of their gizzards."

At my expression of surprise that the turkeys would still be alive if they'd ingested the gems, Stella explained, "No harm done. Birds need gravel in their gizzards to help grind the food. Diamonds are real hard, which makes them ideal for the purpose. They won't need to replace their grit for quite some time."

Mindy set down her lemonade glass and picked up one of the turkeys, cradling it in her lap and scratching its breast. The bird closed its eyes in what one could only assume was turkey bliss.

"I've had Daisy and Tulip since they were chicks," she said. "They're my pets. They were never intended for slaughter."

She had run away Christmas Eve, she said, intending to seek refuge with friends in San Diego.

"Along the way, I realized Steve was following me. I couldn't call the police. I was afraid that if they found out about the diamonds, they would confiscate Daisy and Tulip. That's why I called you. When you didn't answer, I called Stella."

Stella took up the story. "It was important to get the birds off the road, out of harm's way. Thanksgiving is the worst time of the year for turkeys, but Christmas runs it a close second. When Mindy called I told her to bring Daisy and Tulip here where they'll be safe to live out their lives in peace. No one will be able to distinguish one from another once they join the flock."

I said how much I admired her dedication to an apparently lost cause.

She smiled. "We do have our supporters. But it's a hand-to-mouth existence. I never know where the next penny's coming from."

Mindy stiffened. Shading her eyes against the sun, she watched as a gray Dodge van approached and pulled into the parking lot alongside the Pinto.

"It's Steve," she said. "He mustn't find us here."

"It's too late for that," I said. "He's already seen your car. We'll just have to try to explain things to him."

But my trust in sweet reason was short-lived as I saw Steve reach back into the van and slip a handgun into his waistband before heading up the hill.

"Quick," I said. "Into the barn."

They needed no second telling as I hustled Mindy, Stella, Watson and Bear, Tulip and Daisy, out of sight, privately thinking that if worse came to worst, we might just have to hand over the turkeys. I was about to prepare Mindy for that possibility when a pistol shot rang out.

Mindy screamed. "He's going to kill us."

"No he's not," I said with more conviction than I actually felt, thinking that Daisy and Tulip might not be the only casualties of the day.

Through a crack in the barn door I watched Steve approach, firing the pistol as he came and shouting, "Come on out, Mindy. I know you're in there."

I had to think quickly. "Do as I say," I told Mindy and Stella. "Keep back as far out of sight as you can, and take the turkeys with you. Watson and Bear will stay with me."

I removed the dogs' leashes and held Bear loosely by the collar with one hand, while keeping a firmer grip on Watson with the other. She would be held in reserve, ready to run interference if necessary.

"Bear," I told the furry ruffian, "we're counting on you."

Steve was getting closer. Soon his bulk blocked daylight from the crack in the door. My heart pounding, I moved farther along the barn wall.

Suddenly the door was thrown open, and Steve's tall body filled the entrance.

I had only a few seconds to act before his eyes adjusted to the gloomy barn after the brilliant sunshine.

"Now, Bear," I whispered. "Go!"

Bear leapt forward in a rush and, displaying the same enthusiasm with which he had greeted me back at the motel, pinned Steve against the door.

The element of surprise was on our side. Caught off-balance Steve dropped the gun, at which point, in a remarkable display of teamwork, Watson leaped forward and lay down with her front feet on the gun, her teeth bared in a most unbecoming snarl, just as she'd learned at guard dog school.

"Stay, Bear," I ordered, as Steve, in language that I would never repeat, demanded that I call the dog off.

"Mindy, you stay back there," I shouted. "Stella, go and call the sheriff."

But on looking through the open door I breathed a sigh of relief. "Never mind. Here's the deputy. Tell him he's got some business to take care of before he gets his Christmas dinner."

Watson and Bear remained at their posts until Steve was in handcuffs and the deputy's backup was on the way.

Later, amid more tears, Mindy said her goodbyes to Tulip and Daisy. And as we headed down the hill to our cars I called back to Stella: "Keep a close eye on their droppings for the next few weeks. You might just come across a big payoff. The reward ought to keep this place going for quite a while."

The Reunion

Lillian M. Roberts

LILLIAN M. ROBERTS writes the Andi Pauling, DVM, series of veterinary mysteries. (The series debut—*Riding
for a Fall*—was shortlisted for an Agatha Award.) Ms.
Roberts lives in Palm Springs, California, with three cats,
two parrots, and a very tolerant mastiff named Moby. Her
short story "Manor Beast" appeared in the *Canine Crimes*
anthology.

Christmas in Palm Springs is a bit of a letdown.

Like most people who live here, I am from Elsewhere.
In my case, Elsewhere means the Midwest, but the specif-
ics don't really matter. The point is, almost every Elsewhere in this country is different from Palm Springs:
snow country, ice, power failures, studded tires, sand
and rust damage to the old cars—good reasons to come
to California, of course. But they are the same reasons
why, for a few weeks of every year, I contemplate going back.

On this particular December twenty-first, it was so
hot even the plastic snow that merchants sprayed onto
their display windows was melting. This was unusual.
Most years it's chilly. One can at least gaze up at Mount
San Jacinto and *see* snow. Those who are so inclined
can even take a short tram ride to its top and toss a
snowball or two. The serious will cross-country ski,
though I've never tried it myself. But I digress.

There it was, four days till the big day. The usual population exchange was occurring. Our boarding kennel
was full of dogs and cats and birds, along with two

ferrets and an iguana, whose owners had ventured north for the season. A similar number of tourists had descended into town, so the shops were full to capacity and the shelves more or less barren by now. I'd done the usual things—called my pop in St. Louis, visited the local wildlife park to see its light show, sat through an amateur production of *The Nutcracker*, and hosted a buffet and gift exchange party for the staff. But I just wasn't into it. The constant noise of carols ("Winter Wonderland"? "Frosty the Snowman"? Oh, please!) was as irritating as fingernails on a chalkboard. The traditional holiday slow period at the clinic did nothing to help. Signing health certificates so others could take their pets with them to visit family in Colorado and Oregon didn't exactly improve my mood.

"I should have gone to visit Pop," I said to Trinka, over coffee in our shared office. That's Trinka Romanescu, DVM, my partner at Dr. Doolittle's Pet Care Center.

Trinka, who was drinking water from a plastic bottle (even the water is from Elsewhere), shrugged. "I don't see what the big deal is. It's not like you're religious or anything."

Trinka trots out her half-Jewish heritage when she wants to disparage some Anglo–European tradition.

"You'd get it if you wanted to," I said irritably. "Just open your eyes. It's a feeling. A whole season. It's magical! It's a time to spend with family. Time to do good deeds!"

"If you ask me, it's the worst time of year. Everyone's on edge. We're broke. No one brings their pets in to the vet this time of year. Those who do come in whine about how we're depriving them of Christmas by expecting to get paid—like it's my fault they let Fluffy out and he got run over!"

I had to smile, because I knew the case she was talking about. But under the smile was a stubborn determination not to let her be right. In most things, Trinka

was the pragmatist, the optimist. Despite her protesta-
tions, I could see that the mood was affecting her, too.
"At least you get to visit your brother and his family in
San Diego."

"If it bugs you so much, why don't you go out and do
some charity work?"

Why, indeed. How does one go about volunteering at
such a late date?

"Merry Christmas, everyone!" Marie Coulson bustled
into the room, carrying a plate piled high with home-
baked cookies, bars, and sweets all decorated with red
and green icing or sprinkles. They had been arranged
with obvious care on the tray before the whole thing was
swathed in plastic wrap.

Marie was hard to explain. She had brought her ancient cat, Callie, in for its final visit about a month earlier. We knew her husband had died a year or so before
that, and she had no children. Still, even while in mourning her basic cheerfulness showed through. Now, with
her only pet gone, I fully expected her to show up with
a new cat. She had showed up, all right—but as a kind
of hospital volunteer, visiting the boarded animals with
treats and pats, pitching in to clean a cage or answer a
phone as needed. She said it was out of gratitude for
our good care of Callie, but we had done nothing special for the cat and had charged her our usual fees. I
suspected she simply needed someone to take care of.

I was reaching for my second cookie, tree-shaped with
green sugar and tiny gumdrop ornaments, when Sheila
buzzed us on the intercom. "Doctor?" she said, not speci-
fying which of us. "Could you guys, like, come up here?
I think you might have a patient."

Trinka and I exchanged glances. We both went.

The "patient" was a medium-sized terrier. A gray-
and-brown mutt with long wiry hair that would have
looked unkempt even when clean and brushed. He was
neither at the moment, just shaggy and tangled, with fox-
tails and bits of grass and sand and even gravel mixed

into his coat. To describe him as forlorn would have been an understatement—his tail hung limply, his body sagged, his head lowered dejectedly.

Despite all this, his anxious eyes regarded us with something akin to hope. At least until recently, he had had reason to expect kindness from these godlike beings who walked upright.

Trinka and I moved to where he stood in the middle of the floor, instinctively going over him.

"He's so thin!" Trinka said. (Trinka should know— she errs on the scrawny side herself.)

"Where's his owner?" I asked, for the little dog was unaccompanied.

Sheila shrugged. "He just showed up. I heard a scratching, looked up, and there he was, outside the door."

"No collar," I pointed out. But there was an indentation where the hair was worn short around his neck.

"Dumped," Trinka decided. Every so often someone would leave a dog or a box of kittens in the parking lot and drive away. Once, Sheila had gotten a license plate number and the creep was arrested and fined, but that was small comfort.

"Maybe so, but not today. He's been on his own for a while," I said. "His toenails are worn to the quick."

Sheila said, "Maybe he used to be a patient and recognized the building."

"Poor little guy," Trinka said, scratching him behind the ears. "Most of our patients don't think of us as their saviors, you know."

She was right about that; a lot of animals associated us with shots and thermometers. But they might also think of it as a place their owner might turn up.

"Well, let's get him some food and water and see what we can do for him."

Marie was already seeing to it.

He drank a whole bowl of water, wolfed down a can of food, then drank some more water. We offered him a blanket in a cage, and he settled down with an audible sigh. He looked up at us once, wagged his tail twice, then rolled onto his side and was instantly asleep.

Trinka and I exchanged apprehensive glances. "What do you think?" I asked, recalling past strays abandoned on our doorstep. Kittens and puppies we could usually find homes for—which, of course, was why people dumped them here. A young, healthy dog was more challenging but could often be adopted. But the older animals . . .

"Got room for another one?" she said.

"I've got the legal limit." Four dogs. Plus six cats I figure no one had to know about. "It's your turn."

She shook her head. "Ajax would eat him for lunch." Her old white shepherd didn't tolerate interlopers.

We sighed in unison. I noticed Trinka was gazing speculatively at Marie, as I was. But Marie just said, "The poor little darling. I wonder how he knew to come here?"

"I'll at least scan him, what the heck."

"Oh, right . . . he looks like someone would spend the money for a chip," Trinka said cynically. For several years the clinic had offered permanent microchip implantation, a device the size of a grain of rice, injected under the skin. It could be detected at any shelter should the pet turn up lost. But those who sprang for the cost took better care of their pets than this.

However, when I ran the scanner over his back, it beeped and a number came up.

"Hey! Look at this!" I copied the number onto a sticky-note and took it up front. Before calling the registry, I decided to check our computer's database to see if it was one of ours. It was.

"I don't remember this dog," I said.

Trinka just shrugged. Trinka had been with the practice a little under two years. The implantation date was nearly three years earlier, and we hadn't seen the dog since. Probably the owner had absentmindedly checked the "yes" box on an anesthesia release and forgotten about it. That didn't mean he would want the dog back now, but at least we could let someone know we had the dog—in case his stray status was in fact accidental.

I picked up the phone and dialed. As it rang I became conscious of the hopeful expressions of the people in the small crowd gathered around me. Didi, our technician, had returned from lunch and been apprised of the situation, so there were five of us waiting to see who would answer.

After six rings, no answering machine or voice mail or anything, I was ready to give up when a tremulous voice said, "Hello?"

"Mr. Thomas Atkins?"

"This is Tom Atkins. Who's that?" The voice was that of an old man. Very old, beaten down, sick maybe.

"Mr. Atkins, this is Dr. Andi Pauling at Dr. Doolittle's Pet Care Center. We have Willie-Boy."

I heard a sharp gasp. "Willie-Boy? You have my Willie-Boy? But Branson said—"

Suddenly a new voice spoke—younger, sharp, a little mean. "Who is this?"

I repeated my name and my errand.

"I don't know why you're bothering us, but you have no right to do this!"

"What do you mean? The dog is right here!" I shot Trinka a puzzled glance, and she rechecked the microchip number again. There was no mistake.

"Sir, this dog showed up in my clinic this morning, bedraggled and exhausted and with no collar. He has a microchip that identifies him as Willie-Boy belonging to Tom Atkins. Now, if you don't want the dog—"

"Yes, yes, of course that's all right," the voice said, its earlier sharp anger now replaced by mild irritation. "Everyone makes mistakes. But please don't call here again." And the line went dead.

"That was weird," I said, putting the phone down. "It's like we were having two different conversations." I got a new dial tone and hit Redial. Got a busy signal. Tried again with the same results.

Trinka said, "If the phone number's right, the address might still be valid."

All five of us exchanged glances. Should we try?

"The man who answered the phone said he was Tom Atkins, the dog's owner. He sounded a little shocked that we had his dog. The other guy, the one who grabbed the phone away—he wasn't someone I want to deal with."

"I'll go!" It was Marie, our perpetual volunteer.

Trinka grinned. "We'll all go. After work."

Though we could probably have closed early without anyone noticing, we waited until five. That gave us a chance to bathe and brush the little mutt. Didi presented him with a new collar from the rack out front. Trinka started to protest the donation, but I glared at her and said, "Throw in a leash, too."

"You gonna clean his teeth for free, too?"

I pretended to consider it. "Well . . . they sure could use it. Too bad we don't have a signed consent form."

Still, a shaggy wirehaired mongrel cleans up just so well, and the Willie-Boy we led out to my car that afternoon didn't exactly have a bounce in his step. He followed the leash willingly enough, lifted his leg on the bush outside as if from long habit, and after a moment's hesitation climbed agreeably into the passenger side of the Miata. But even after a nap and a bowl of food, he looked worn-out and dejected. I hoped we weren't letting him in for even greater disappointment.

Since it was the end of the day we took four cars, Trinka leaving her Harley to ride with Marie. We made quite a caravan.

Didi's Thomas Guide got us to a side street near the foot of the mountain. It was only a few miles from the clinic, but far enough for a directionally challenged mutt to get himself lost if he wandered off on his own.

Despite the evidence, I allowed myself to hope this was
what had happened.

It was a nice house but needed paint and gutter work.
The landscaping was uninspired—grass, oleander, and
one palm tree overdue for trimming—and weeds pro-
truded through cracks in the concrete driveway. Either
the inhabitants hired a cut-rate gardener like I did, or
did just enough themselves to keep the neighbors from
complaining.

I climbed two steps to a wide concrete stoop and
knocked on the door. Nothing happened. I knocked
again, then a small sound told me there was someone
on the other side. I gazed at the peephole, waiting.

Behind me, Willie-Boy whined. It was the low, eager
sound of a dog trying unsuccessfully to restrain himself.
I looked back to see him pulling at the leash. He was a
dog transformed. His tail was curled over his back, his
head was up, his mouth open in a panting grin. He
glanced at me, as if wondering what was taking so long,
then returned his gaze to the door.

I knocked once more.

Finally, it opened.

I found myself facing a man who did not match the
voice that had first answered the phone. That had been a
creaky voice—old or sick or both. This man was maybe
mid-forties, overweight in a lazy, self-indulgent way. He
had a pinched face with small, mean eyes.

For a moment I stood mutely, certain that we had the
wrong house, that Thomas Atkins had moved, perhaps
given his dog away to someone who had failed to notify
the microchip registry of the change of ownership. But
then Willie-Boy growled.

Turning, surprised, I saw the formerly sweet-tempered,
patient little terrier bristling. Hair up, back in a straight
line, he bared his teeth and produced an admittedly un-
convincing rumble. I followed his gaze back to the man
standing before me.

"Mr. Atkins?" I said, knowing this was not he. This

must be the man who had hung up on me. Branson? Something was definitely wrong here.

"You have the wrong house." He started to shut the door.

I surprised myself by jamming my foot against it. "I don't think so," I said. "I want to see Mr. Atkins."

Instead of becoming indignant, or shoving harder at the door, or threatening to call the police—all things I myself might have done in the same circumstances—he seemed to have no idea what to do. He stomped one foot, placed his fist on his hip, and sighed in exasperation. "My uncle doesn't want the mutt!" he said, casting an uneasy glance at Willie-Boy.

Behind me, the dog barked once and strained against his new leash.

"Then let him tell me so himself." I felt vaguely shocked at my own persistence, but the prickling on the back of my neck told me something was very wrong here. And I was outraged on behalf of the dog. There are times when a beloved pet can no longer be kept, but there are humane ways of addressing that situation. Dumping the dog on the street is not one of them. Mr. Atkins had been a client at one time, and if he had orchestrated such abandonment, it wouldn't necessarily be a bad thing to make him own up to it.

"He's napping! I'll tell him you were here. Now go away!"

I hesitated, not adept at barging past people and really not sure what to do next. The door began to close, and I knew that if it did so I would not be able to get it to open again.

Maybe the dog sensed that his chance was slipping away and broke free, or maybe Marie let him go. At any rate Willie-Boy came flying past me, leash trailing. He snarled viciously, startling the man in the doorway enough that instead of slamming it, he stepped back. The dog did not attack him, as I half expected. Rather, without a backward glance, he dashed past him into the house.

Forgetting us, the man shouted in outrage and dashed after Willie-Boy.

The five of us exchanged glances. "Is that it?" Didi asked. After all, we had set out to take Willie-Boy home, and home he clearly was.

"I don't know," I said. "Whoever that was, doesn't seem too glad to have him back. I'm afraid he'll just dump him again. Or worse."

Trinka said, with a completely straight face, "We've come this far. There could be a medical emergency involving that dog. We have an ethical duty to go in there and make sure he's all right."

Suppressing a smile, I took a quick visual poll. Everyone seemed inclined to follow the dog inside the house. "He left the door open," Sheila said. "That's, like, such an obvious invitation."

We went in.

The house felt smaller than it probably was, darkened by drab carpet and wallpaper. The tightly drawn drapes that blocked out the sun felt severely out of place in southern California, land of vertical blinds and creative use of light. The air was stale and a little rank.

We hadn't seen where Willie-Boy went, but there weren't many places to choose from. We passed through the dingy living room, noting a small cramped kitchen to our left. Beyond was a short hallway, with a couple of closed doors—closets and a bathroom, I surmised—then two small bedrooms on the left and a larger one at the end on the right.

Voices led us to one of the smaller bedrooms. Our group crowded into the cramped space. It was dingy from lack of light, and the stale odor intensified here. The querulous voice from the telephone was saying, ". . . told me he was dead!"

It was a heart-wrenching reunion. Willie-Boy romped on the bed, tail waving, legs practically dancing, as he licked his master's face. The old man, who did look vaguely familiar now that I saw him, alternately held the dog at arms' length and clutched him in a feeble embrace. The shine on his cheeks might have been dog kisses . . . but was probably tears. I noticed a dark bruise on his right bicep, another one in the yellow stages of healing on the left. Illness? Abuse? My stomach knotted with unease.

The man who had answered the door—Branson, I guessed—literally stomped in frustration. "That mutt isn't welcome here! I'm warning you, Uncle Tom! Either that dog goes or I go!"

The old man began sobbing in earnest. He hugged and patted the dog. Willie-Boy settled down complacently in his lap, gazing with unmistakable menace at Branson.

I looked at Trinka and she nodded. "Excuse me," she said to the younger man, "Could I speak to you in the other room?"

"This is a family discussion. You are not invited!" he said.

"I might be able to suggest a solution for . . ." She jerked her head toward the dog, giving the impression she sympathized with Branson.

He hesitated, fists on his hips, then sighed theatrically and followed her into another room. Didi went with her.

As soon as they were out of earshot, I approached the bed.

"Mr. Atkins, I'm very sorry for this intrusion. I don't know if you remember me. My name is Andi Pauling, and I'm the veterinarian who implanted the microchip under Willie-Boy's skin. Today he wandered up to my clinic, and we looked up his number and called you. Frankly, we thought the dog had been abandoned but it's so close to Christmas and, well, we wanted to give him a chance. But if you can't keep him, well . . . I can see about trying to find someone who could."

His arms tightened protectively around the dog. "Branson took him away, about a month ago. He said—he told me he'd had him destroyed. Said it was . . . punishment. I've been so lonely ever since. I don't know what to do. I've been sick; I can hardly get out of bed. Branson's the only family I have left, and I need him. But oh, my, I've missed this dog."

"Mr. Atkins, I . . . I don't know how to ask this." I stared at the bruises on his arms. Blood thinners and various diseases caused people to bruise easily. Was I jumping to the wrong conclusions? But these were so symmetrical. I decided to just get it over with. "Does Branson . . . hit you?"

The devastation that crossed his face told me I shouldn't have been so blunt. But it also answered my question. I stammered an apology, torn between dropping the subject and wanting to help.

Then Marie stepped in. "Excuse me, Dr. Andi," she said gently. I gladly yielded.

"Do you have other family?" she asked Mr. Atkins.

He shook his head desolately. I felt his humiliation. I looked away. In the other room I could hear the angry sounds of Branson trying to throw us out and Trinka blocking his way.

"Is this your home?" A nod. "Not Branson's?" Another nod.

Marie and I exchanged glances. How had the younger man taken over?

"He moved in about two years ago," the old man said, as if reading my thoughts. "He's my sister Jo's boy. She died not long before that. Branson was . . . between jobs. I'm the only family he has left, so he said. It seemed only right that I take him in. Till he got back on his feet . . ." He trailed off, apparently lost in memories.

"He's had enough time for that, don't you think?" I said more harshly than I'd intended. It earned a reproachful glare from Marie.

"Then I . . . my health . . . First I couldn't keep anything down. My skin turned bad. Just look." He held up a gnarled hand. The fingernails curled inward, with lines of discoloration across them. His skin had a waxen cast and hung from his arm loosely. "I needed him, to take care of me."

"And so he stayed," Marie concluded. "It must have seemed fortuitous that he was here."

Mr. Atkins nodded absently. "Yes. Yes, at first. But now . . . now, I just wait here to die. If I'm good, he'll let me have some TV. If I'm bad . . ." A feeble shrug. His hand caressed the dog's ears almost convulsively. "I don't suppose he'll let me keep old Willie-Boy here. Will you see that he's cared for?"

This last was directed at Marie. A strange connection had formed almost instantly between the two of them. He seemed to have forgotten me altogether.

But something was nagging at me. Something about the list of symptoms. Risking stepping on my own tongue yet again, I said, "How did your sister Jo die?"

His eyes shifted to me. "Same thing that's got me, seems like. Same symptoms. No one ever did figure it all out."

"And what do the doctors think is wrong with you?"

"I haven't been seeing doctors. Branson . . . It's no use anyway. They ran all their tests on Jo, there at the end. Never did figure it out, and she died just the same."

Marie stared at me. I waved a hand, not ready to tell her what I was thinking. It was too weird.

Mr. Atkins's voice sank to a whisper. "The only consolation is that he won't get anything when I'm gone. I'm leaving it all to the Humane Society."

I smiled involuntarily. Not only did I applaud his bequest, but I was relieved to see that he still had some fight left.

"We're going to make sure you get some medical attention," I said firmly. "And then we'll talk about Willie-Boy."

I was dialing 911 on Marie's cell phone when Branson returned. He actually reached to try to take the phone away from me but froze when I spoke into it. "I want to report a possible attempted murder," I said. "And the victim needs help. Please send an ambulance." And I stared into Branson's eyes as I gave the address.

I was watching him closely. His eyes grew enormous, and as I hung up, his shoulders slumped. Then he turned and quickly left the room.

On Christmas Eve, Marie and I picked Mr. Atkins up at the hospital. We took Marie's big, boxy Cadillac. Willie-Boy, his ribs already less prominent, lounged in the backseat.

"I'm already feeling better," Tom said as an orderly wheeled him out. And his eyes held a shine that had been missing earlier. To me he said, "Marie's been filling me in. I know Branson's in jail. How did you know to ask them to test for arsenic?"

I glanced at the floor, embarrassed to admit the truth. "It reminded me of a case I'd read about."

"Another case? Someone . . . someone poisoned a dog?"

"No, not that kind of case. It was, well . . ."

Marie laughed. "Oh, dear! It was one of those mystery books you're always reading, wasn't it?"

I smiled ruefully and admitted that it was. "The symptoms are classic, but only if you have reason to suspect it. The police found the ant spikes under the kitchen counter. Branson might have convinced them he was really trying to kill ants, but he'd pried several open and hadn't gotten around to emptying the trash containing the evidence. And they'll probably find traces of it in the powdered sugar they took away."

"Of course. I wondered why he was so fond of French toast. All the trouble it took. The sweet taste hides the bitter poison."

Tom chose to sit in the backseat, with his dog. "Willie-Boy," he kept muttering. "The real hero of the day. How did he know to find you?"

Marie and I exchanged smiles. She dropped me off at the clinic. Tom would be recuperating at her house. I would drop by the next day with a few gifts.

I'd lost a volunteer, but gained a Christmas.

Good Dog Wenceslas

Melissa Cleary

MELISSA CLEARY writes about Jake, a German shepherd and former police dog with a flair for crime-solving. The latest novels in this series are *And Your Little Dog, Too* and *Old Dogs*. Ms. Cleary also contributed a story to the first *Canine Crimes* anthology: "You'll Never Bark in This Town Again."

Jackie Walsh decided that if she never saw another packaged turkey again, it would be years too soon. She picked up a plump twelve-pound bird from a box of dozens, set it into a cardboard box labeled with the recipient's name, checked the name off the list on her clipboard, then repeated the procedure for at least the hundredth time tonight.

It should be no problem keeping the birds cold, she supposed. Every time someone opened up the big doors of the parish hall to take filled boxes out to the waiting vans and trucks lined up along the curb on Michigan Avenue, blasts of icy air blew in accompanied by flakes of snow. The flakes had been getting bigger and thicker for the last hour.

Jackie's teenage son, Peter, was visiting his father this Christmas vacation, which didn't exactly thrill her—she'd never spent a Christmas without Peter in fourteen years. Jackie would ordinarily have distracted herself with work, but she couldn't go back to her job teaching film classes at Rodgers University until after the new year. Her mother's attempt to get her out of her slump and into the proper holiday spirit by volunteering her for the St. Wenceslas Parish Holiday Dinner Drive had only succeeded in making Jackie sadder.

Jackie's mother was a feisty Irish American woman named Frances Cooley Costello, and when Frances Costello said you were going to come to church on Christmas Eve and pack boxes, you went and you packed. Frances meant well, but her plan had backfired through no fault of her own. The sheer number of people being provided a box of holiday groceries by St. Wenceslas volunteers alone made Jackie realize how many people in Palmer, Ohio, could not afford to buy a Christmas dinner for themselves and their families. She looked around at the parish hall floor, nearly wall-to-wall with cardboard containers of food, and realized that she could stuff dead turkeys into boxes for the rest of her life and not ever make a real difference in the life of a single person who needed it.

She sighed deeply, and her German shepherd, Jake, perked up his enormous black ears and cocked his head at her as if trying to figure out what her problem might be, and how it related to him. Jake's problem at the moment was the two-year-old who had hold of the shepherd's bushy black tail and was swinging it around and around like a furry jump rope. "Be nice to the doggy, Trevor," called a parent from somewhere in the maze of boxes, but Trevor was pretending not to hear. Jake was a retired police service dog who had once worked for the Palmer Police Department, but nothing in his years of training had prepared him for small children.

"It's a hopeless world, Jake," Jackie told her dog, but as usual he declined to comment. A second toddler had wandered over to him and had him locked in a baby bear hug. Jake put his head down between his paws and adopted a look of pained resignation. Jackie went back to distributing turkeys and tried to brighten her spirits by humming along to "Angels We Have Heard on High," which was currently playing over St. Wenceslas's public address system. It wasn't working.

"How's it going so far, Ms. Walsh? Have we gotten through our five hundred turkeys yet?" That was young Father Morelli, the new assistant pastor.

"Not quite, and call me Jackie, Father, please," she told him, straightening up from depositing yet another turkey in yet another box. "I know you don't see much of me around here . . ."

"I wasn't going to be the one to say it," said Father Morelli with a smile, "though Father Schumann might."

Father Schumann was the cranky old priest who had served St. Wenceslas as pastor for the last forty years. Actually, Jackie had known him since she was six, which was a bit over thirty-two years now, and as nearly as she could remember, he had been a cranky young priest as well.

"What's that?" Father Schumann appeared out of nowhere, a trick for which he was justly famous. Fat flakes of snow glistened on his black jacket. He rubbed his hands together and shivered. "Where did all this snow come from?" he asked. "It has been almost warm for weeks, and now this!" He looked back and forth between Jackie and Father Morelli. "Did I hear my name spoken just now?" Father Schumann retained the ghost of a German accent and an old-world manner from his boyhood in Munich. The older ladies of the parish found him charming, Jackie's mother included.

"Only in the most glowing terms, Father," Jackie assured him. "Father Morelli and I are impressed by the size of your holiday dinner drive this year."

"Thank you, Jackie," said Father Schumann. "Perhaps the scope of St. Wenceslas's charitable activities wouldn't come as such a shock if you came to mass on occasion."

Jackie glanced over at Father Morelli in time to see his eyes roll up toward the ceiling. She bit her lip to suppress the giggle that threatened to get her into even deeper hot water with Father Schumann.

"I think we ought to be happy to have Jackie here

when we can get her," said Sister Mary Pat, walking up to the three of them with her usual cheerful expression. "So many of our regular parishioners can't be bothered to get involved when there's real work involved. Thanks for showing up tonight, Jackie."

"I wish I could take credit for being a good person," Jackie told her, "but it was all Mom's idea."

"Is Frances here, too, then?" Sister Mary Pat wanted to know.

"I believe she's supervising the toy and clothing boxes in the church foyer," Jackie told her, "and I hope she's warmer in there than we are in here."

"We're warmer than some are tonight," Father Morelli reminded them. "But just the same, I think I'll put on my heavy coat before I take another box outside."

"That reminds me," said Father Schumann. "Mr. and Mrs. Polinowski had to go home, and the snow is really picking up out there. I need some more people on the box line outside to get the trucks packed before it gets too deep. Jackie?"

"Sure thing, Father," said Jackie dutifully. She could always get warm again when the last truck had pulled away, she supposed. "But who's going to pack the rest of the dinner boxes?"

"Why, I will," said Father Schumann. "I am always glad to help."

And you are always glad to get out of the cold, Jackie thought, but was careful not to say it. "I'll just go on out then" was what she did say, picking up her coat and scarf from the floor among the boxes.

"I'll go with you," said Sister Mary Pat.

"You can go, too, Father Morelli," said Father Schumann. "Don't forget your coat."

"We'll see you out there, Father," Jackie said to Father Morelli. "Come on, Jake."

Jake got carefully to his feet with a look that Jackie assumed to be gratitude. "Come back, doggy!" said Trevor, but this time it was Jake who was pretending not to hear. Jackie picked up the end of Jake's leather lead that was trailing on the floor behind him and looped it over her wrist. They walked behind Sister Mary Pat toward the heavy double doors that led outside, and were nearly bowled over when the doors swung inward. "Hey, Sister," called one of the bundled-up volunteers who was coming inside, "you won't believe what's outside in the crèche. It's a genuine dog in the manger!" They walked past, laughing, on their way to pick up more boxes.

"This I've got to see," said Sister Mary Pat. She stepped out the door, and Jackie followed, leading Jake. A gust of wind blew stinging snow into Jackie's face and made her clutch her coat around her, shivering. This storm had arrived unexpectedly on the heels of a welcome mid-December mild spell, and white Christmases aside, she wished it had stayed up in Canada a day or two longer. She wrapped her warm scarf twice around her neck and buttoned up the coat as she followed Sister Mary Pat to the crèche on the church lawn.

St. Wenceslas's crèche was the most elaborate and beautiful in the city. It had been donated by a wealthy parishioner, a hand-carved and hand-painted life-size wooden holy family complete with wooden shepherds, wooden wise men, and assorted wooden livestock. It had been shipped over from Father Schumann's native Germany years ago and set up on the front lawn of the church every December for nearly as long as Jackie could remember.

A striped canvas pavilion kept the worst of the weather off the painted figures, and a row of floodlights lent the scene an aspect closer to Hollywood than Bethlehem. Near a bearded shepherd and a richly robed wise man, Jackie saw Joseph standing calmly behind Mary, who was kneeling with her arms outspread, gazing in adoration at . . . a dog.

A small, wirehaired white dog of uncertain and no doubt complicated lineage was curled up into a ball at the feet of the baby Jesus. When he saw Jackie and Sister Mary Pat, he raised his head and whined but made no effort to vacate the spot. Jake barked once, half-heartedly, but the big shepherd didn't seem overly excited about the small intruder.

"What should we do?" Sister Mary Pat whispered as though they must avoid being overheard by the little dog.

"It doesn't look like it's going to hurt anything," Jackie whispered back.

"No, but if Father Schumann sees it . . ."

"If I see what?" asked Father Schumann, appearing as suddenly as before, and when Jackie saw the look on his face she understood why Sister Mary Pat had been whispering. "Oh!" he said when he saw the dog. His mouth opened in alarm. "Oh, my!"

Father Morelli came out of the church doors. "What's happening?" he asked.

"There's a dog!" said Father Schumann. "It's in the manger with the Christ Child! Sister, remove it immediately!" he commanded.

"Aw, he's just a little dog," said Father Morelli. "What harm can he do?"

"Dogs chew," said Father Schumann, wagging a finger at Father Morelli. "They scratch and chew and do far worse things. We can't allow it to harm our beautiful crèche!"

"Well, I'll see if I can get the little guy to move," said Father Morelli. "I don't know where he's going, though, in this weather." He walked slowly toward the manger, holding out his hand. "Come here, little guy," he coaxed. The dog didn't move but looked up at Father Morelli, as though interested in what the hand might be offering him.

"Shoo!" shouted Father Schumann at the top of his lungs as he waved his arms in the air. "Get out of here!"

At the sound of the shouting, the little dog bolted from his spot by the baby Jesus, nearly upsetting the manger as he jumped down and raced away into the snow-covered alleyway between the church and the old hotel next door. "You scared him off!" said Father Morelli.

"That's exactly what I meant to do," said Father Schumann. "He should not be here. He should go home."

"But what if he doesn't have a home?" asked Sister Mary Pat. "Where will he go then?"

Father Schumann gave her a look that clearly said it had never occurred to him before, and he didn't want to be held accountable now that it had.

"Oh, worse!" exclaimed Father Morelli, bending over the manger.

"What's worse?" Jackie asked him, coming closer with Jake at heel.

Father Schumann put his hands over his face. "I knew it! He has already chewed our precious Christ Child!"

"No, that's not it. Look!" said Father Morelli to Jackie. He pointed to the recently vacated manger, now occupied only by a chubby wooden Christ Child and a thick layer of straw. Jackie came closer and saw what Father Morelli was pointing at: the straw was spotted in several places with blood.

"He's hurt!" said Father Morelli, turning around to give Father Schumann an accusing look.

"How could I know that?" Father Schumann asked. "I was only trying to protect our Christ Child!"

"Don't worry, Father," Jackie told him. "Jake and I will find the little guy."

"Your Jake is a search and rescue dog?" Father Schumann's white eyebrows shot up in surprise. "I thought he was a police dog!"

"It's a hobby of his," she said. "What do you say, Jake? Shall we go to work?"

Jake knew the words *go to work* as well as he knew *eat* or *walk* or *ride*, his all-time favorites. His ears perked up and he looked back and forth between Jackie and the others, waiting for further instruction. "Over here, Jake," Jackie told him, and led the shepherd to the manger. She picked up a handful of the blood-spattered straw and held it out for him to smell.

Jake sniffed at the straw, then barked again, eagerly this time, and pulled on his lead. "Here we go!" said Jackie over her shoulder as her dog pulled her off in the direction they had seen the white dog disappear, between the church and another tall building. She followed as fast as she could in the deep snow.

The snow had slackened since they came outside, and it was still possible to see a few flecks of blood leading into the mouth of the alleyway, away from the comforting lights of Michigan Avenue. Jackie pulled Jake up a bit, uncertain how eager she was to go trudging through a dark alley for an animal who might or might not still be there. "Well, I've got you to protect me, don't I, Jake?" she asked her dog. He barked and pulled at the lead. "Okay, then," she said. "Let's go."

Father Morelli and Sister Mary Pat caught up with her. "Can we help?" asked Sister.

"You probably can't hurt," Jackie told her, and the three of them followed along after Jake as he dashed from one side of the alley to the other, following the trail. Behind them, they could hear Father Schumann panting to catch up.

"We should be able to find him in here without too much trouble," said Father Morelli. "This alley is a dead end."

Tall brick walls loomed on both sides, blocking out what little moonlight there was. It was too dark in the alley to see the blood trail, and Jackie couldn't be sure whether or not she could see paw prints. Jake didn't need the visual cues necessary to humans, however, and he continued to sniff and take off in different directions, following a trail only he could sense.

Jackie glanced around uneasily at the dark shapes she could perceive against the walls of the buildings and on the ground. Some were immediately identifiable as trash containers and empty boxes, but others defied any comfortable definition. They seemed to want to take on more ominous shapes as she moved past them, trying not to let her imagination run wild.

Jake ignored them all in his focused search for the little dog until he ran up against the tall cyclone fence where the alley ended. Frantically, he ran back and forth, trying to pick up the strongest source of scent, for that would tell him the direction his quarry had gone. Finally he stopped in his tracks and whined in frustration.

"Did you lose him, Jake?" Jackie asked.

Jake whined again and sniffed the air.

"Maybe he got to the dead end and ran back out again," said Father Morelli.

"But wouldn't we have seen him?" asked Sister Mary Pat.

"We should have, but maybe we didn't. Anyhow, it's worth a try," Jackie said. "Come on, Jake, let's go the other way and see if you can pick up his scent again." She led him back toward the mouth of the alley, but halfway there he stopped and started pawing something dark on the ground.

"What's that?" asked Sister Mary Pat.

"It's only a pile of rags, I think," said Father Schumann.

Then the object moved, and a low moaning sound emerged from it. Jake stood back and barked at his mistress.

Father Morelli pulled his keys from his pocket and switched on a small flashlight that was attached to them, then shone it on the object of Jake's attention. In the dim light of the flashlight's beam, the pile of rags resolved itself into the crumpled form of a man, and the dark stain that spread from his head and down onto his face looked a lot to Jackie like blood.

"Where's my wife?" the man asked, weakly. "Where are my kids?" He pulled himself up to his hands and knees. His clothes were soaked through, and he trembled violently from the cold.

Father Morelli leaned down and helped the man gently to his feet. "Take it easy," he told him. "It looks like somebody hit you over the head. Do you remember who hit you?"

"I'm okay, but you need to find my wife and kids," said the man to Father Morelli.

"We must also find you an ambulance," said Father Schumann. "It is only a few feet to St. Wenceslas. Right around the corner. From there someone can call one for you."

"Find my family," the man repeated, but his voice was weaker now. "Please."

He sagged against Sister Mary Pat, who flung his arm expertly over her back and shrugged herself up to support his weight. "You're nearly frozen, poor dear man! I'll get him back to the church," she said to the others. "You three go find his family." She walked slowly out of the alley with the man leaning heavily against her. They watched her proceed to the corner of the church and out of sight.

"Where do you suppose . . ." Father Morelli began, but just then Jake leaped forward again and took up the trail. This time he dragged Jackie through a half-open door in the building across the alley from the church. Jackie stepped through the door and stopped, pulling Jake's lead to keep him from dragging her any farther. Inside the building it was completely dark, and Jake was nearly invisible at the end of his lead. Anything beyond Jake was the great unknown.

"Hello?" Jackie called, but the darkness swallowed up her voice. Just as well, she thought, since she didn't know if she was announcing herself to friends or foes. The man outside had been hit by someone, she reminded herself.

A pale beam mitigated the darkness slightly, and Jackie saw that Father Morelli had turned on his little flashlight again. He played it around the room they had entered, picking out an area of floor just ahead of them. "This won't help us see very far," he told her, "but it should keep us from tripping over our feet."

Jake tugged at the lead and walked forward. Jackie followed, with the two priests behind her. Father Morelli aimed the flashlight's beam over her shoulder and onto the floor.

"Are those blood spots?" he asked in a whisper, indicating some dark spatters on the floor.

"They might be," Jackie said, "but they could just as easily be dirt. What is this place, anyhow? I thought there was a hotel here."

"This is the old South Palmer Arms Hotel," said Father Morelli.

"It has been condemned and will be torn down soon," added Father Schumann. "They boarded up all the doors and windows months ago, or so I thought."

That explained the extreme darkness inside, Jackie thought. She wished whoever had removed the boards from the alleyway door had opened up a couple of nearby windows, too. Any light at all would have been a help right then. At least it was warmer in here where the wind couldn't reach.

Jackie tried to keep up with her dog as he pulled her along, moving in the zigzag pattern she'd seen him use before when searching for an elusive scent, while Father Morelli tried to keep the flashlight just ahead of him. Then he stopped and pulled her in a completely new direction. From far away, she could hear the faint sound of someone crying.

"It's a child!" Jackie said to her companions. "Find 'em, Jake!" she told her dog, and he led her across one end of a large open area that might once have been the hotel's lobby, then up two flights of stairs and down a long hallway, moving toward the sound of the crying, which grew steadily louder and clearer as they approached. They stopped behind a door like a dozen other doors along the darkened corridor. This one was standing partly open. Jackie pushed on it, and Jake led the way inside.

The crying stopped abruptly. Father Morelli scanned the room with his light, which came to rest on the tear-streaked faces of two small children dressed in layers of clothing and overcoats. They stared at Jake, then at the three adults who towered over them. "Our mommy's with the bad man," said the smallest one—a girl—in a voice barely above a whisper. "Can you help her?" asked the older one.

Jackie knelt down to the kids' level. "Does the bad man have a gun?" she asked them.

The boy shook his head. "He has a knife," he said. "He wants our house money."

"We're going to have our own house again," said the little girl.

"How long has the bad man been here?" she asked them.

"A few minutes," said the boy. "He took our mom to find the house money where she hid it, and Mom told us to run away, but we didn't want to go outside, so we came in here."

"Do you know if there's anyone else in the building?" Jackie inquired.

"Just a little dog. He came in here just a minute ago, but he ran right back out. He had blood all over him."

"I want the doggy to come back," said the girl.

"Well, we're going to find your mother and the dog if we can," Jackie told them. "And Father Schumann and Father Morelli are going to take you back to St. Wenceslas where your father is." She turned her head to look at the two priests. "You can call the police from the church. Jake and I are going looking for the kids' mother."

"You cannot stay here, Jackie," said Father Schumann. "You might be putting yourself in danger."

Jackie stood up again. Her knees were shaky and her

heart was trying to thump its way out of her chest, but she knew what she had to do. "Someone else might already be in danger," she told him. "And there might not be time to wait for the police."

She turned back to the children. "Do you have anything here that belongs to your mother? Some clothes?"

Both children shook their heads. "Our clothes are in another room," said the boy.

Jackie turned to her dog. "We haven't got much to go on, but I know you can do it. You've got to find her, Jake. Let's go to work."

Jake barked. Father Morelli handed Jackie his flashlight. "We can find our way back to the alley door without this," he told her. He took the children's hands.

"It's all right—we know the way," said the little girl.

"Father Morelli, can you handle both the children?" asked Father Schumann. "I'm going to go with Jackie."

"Father, you don't have to . . ."

"I cannot leave you here alone," said the old priest. He held up a hand to ward off any further argument. "Now let us hurry and find the mother."

Jackie followed Father Morelli and the children out of the room and turned in the opposite direction to the one they were taking to leave the old hotel. "Which way should we go, Jake?" she asked the dog. She shone the beam of Father Morelli's flashlight into the gloom. A streak of white near the floor entered the hallway from one room and sped away into the darkness. It was the little white dog. Jake whuffed and followed.

"He's not just going after that dog, is he?" asked Father Schumann. "Does he know he is supposed to be looking for someone else now?"

"Father, I only wish I knew," Jackie told him. "We have to trust Jake now. The only thing we can do is follow and hope."

"No, we can follow and pray," said the priest.

"You're in charge of praying," said Jackie, "and Jake's

in charge of tracking." I wish I knew what I was doing here, she thought to herself, but decided against saying it.

Jackie kept the light in front of them as best she could, but not only was Father Morelli's flashlight growing dimmer by the minute, but Jake's breakneck pace had them heading into total darkness every few seconds, unsure what might lay ahead. Or Jackie was unsure—Jake seemed utterly confident. At least there wasn't a lot of debris lying about in their path.

As her dog led her along, Jackie thought, but once or twice was certain, she saw a rat scurry out of the approaching beam of light.

"Jackie, slow down!" Father Schumann called from behind her.

"Tell it to Jake, Father," she called back over her shoulder. She had wished Father Schumann weren't so insistent on coming along back there in the room. She had to admit she felt less alone and less afraid of what she might find at the end of their search with another human being present.

Still, she would rather the human being in question be Father Morelli or Sister Mary Pat than the dour, disapproving Father Schumann.

At the end of the hallway Jake stopped and turned both ways for a moment, then caught a scent and took her down a flight of stairs covered with threadbare carpeting. Jackie shone the beam on the steps and hoped they were all intact, which turned out to be the case. As Jake took a turn at the bottom of the steps, Jackie heard the faint sound of human voices coming from nearby.

"I heard your kid talking about the money, so I know you've got it," said a rough male voice, echoing through the empty spaces. "You'd better find it and hand it over before I find those kids."

"My kids aren't anywhere around here," said a woman's voice. Jackie felt even more relief than fear. They were almost on top of the man with the knife, and the children's mother was still alive. The uncertainty lay in what was coming next.

They moved forward as quietly as they could manage, turned a corner, and emerged into a large area with shafts of moonlight penetrating the gloom. Some of the window boards had fallen or been pried off, and Jackie could see the moon—just past full—with a few wispy clouds skipping across its surface. The storm had blown over at last.

The room appeared empty, but the tension in Jake's body told Jackie they weren't alone, and the awful silence where only moments before she had heard a voice told her that whoever was in here was watching them. Slowly, she reached down Jake's heavy leather lead until her hand rested on the clip that separated the lead from Jake's collar. Then she raised the flashlight's weakening beam from the floor and scanned the room.

They were on a mezzanine just above the lobby of the hotel. A few old pottery planters, broken and fallen over, were all that was left of the furnishings that once filled it. A waist-high railing ran along one side, overlooking the lobby floor, and at the far end of that railing, half-hidden by shadows, was a man holding a woman with a knife to her throat. Jake growled when he saw the knife and the situation, two things he had learned to recognize in his former career as a police dog. Jackie jerked firmly once on his collar to signal him that it wasn't yet time for action.

"Get the hell out of here," the man told them. "I just came for the money. Once I have it, I'm out of here."

"That's our house money," said the woman. "I'm not going to tell you where it is." Her eyes were wide with fear, but her voice was firm and determined.

"We are not armed," said Father Schumann. "Let the woman go."

"I know you're not armed," the man replied. "If you had a gun you'd be waving it around. Besides, you're a preacher or something."

"I'm Father Detlef Schumann, pastor of St. Wenceslas church, right next door. Please let us have the woman. Then you are free to look for the money as long as you like."

Jackie thanked whoever might be listening that Father Schumann hadn't decided to threaten the man with the police, who would certainly be here soon. Soon enough? She knew she couldn't count on it.

"No!" the woman cried. "He can't have our money. We're going to rent a house!"

"Your life is more important than a house," Father Schumann told her. "Tell him where the money is, and he'll let you go."

The woman only shook her head, tears running down her cheeks.

"She'll tell me where the money is, all right," said the man. "But if push came to shove I could find it without her, so if you don't back out of here right now I'm going to cut her throat. You might be thinking I won't, but you just don't know me." He pressed the knife closer to the woman's neck. She whimpered in fear. "She wouldn't be the first."

Jackie believed him. Now she had to make him believe her. She began to back away.

"Jackie, what are you doing?" Father Schumann whispered to her.

"I guess we're leaving," said Jackie.

"But . . . !"

"We've got to leave, Father," said Jackie, and hoped the priest could see she meant business. "If we don't, he'll kill her." Jackie was pretty certain the man planned to kill the children's mother one way or the other, once he found the money he was looking for. She and Jake had seen his type before.

"We're leaving now," she said to the man. "This is none of our business."

"You're damned right it's not!" the man shouted, his voice cracking at the end. "Now get the hell out!"

Jackie took Jake's collar firmly in one hand and led him through the doorway. He was quivering with frustration, but there was nothing she could do about it right now. She had to make the man relax, and she prayed he would when he saw them leave. Praying might be Father Schumann's department, but what the hell—maybe he could use some help.

As Father Schumann came through the doorway behind her, Jackie switched off the flashlight, then turned Jake back in the direction of the mezzanine and unclipped the lead. Without a sound, Jake took off at a gallop and leaped into the air near the railing. Jackie switched the light back on, but it was hard to see anything from here. The man's scream told her Jake had found the knife hand, even in the dim light. The crunch of bone that followed told her that the ex-police dog was taking no chances with this perpetrator. She fought down a surge of sudden nausea.

The man screamed again and fell back against the railing. The woman fell down onto the floor and began to crawl toward the doorway as Jake and the man struggled. Jackie ran into the room. "Jake, off!" she shouted, just as the man lost his balance and fell backward into the blackness with Jake still clamped on to his ruined arm. There was a short, terrified scream, a hard thump, then silence.

"Jake!" Jackie ran to the railing and looked over, but couldn't make any meaning out of the jumble of dark shapes on the lobby floor, even with the help of the flashlight, which was growing dimmer by the second. She turned and pushed past Father Schumann, who was coming to the aid of the children's mother, then ran down the stairs and out onto the floor under the mezzanine railing. Something was rising up from the floor. She played the light in that direction.

Jake rose up from the body of the man on the floor and stepped away. He seemed to know there was no more danger in the still, twisted form. He walked around the man—now only an obstacle between him and his mistress.

Jackie knelt down and hugged her dog. "Jake, you're wonderful!" she told him. "You're the best dog anyone ever had!"

Jake whuffed. It wasn't the first time he'd heard that sort of praise, and the way Jackie figured it, he probably knew he deserved it.

"Jackie, is Jake all right?" Father Schumann called down from above.

"He's fine, Father," Jackie called back.

"And the man?"

"Dead." Jackie swallowed hard. "Is everything okay up there?"

"Everything is fine. And we have a little surprise, as well."

From above came two short, high-pitched barks.

"Well, you didn't find the dog in the manger," Jackie told Jake, "but it looks like he found us."

"So I missed all the fun again," said Frances Costello, shaking her head. "Why didn't you come get me when all this started?"

"Things sort of got away from us, Mom," Jackie explained. "More hot chocolate?"

"Of course. But don't think it's going to make up for not bringing me along on your adventure."

Jackie picked up the steaming pan of chocolate from the stove in the church kitchen and poured cups for her mother, Father Morelli, and Sister Mary Pat.

Father Schumann was busy putting little Wenceslas to bed in a pile of his old sweaters, after finding some dog food in the donated items for the holiday drive, and taking food and water bowls from the kitchen cupboards. The two of them were hitting it off just fine. Father Schumann seemed to have found something more gratifying to worry about than the welfare of wooden statues, and it was doing him a world of good.

The blood on the dog's fur had apparently belonged to someone else—presumably the children's father, who had been taken to the nearest hospital for a few stitches to close the wound the prowler had given him. Father Schumann had paid for a cab and a hotel room for the man's family, and told them he'd pick them up himself tomorrow for Christmas dinner at St. Wenceslas. The family had arrived a few weeks before in Palmer, down on their luck, and had been squatting in the old hotel. Then the father had gotten a job, and they had been trying to save enough to rent a place to live. Father Schumann was sure he could find someone among his parishioners who could help with that goal.

"It's hard to believe how bored and depressed I was only a little more than an hour ago," Jackie told them. "I was certain that nothing I did could possibly make a difference."

"We've seen a big difference made here tonight," said Sister Mary Pat.

"And I think you and Jake have to take a lot of the credit for it," said Father Morelli.

"Thanks, Father," said Jackie, "but all I did was follow Jake. He's never led me astray yet."

Jake lay at her feet, legs twitching in a canine dream of chasing rabbits or sheep or just possibly a small white dog.

"And we all followed Wenceslas," Jackie added. "He's the one who seemed to know all along exactly where we were needed."

Habits

Jeremiah Healy

JEREMIAH HEALY, a graduate of Rutgers College and Harvard Law School, was a professor at the New England School of Law for eighteen years. He is the creator of John Francis Cuddy, a Boston-based private investigator. Mr. Healy's first book, *Blunt Darts*, was selected by the *New York Times* as one of the seven best mysteries of 1984, and his second novel, *The Staked Goat*, received a Shamus Award. His later works include *So Like Sleep*, *Rescue*, *Invasion of Privacy*, *The Only Good Lawyer*, and *The Stalking of Sheila Quinn*.

"As my brother Earl would put it," said Joe Bob Brewster from the rocker on his porch, "you're having a day of bad biorhythms."

Chief Lon Pray looked up from the window of the town police cruiser at Joe Bob, a paperback book open in his lap and a sleepy hound dog named Old Feller twitching his tail under the chair in time to the rocking of his master. Pray couldn't recall ever meeting Joe Bob's brother, who'd moved away before Christmas a year before, but he had been introduced to a couple of the Brewster sisters, and they varied from Joe Bob's carroty hair and stocky frame about as much as one pumpkin from another. Unfortunately, though, issues of family tree—or Yule Tree—weren't what brought Pray back to Joe Bob's dusty front yard for the second time that December morning.

The chief said, "You still haven't seen anything, then?"

"Uh-uh," from the man in the rocker. "You ain't turned up nothing from all those roadblocks?"

"Nothing like the three that hit the bank, anyway."

"Well," said Joe Bob, "I sure didn't hear them running down behind the house here," flicking his head to the rear.

Three men, in masks, had hit the bank just as it opened that morning. Pray had seen his share of armed robberies while working as a detective on Boston's force up north. But instead of a getaway car with a wheelman out front, these guys had run across the street and down a path through the wooded hillside half a mile above Brewster's ramshackle home. They'd apparently stashed a pickup truck on a fire road about midway down the slope, because the one witness who'd had the courage to run after them saw it pulling away in the distance when he reached the fire road himself.

Only thing was, Pray had contacted his patrol units within two minutes after the bank manager had called it in, and the county sheriff within two after that. This part of the state—that Pray had found himself just by driving south from Massachusetts one brutal February until he started feeling warm—had paved routes laid out like a grid pattern at intervals of roughly three miles, so setting up roadblocks had been both practiced in the past and easy in the present.

Except that while quite a few pickups had been stopped, none had contained three men, their handguns, or thirty-six thousand in cash.

"Besides," said Joe Bob, "Old Feller would of tore them to pieces."

Pray tried to refocus. "What?"

Joe Bob seemed hurt, leaning down to scratch his dog between the ears. "Old Feller got wind of three strangers barreling in here, Chief, he would of tore them to pieces."

"Right." Pray tried to keep the sarcasm out of his

voice, especially given that he hadn't seen the hound burn twelve calories total in the five months he'd been driving past the Brewster house to the restaurant where he took most of his meals.

"Well, if you do see or hear anything, call the office."

"You gonna go around to everybody else you already talked to once?"

"Can't think of anything else to do," replied Chief Lon Pray, putting the cruiser in gear and pulling away.

"Like I told you before, Chief," said Mary Boles from behind the bank desk—a nice holly wreath centered on its front—"it had to be somebody who knew we had extra cash on hand to cover the mill's Christmas bonuses."

Watching Boles, a plump black woman in her forties, Pray fidgeted in the customer chair, finding it uncomfortably like the client chair in his divorce lawyer's office back in Boston. "Isn't that pretty widely known, though?"

"In town, yes. Even in the county. But robbers from any distance away? I don't see how they could know that today was one of maybe three times a year there'd be enough cash in the vault to be worth stealing."

From Pray's experience, armed bank robbers were the most dangerous felons around exactly because they didn't know very much or plan very well. But, he had to admit, so far these had planned well enough to fool him.

"Mary, can we go over what happened in here this morning?"

"Again?"

"Please?"

"Okay." The manager seemed to compose herself for reciting a particularly distasteful poem. "I'd just opened the front door from the inside, and Eugene was just unlocking his drawer at the teller's cage, when the three men burst in."

"And Josh?"

Boles blushed at the bank guard's name. "In the bathroom, like I told you before."

"Then what?"

"These three men came busting through, like they knew the precise moment I'd be opening up."

That didn't seem to Pray like much of a clue, but he nodded to keep Boles talking.

"The one man, he stuck a gun in my face and walked me backward to the vault. The second one rushed past us, and I heard him tell Eugene not to press any button, or he'd die with his finger on it."

"What about the third man?"

"He ordered me to open the vault, which of course was where we kept the money after the armored car dropped it off yesterday."

"And you did."

"Open it? Damned right, with that spooky first man pressing his gun to my cheek." Boles went to rub the spot.

"Mary, the man who stayed on you, he never spoke?"

"No."

Pray always felt uncomfortable asking, much less repeating, the next question, but it was necessary. "And you don't know the race of that man?"

She shook her head. "Like I said before, they all wore masks and gloves, long-sleeved shirts, and pants. But from the voices of the two who spoke, I'd say they were white, so I'm guessing two grains of salt didn't ask a peppercorn to join them."

Pray grinned, getting the impression Boles was trying to make him feel at ease for having to ask the question at all. People rarely behaved so considerately up north when probed by touchy questions.

"Anything else, Chief?"

"Yes."

"What?"

"Eugene."

"I had to send him home," said Mary Boles. "Poor boy was shaking like a leaf."

"How about Josh, then?"

"Mary has her habit of opening on time," said Josh Stukes. "I have mine of relieving myself just then."

Pray blinked at the doughy, fiftyish man with sandy hair. "You couldn't wait till the first few customers came through?"

"Chief, you never worked in a bank around Christmas, let me tell you. There ain't never a time nobody's coming through the doors, so one time's as good—or as bad—as another."

"Give me the sequence again, then, as you remember it."

"All right." Stukes pointed toward the rear of the bank lobby. "I was just finishing, and the flushing kept me from hearing anything. When I opened the door, I got the muzzle of a Ruger forty-four stuck in my face."

"And you knew it was a Ruger . . ."

". . . account of that's what I have next to my bed, for home protection." Stukes pointed again. "This feller with the cannon walked me over to where they already had Eugene and Mary, kneeling on the floor, noses against the wall, and I joined them."

"And that was it?"

"Mary already had the vault opened by the time I got out there, and all I heard was the one feller telling us all to be quiet and nobody had to get theirselves shot. So I was quiet as a little mouse." Stukes suddenly grinned, but not pleasantly. "Speaking of mice, you gonna talk to Eugene again?"

Very evenly, Pray said, "Yes."

"Hope for your sake he changed his undies first."

* * *

"Chief, I really don't know what else I can tell you about that frightful experience this morning."

Lon Pray watched Eugene Cornwell cradle a small dog in his arms. The dog was a little mop of brushed hair and cute as a bug, the living room decorated tastefully even without the handsome tree and draped bunting of pine branches.

"Eugene, I won't know what'll help me either till I hear you tell it again."

Cornwell closed his eyes, then opened them. "Very well. I was behind my cage, just opening my cash drawer for the morning and arranging the currency and coins, as is my habit. Suddenly, I heard a stampede sound from the front door. I looked up to see these horribly dressed men barging past Mary, one stomping up to me and pointing a monstrous gun right here." Cornwell's index finger reluctantly left the dog and tapped the owner's forehead over his nose. "They say your whole life is supposed to flash by in front of you? Well, I swear my only thought was, 'Who would take care of Florinda?' " Cornwell's finger returned to the dog, and his forehead dipped to touch the same spot on the dog, who licked it appreciatively.

Pray waited a moment. Then, "You did hear the men speak?"

"At least one of—no, two of them. But I was too terrified to recall anything they actually said."

After striking out again on race, age, and idiosyncrasies, Lon Pray concluded with, "Anything else you remember?"

"Yes," said Eugene Cornwell, "I remember that the reason I relocated here after college in Richmond was to be able to feel safe in a small town."

"That was still pretty brave of you, Luis."

Pray noticed that his words made the thirteen-year-old in the Atlanta Braves jersey stand a little taller, the wiry dog at his side whuffing.

"Without Mrs. Boles and her bank, we do not have our life here."

Pray knew that the Cortez family had moved in over the store they were running after Luis's parents had decided the migrant life left a lot to be desired. But he also knew how impossible becoming shopkeepers would have been if their loan request had been turned down.

"Luis, can you tell me again what you saw?"

"Sure thing. I am outside our store, washing down the windows from the dust that seems to come during the night from nowhere. I hear the sound of people running, so I turn to see three men crossing the street from the bank, guns in their hands but not shooting at anybody. I drop my window brush into the pail, and I wait until they cannot see me before I run after them."

"You get any kind of look at their faces?"

"Like I tell you before, they have masks over them, and gloves on the hands, too. But the way they run, I think they must be white."

"Why?"

Luis Cortez scuffed at the dust with the toe of his sneaker, causing the dog to stick his nose down there and paw the ground himself. "Because they do not run so very well."

Pray tried not to grin this time. "Go on."

"I am coming after them down the path through the woods. I can hear them in front of me, making noise with their feet and hitting the branches with their arms, maybe, but not talking or nothing. Then I hear the sound of a car engine starting, only when I get to the edge of the fire road, I can see that it is a pickup. By this time, though, the truck is too far away to see anything but that it is dark in color."

Which was what Pray had put out over the radio to his officers and the sheriff's deputies. Too bad half the vehicles in the county were pickup trucks, and half of those were blue, black, or brown.

"Nothing else, Luis?"

The boy and his dog pawed at the ground in unison. "Just that when I tell my mother what I did, she slap me hard enough to loosen a tooth."

Chief Lon Pray tried to tell himself that, as a parent so close to Christmas, he wouldn't have done the same thing. Tried and failed.

"Anything?" said Pray.

Edna Dane, one of two uniforms on the roadblock, reached into her cruiser, a short pony-tail bobbing against her neck under the Stetson. Coming out with a clipboard, she looked down at it. "We've had fifty . . . five vehicles so far. Twenty passenger cars, three semis, two buses, five panel trucks. The balance were pickups, seven of them dark in color. We called them all in to Dispatch. None with more than two men in it, and no wants or warrants on any of the trucks or occupants."

Pray squinted past the other uniform, standing hip-cocked with the butt of a riot pump gun resting on his thigh. The pavement was otherwise empty in the noon-day sun, people either working or doing holiday shopping at the mall ten miles away.

Dane said, "I'm guessing you haven't had any better luck at the other roadblocks or you wouldn't be here with me."

Pray turned to her. "You grew up in town, right?"

"Born and bred, except for four years of Criminal Justice over to the university."

"Answer me this, then. Three men hit our bank at opening, and then run for it instead of driving away. But they get into a pickup on a fire road barely ten feet wide that would leave them no way out if just one of our cars—or hell, a county surveyor even—happened to be on the road at the same time. Now, why would a gang risk that?"

Edna Dane smiled, and Lon Pray thought he could see the teenager she'd have been a few years back shining through. "I guess if I knew that, Chief, you'd have stopped fifty-five vehicles this morning, and I'd be worried sick over what you didn't find."

Chief Lon Pray stopped at his own house—a small ranch he rented on the edge of town—to let the dog out, as he did each day around lunchtime. Everybody else in the area just seemed to let their pets roam free during the day, and probably, Pray thought, in time he would, too. But back in Boston, before making detective, he'd tried unsuccessfully to comfort one too many kids kneeling in streets, crying uncontrollably while they in turn tried to will their pets back to life after being hit by passing cars.

And Lon Pray didn't think he could tolerate that happening to Grizzly at this time in his life. In Pray's own life, that is.

After his divorce, most of the marital property—house, car, even their TVs—went to the ex or her lawyer. Funny, Lon realized as he unlocked his back door. You thought of her as Sally in Boston but down here as *the ex*. I wonder if other guys—

Which is when Pray was knocked nearly flat.

"Grizzly!"

The combination German shepherd/Irish wolfhound had already bounded by him, loping around the yard like a racehorse around its paddock. Watching him, Pray couldn't stay mad. Grizzly had been the first creature in his life after the divorce, and the chief knew that, in a very basic way, the dog kept him sane.

By the time Grizzly got the pent-up energy burned off, Pray already had washed out his water bowl and filled it with fresh from the tap. Placing the bowl down in the yard, Pray watched Grizzly pad over in that slightly prancing way he had from the Irish side of his family.

Lon decided to let the dog run free for another ten minutes, then grab a sandwich-to-go at the restaurant before wracking his brain again on why the robbers had planned their escape as they had.

And why the roadblocks hadn't turned them up.

But meanwhile, he'd take a page from Joe Bob Brewster's book and just sit on his porch, giving himself an early Christmas present by watching Grizzly enjoy the habit of midday exercise.

Driving by the Brewster place, Lon Pray gave a thought to stopping and asking Joe Bob a third time if he'd spotted anything, but the man was holding up a newspaper instead of the usual book, just the carroty hair visible above the top of the paper. Pray thought Joe Bob must be deep in thought, too, because he wasn't rocking, and Old Feller wasn't in his customary position but rather a full yard away from the chair.

It was five minutes later that Pray, ordering his trademark ham and cheese on wheat with mayo, suddenly registered what he'd seen. Then he put it together with what he'd heard, both as answers to his questions and as statements that had seemingly been offered gratuitously.

And, sprinting to his cruiser, Chief Lon Pray thought he'd figured it out.

Twenty minutes later, the man in the rocker was still holding the newspaper, and Old Feller was still lying a good three feet away.

Which was fine by Lon Pray, now crouched behind a tree rather than sitting behind a wheel.

Pray waited for three minutes more, until he heard the shrill whistle from the back of the house. Then he leveled his Glock 17 and yelled over the sound of breaking glass. "Let that paper fall from your hands without lowering them!"

Old Feller looked first toward Pray, then to the rocker. The paper trembled, but didn't fall from the fingers holding it.

"Be smart!" yelled Pray a little louder. "Nobody's been shot yet. Don't make yourself the first."

From the back of the house, Officer Edna Dane's voice rang out with, "Clear in the house. I say again, the house is clear."

Pray yelled a third, final time, "Last chance to see Christmas."

The paper then wafted down, the hands staying in the air and about even with the carroty hair and the face below it that was almost, but not quite, Joe Bob Brewster's.

Chief Lon Pray said, "Just a day of bad biorhythms, Earl."

"Chief, I was beginning to think I'd have to hit you in the head with a hammer."

Lon Pray watched the Santa coffee mug shake as the man holding it shuddered in his rocking chair. "You did everything you could, Joe Bob. It just took me a while to catch on."

"I mean, I lead with my brother, I flick my head toward the house, I even go on about Old Feller and 'strangers.' But all you do is kind of grin and drive off."

"Joe Bob, I just didn't get what you were telling me till I drove past half an hour ago."

"When my brother Earl was out here."

"Right. I'm guessing he wasn't too pleased with your mentioning his name to me."

"He thought he had a tight plan, all right," said Joe Bob, taking a slug of coffee. "Him and the other two hit the bank, then run down to the fire road. One gets in his own pickup that they left there, the other runs with Earl almost to my place. Old Feller didn't kick up any fuss when his owner's brother happens to stroll around from the back and ask how I'm doing. Then Earl tells me that him and his 'friend' are gonna be in the house for a few days, waiting for things to cool down before they call their third friend to come back and pick them up."

"Along with the guns and the money."

"The money Earl never showed me, but he sure did wave that gun under my nose, and I knew I couldn't say anything direct-like to you, or he'd have shot through the window there and killed the both of us."

Pray said, "So you tried to tip me, Earl didn't like it, and he came out onto your porch here to impersonate you."

"Which was pretty smart of him, what with my habit of sitting out here." Joe Bob took another slug from the mug. "Only my book wasn't big enough to cover his whole face, so he had to use a newspaper, which I doubt you've ever seen in my hands. That was what tipped you, right?"

"That plus some other things. I wondered how out-of-towners would know about the mill money and the fire road. I also wondered why the third man in the bank never spoke."

"Simple," said Joe Bob around another sip of coffee. "Old Mary Boles might've recognized his voice."

"Another thing was, when I drove by a little while ago, your brother wasn't rocking in the chair like you do."

"Earl tried that, but his rhythm was all off, and he caught Old Feller's tail underneath."

"That's the last thing."

"What is?" said Joe Bob.

Pray gestured toward the sleepy hound. "Old Feller wasn't switching his tail under your chair, and that seemed to me oddest of all."

"Habits."

"What?"

"Habits," said Joe Bob Brewster. "We all have them. Sometimes they hurt, but sometimes they help, too."

Chief Lon Pray found himself nodding in time to Old Feller's tail.

Eye Witness

David Leitz

Author of numerous short stories and the Max Addams
fly-fishing mystery novels, DAVID LEITZ splits his time
between a 250-year-old farmhouse on the north coast of
Massachusetts and a cabin in the woods of southern
Vermont. For more information about Mr. Leitz and his
writing, see www.whitefork.com.

"I wish I was half the man my dog thinks I am."
Anonymous

I watched him murder her; his bare left knee pressed
hard between her soft, white, flopping breasts, holding
her down as his thumbs pushed knuckle-deep into her
neck. Her face turned blue, her mouth gaped, and her
long legs kicked around his naked hips like she was
running somewhere.

And as usual, I yawned.

I was used to it. I'd been watching him do it all
week; hump her and then flip her to her back where
she would twist and claw as he climbed roughly to her
chest, straddled it and, throttling her neck with one
hand, leaned over her face.

They were like that; violent in their lovemaking ...
growling, biting, slick with sweat when it was over ...
only this time she didn't cough or laugh or even slap him.

She just sprawled there on the bed of twisted
sheets. And smelled of death.

He walked to his chair by the now-dead fire, wrapped
his bony shoulders in the afghan, and sat. Then he lit a

cigarette, exhaled at the ceiling, and scratched me behind the right ear. "I think I've got a problem, Jack, old buddy," he said to me. "A big problem."

It was the first time he'd touched me in days. I licked his hand. It was strangely warm and tasted of her.

He pulled it away. "Jesus, Jack."

After he finished his cigarette, he flipped the butt into the fireplace and we both slept.

When I awoke, he was gone. So was she. The bed was stripped to the mattress, the pillows were on the floor, and I could hear voices in the downstairs hall.

"It just got out of hand," I heard him say. "We went crazy. It was like she was begging me to do it."

"I told you she was a bad one," a man's voice I'd never heard before said. "I told you. When she first started coming here I told you she'd find a way to fuck you over. Didn't I?"

My man didn't answer.

I got to my feet, stretched, shook, and went to the big carved door. It was ajar but my nose wouldn't fit in the opening. I couldn't open it.

I whined.

They were still talking and couldn't hear me.

I barked. Two short, sharp ones like I use when I get trapped in the kitchen bathroom after drinking from the toilet bowl. I barked again.

"Shit," my man said. "I must've shut Jack in the bedroom." His feet started up the stairs.

"The bedroom . . . ?"

"Yeah. The bedroom." The footsteps were almost to the top of the stairs.

"You telling me he was there?" Now I heard the other man start up the stairs. He was heavier. "The fucking dog saw you do it?"

They were in the upstairs hall now. "She seemed to get more turned on when he watched," my man said.

The door opened before I could get out of the way,

and it caught my left foot as it swung in. It startled me more than it hurt and I yelped.

"Damn it, Jack," my man yelled. "You want out so bad, then let me open the door."

I held up my paw and whined. Now it was starting to hurt. I backed away on three feet.

My man held the door open with his hip, leaned, and grabbed me roughly by the collar. "Get out of here, Jack." He jerked me toward the door and threw me out into the hall. "Get out, damn it."

I yelped again. What had I done? I didn't like being yanked and thrown around. Or yelled at. Not by my man.

The other man in the hallway was bigger—wider than my man as well as taller—with long red hair and a darker red beard. He smelled like cheese. As I limped by, he kicked at me. "Fucking dog," he said. "What the hell do you need with a fucking dog?" I tucked my tail, sidestepped his second kick and, forgetting my paw, ran for the stairs. As I went down the steps two at a time, the big man was laughing.

My man grunted something I couldn't hear as I hit the downstairs hall running, skidded on the hardwood floor, and hung a sharp left into the long hall to the kitchen, through the swinging door to the safety under the table. I put my head on my paws and listened to them come down the stairs. I was puzzled. It was getting worse. Now my man had yanked me. And yelled at me.

"Who knows she was here?" I heard the big man say.

"Her office, of course."

"Dinkletter knew she was coming over here?"

"I told you, she was doing our books. Dinkletter is the one who assigned her."

They were in the front hallway now. The big man sounded angry. "Then they're going to look for her here, aren't they, Bill? Jesus fucking Christ, Dinkletter's going to call the cops when she doesn't show up tomorrow. They're going to be all over this place."

"I know. I know."

"You've got to call him."

"Dinkletter? Why?"

"To complain. Tell him she didn't show up today. You're pissed off. That kind of crap. You know."

"It's after hours. No one'll be there."

"All the better. Leave a voice mail."

"I don't think I can . . ."

"You've got to, Billy boy. And you've got to do it now."

My man mumbled something, and I heard them walk into the study. I ducked out from under the kitchen table, pushed back out into the hallway and, trying not to click my toenails on the hardwood floor between the Orientals, I followed.

I stopped just outside the study door and sat, holding in my tongue, attempting not to pant. It was getting hot in the house. "Mr. Dinkletter?" I heard my man say, obviously now on the phone at the big cherry desk over by the long windows. "This is William Wadsworth III. Wadsworth Industries. I . . . ah . . ." He was talking to an answering machine. ". . . ah, I'm calling because Jenny Darrel did not keep her appointment at my home office today."

"Be pissed," the big man whispered.

"I'm a busy man, Dinkletter." My man's voice became angry. "Wadsworth Industries pays your firm a handsome fee every winter to audit our books and I expect your services to be commensurate with that sum. I also expect a full explanation and apology from you and Miss Darrel first thing in the morning." He slammed down the phone. "How was that?"

"Not bad," the big man said. "Now, where's her body? We've got work to do."

I ducked back down the hallway to the kitchen and returned to my place under the table. I had to pee now, but it would have to wait.

They pushed through the door a few seconds later, and I watched their feet cross the room to the walk-in freezer door. "I can't believe you put her in the freezer," the big man said, standing back as my man swung the heavy door open. I could smell the cold. And her.

"I didn't know what else to do with her," my man said. They entered the freezer.

"Nice," the big man said. "Real nice. Look at those knockers. And what a soft . . ."

"Don't touch her."

"Why not? She doesn't give a shit."

"It's bad enough."

"These the sheets from the bed?"

"I wrapped all her clothes in there, too."

"You sure you got everything?"

My man sighed. "Everything except her car."

"We'll do her car when we get rid of everything else," the big man said. "I'll drive it. You can follow me in yours. We'll leave it down in Burly Town with the keys in it. It'll be a stripped shell by morning. Now . . . where are we going to make the beautiful Miss Darrel more manageable?"

"Do we have to? I'd rather just bury her and be done with it."

"We are going to bury her," the big man said. "Here, give me a hand. Take the legs." They were bringing her out into the kitchen. Their feet shuffled along the floor.

"I mean, bury her in one piece." I heard my man grunt with exertion. "Watch her head."

"Screw her head," the big man said. "I asked, where are we going to do it?"

"Outside. In the potting shed," my man said. "Next to the garage. There's a table in there."

"You have the things I told you to get?" The big man let one of her arms go and opened the door to the back-yard. Her hand flopped on the floor.

"I hope. The gardener keeps stuff in there."

"He better have some good saws. Pruning shears wouldn't hurt either." He picked up the dangling arm. "Turn off the light."

My man switched off the kitchen light and they jostled her out the door. I took advantage of it remaining slightly open and pushed out, scooted down the steps and out into the yard. I really had to pee now.

They didn't see me and, as my urine puddled in the grass, I watched their dark shapes lurch to the potting shed, wrestle the body inside and then the door closed. The single fluorescent came on, for a second illuminating the yard like moonlight and then the red haired man pulled down the shade.

I couldn't get back into the house so, for a while, I lay on the stoop with one ear up and listened.

The big man swore. My man swore. A clay pot fell and broke. Then there was the sound of the little electric chain saw the gardener used to prune the peach trees in the fall. "Hold her still," the big man growled.

"Oh, Jesus," my man said.

The whine of the saw intensified. "Damn it, Bill, I said hold her steady. Not that way. There. Like that."

"Oh, Jesus," my man said again.

"Damn," the big man said, grunting with effort. "That guillotine the French had must've been sharp."

I sighed and closed my eyes. I must have dozed because plastic garbage bags crinkling was the next thing I heard.

"You pack both hands?" I heard my man say.

"Of course."

"You're sure? I only remember seeing one."

"Damn it, Bill, do you see any hands laying around in here anywhere?"

"I just want to make sure we get everything."

Then my man backed the Mercedes out of the garage and they loaded the ten plastic bags into the trunk.

"Now, let's get out of these clothes," the big man said.

"Take a shower. I hope you've got something that'll fit me."

I watched them strip naked in the yard, bag their blood-soaked clothes, and put that bag in the car trunk with the others.

I got up off the stoop as they approached.

"You put a shovel in the car?" the big man said.

My man nodded. They were at the stoop now.

"I don't trust this mutt," the big man said as I dodged away from another kick. I ran into the yard and stopped, braced to run again if he chased me. "We'll get rid of him tomorrow."

"Get rid of him? I wish . . . but he was my father's."

"Your father?" The big man laughed and opened the door. "Your father's as dead as Miss Darrel out there. He doesn't give a shit." He scratched his naked crotch.

"Father's will stipulated that Jack be . . ."

"Will, schmill, Bill. You gotta get rid of him. Look at him. I don't like the way he looks at us. He knows what's happened. He'll tell sure as shit."

My man swatted a mosquito on the back of his neck. "How's he going to tell anyone?" He laughed.

"I don't know," the big man said. "He will, though. Lassie used to be able to tell Timmy. Remember?"

"I don't think I have the stomach for it."

"You can kill a gorgeous girl like that," the big man said with a laugh, "but you can't do a fucking dog?"

"I told you, her death was . . ."

"Okay. Okay. I'll take care of old Jack for you to-morrow. How's that?" The door slammed behind them. My man said something, but most of it was too muffled behind the door to make out.

Since there was nothing I could do about any of it right then, I trotted out to the potting shed and nosed myself inside. I had only been able to imagine what they were doing and wanted to smell for myself. The stench of death and blood and bone was fog-thick in the humid little building and I recoiled, instinctively backing away from it. My rump rammed the door. The latch clicked before I could turn. I was locked in.

I started to bark my locked-in bark but thought better of it. I didn't want to be yanked again. Or kicked. Or yelled at. So, I lay down by the door and put my nose close to the damp dirt floor where the odor of death was thinner.

I was confused. Why was my man so angry with me? It seemed as though he had been getting less and less patient with me over the past several months. And he hadn't been feeding me. Not every day anyway, like usual. He had been fine for a while after the father died. Let me ride in the Mercedes. Even took me to the country once ... He didn't let me out of the car, but it smelled nice though the crack in the back window. But then, he started to change. He fired the gardener and cook. Yelled at them like he was now yelling at me. He was on the phone a lot. He stayed up late. Drank from a bottle. He would still be in the study—sometimes on the floor—in the morning when I went to look for him to put me out. And then the girl began coming to the house. She was nice to me. Always brought a dog biscuit in her purse and didn't mind when I sniffed at her crotch. And my man was nicer. And now this. I sighed. Who was the big man with red hair? He didn't like me and was making my man angry at me again. If only I knew what I was doing wrong, I thought. If only I could find a way to make my man like he was before. If only ...

I heard the back door open and the two of them come out. I decided not to bark, remembering how angry my man had been when he let me out of the bedroom. And I could only imagine how angry the red haired man would be. So I lay there and listened to them go to the driveway.

"Just follow me," the big man said. "Once I ditch her car in Burly Town, we've got all night to get rid of the rest."

"Where?"

"Where what?"

"Where are we going to get rid of the rest?"

"A little here." The big man laughed. "A little there. A little everywhere."

I listened to the car doors slam, the engines start and then they were gone. A cricket began chirping in the far corner of the shed. Ordinarily I would have hunted it down—I liked their crunchy, sweet taste—but tonight I was too tired.

I closed my eyes and dozed and dreamed of my days with the father. Our trips to the hunting camp. The cold, misty mornings and the distant honking of migrating Canada geese. The smells of the woodsmoke, the coffee, the bacon, the guns, and wet wool. I felt the icy water, my feet swimming, the soft, warm, feathered bulk held lightly in my mouth. And I dreamed about the words of praise. The hugs and long rides home perched high and proud in the front seat. The special treats when the big tree went up in the house.

I heard the Mercedes return several hours later and only my man got out. After he entered the house and clicked the door shut I fell asleep again, this time dreaming of last summer and chasing that musty smelling woodchuck across the yard. I remembered how he had managed to escape me by diving though a hole in the back wall of the potting shed. How I had followed—it was tight—and by the time I had wriggled myself inside, he was long gone down the burrow hole he had behind the bags of peat moss. Over the next several days I had tried to dig him out and might have succeeded but the gardener caught him cockily sunning himself by the rhododendrons, shot him in the eye with his twenty-two pistol, and dumped the big brown rodent in the garbage can with the locking lid. I could barely smell its pungent fur through the thick plastic.

I awoke. Sunlight pressed yellow against the closed

window shade. Flies buzzed at the back of the shed. Sparrows squabbled and scratched along the tin roof. Old Charlie barked on his chain in the backyard three over. I stood and stretched. The smell was worse. Hugging the dark along the wall under the shelf, I went to where I remembered the woodchuck burrow hole to be and nosed behind the peat moss bags. The gardener must have filled it in before leaving, but the jagged opening in the shed wall was still there. I pushed my head through but my shoulders wouldn't fit. It was tighter than I remembered. I backed out and took a few steps away from it. Maybe if I ran at it like I'd done with the woodchuck, I'd fit. I took another couple steps back into the shed—I wanted to get a good running start—and my back left paw stepped on something soft and cold that grabbed at my foot. I yelped and jumped, spinning to attack whatever it was.

It was a hand. Tentatively, I sniffed it. It was her hand. The same one that had dragged on the floor in the kitchen—lying there palm up in the dim morning light. My weight in its center had caused it to clench.

I picked it up by the thumb, carried it to the hole in the wall, and dropped it out into the yard. Then I backed up again and charged. The opening was tight and the jagged sides hurt, but I was free. I turned, scooped the cold hand into my mouth, and ran for the house.

The back door, of course, was closed. Normally I would have barked and pawed at the screen until my man came and let me in, but my mission was to improve his mood and his opinion of me, not irritate him further.

I ran around the house and tried at the front door, but it, too, was closed. Sometimes one of the cellar windows was left ajar in the summer to let in fresh air, so with the hand still clamped in my jaws, I began a slow inspection of the narrow windows along the foundation. As I passed under the long windows to the study, I heard my man's voice through the wall. I sat, pricked my ears, and listened. He was talking on the telephone. "Of course, I'm upset, Dinkletter," he said. "I waited most of the day for her."

There was a pause while he listened to Dinkletter on the other end. Then he said, "Well, I wish you'd listened to your messages before you called the police. Now I have to endure another inconvenience because of your negligence. The New Year is only a few days away."

Another pause and then, "Yes, you do that, Dinkletter. Call them and tell them how unhappy I'm going to be to see them. Of course, a lot of good it's going to do if they're already on their way."

Pause.

"Yes, I'm sure you are, Dinkletter, but it's really too late, isn't it?"

Pause.

"I don't really care, Dinkletter. And make sure you pass on my sentiments to Miss Darrel also. When she shows up." My man slammed down the phone receiver and laughed.

I started for the next basement window when I heard him dialing. I went back to my place under the study window. The hand in my mouth wasn't cold anymore. "It's me," my man said. "I just got off the phone with Dinkletter. He called the cops first thing. Evidently she was living with her sister and the sister called Dinkletter before he had a chance to hear my message." He paused, listening. Then he said, "Any minute now, I guess." He sighed. "I'm ready as I'll ever be." Another pause. "No I haven't seen him this morning. But he'll be around groveling for his kibble. I'll lock him in." Another pause. "Fine. I'll call you when they leave. You can come get him then if it's so important to you." He hung up, and I heard his footsteps cross the room and enter the hallway beyond. "Here, Jack," he yelled. "Here, Jack. Time for breakfast, old buddy."

My stomach growled. Food can wait, I thought,

mouthing the hand. I have more important things to do.

Two more basement windows and I found what I was looking for. After that, it was simple: shoulder it open, leap through to the basement floor, cross over to the back stairs, up to the servants' door—that had a latch not a knob—nose it open, and head for the study via the dining room. I could hear my man calling me as I stood on my hind legs and deposited the hand beside the telephone on the cherry desk. Right next to the big tree he'd put up last week.

Now things will get back to the way they used to be, I thought as I trotted toward the kitchen and the sound of the electric can opener. My man will be happy when he sees the hand—he was so worried about losing it last night. He'll know I found it for him, and it will prove how helpful and loyal I can be. He'll see it and know I would never tell what I know about the dead woman. And he'll scratch my belly and throw sticks for me to catch and maybe even take me to the hunting camp like the father did. But, mostly, he'll never let the big, red haired man take me away, because we'll be friends again.

He fed me a big bowl of canned mixed with dry and sat at the table smoking while he watched me gobble it down. Then he locked me in the bathroom like I knew he would. I didn't mind. He would be letting me out as soon as he discovered what I did for him. I drank from the toilet and then lay down by the door to wait.

The front doorbell rang an hour later. A man's voice introduced himself as police lieutenant Grabel Smolowitz. "And this here is Sergeant Rita Sanchez," he added.

My man invited them inside. "I hope you've found her," he said.

"Her?" Sergeant Sanchez said. "You mean, Miss Darrel?"

"Yes. Of course I mean Miss Darrel. She's missing,

isn't she? I talked to her boss, Mr. Dinkletter, this morning. She was supposed to be here yesterday but didn't show up. My company pays Dinkletter . . ."

Lieutenant Smolowitz interrupted my man. "When was the last time you saw Miss Darrel?"

"Day before yesterday."

"Did she seem normal to you?" Sanchez asked.

"Normal?" my man said. "I guess. I'm not sure what you mean."

"Sergeant Sanchez means, did Miss Darrel seem preoccupied or anxious or actin' strange somehow?"

"She was auditing our books, officer," my man said. "I let her do her job. I didn't sit and look at her all day."

"And what is it you do exactly, Mr. Wadsworth?"

"I manage the family's estate."

Sanchez said, "Uh-huh, I see."

It was silent for a few seconds and then my man said, "I'd like to offer you some coffee or something, but I really have several phone calls to make before our offices in Europe close for the day, so . . ."

"Speaking of telephones," Smolowitz said, "would you mind if Sanchez here used yours? Our squad car radio seems to be on the fritz this mornin' and we shoulda checked in to the precinct half an hour ago."

"Not at all," my man said. "There's one right in the study."

I was on my feet and barking before it was all the way out of his mouth.

"What's up with the dog?" Sanchez said.

"He's probably locked himself in the bathroom again," my man said. "Study's that door right there, Sergeant Sanchez. Go on in. Use line one."

I barked louder. Faster. I leapt at the door.

"Had a dog did that," Smolowitz said. "Drank from the toilet, I mean. Never could understand why he liked that over his water bowl."

"I read in a magazine where it's the height," Sanchez said, her voice now coming from the study. "Dog doesn't have to bend over for the toilet. Easier to drink that way, the article said."

I howled and whined and barked.

"I was you, Mr. Wadsworth," Smolowitz said, "I'd go check on that dog of yours. Reminds me of Lassie, you know? The way he use to sound when he was tryin' to warn little Timmy of somethin'."

If you enjoyed the stories in

CANINE CHRISTMAS,

we invite you to investigate further:

THE PUZZLED HEART
by
AMANDA CROSS

Kate Fansler's husband, Reed, has been kidnapped—and will be killed unless Kate obeys the carefully delineated directives of a ransom note.

Tormented by her own puzzled heart, Kate seeks solace and wise counsel from friends both old and new. But who precisely is the enemy? Is he or she a vengeful colleague? A hostile student? A political terrorist?

The questions mount as Kate searches for Reed—accompanied by her trusty new companion, a Saint Bernard puppy named Bancroft. Hovering near Kate and Bancroft are rampant cruelties and calculated menace. The moment is ripe for murder. . . .

Published by Ballantine Books.
Available at your local bookstore.

CANINE CRIMES

15 canine crimes committed by
a kennel of top writers:

Deborah Adams
Laurien Berenson
Melissa Cleary
Amanda Cross
Brendan DuBois
Jonnie Jacobs
Dean James
Taylor McCafferty
Jeffrey Marks
Anne Perry
Lillian M. Roberts
S. J. Rozan
Polly Whitney
Valerie Wolzien
Steven Womack

Published by Ballantine Books.
Available at your local bookstore.